# RIKA'S

'Your skin is unmarked. No tattoos, no scars.' Pia pointed to the criss-crossing ridges up her own arms. 'It won't remain so soft and velvety smooth, Rika. Not if you're serious about joining us in battle today.'

'No –' Rika's tongue quivered at her lips in hesitation. She privately liked the mixed textures on Pia's skin, the way the fresh scars faded from livid purples to mere bruises of colour, then finally became ornate spirals of chalky, fine lines. Now in the heat, for example, a film of sweat was forming on the curves of Pia's biceps, just beginning to run on to the old scars. She drew in her breath. Suddenly she had an urge to duck down her head and lick at the moisture, an urge to taste the salt and sweet of Pia's skin.

# RIKA'S JEWEL

## ASTRID FOX

First published in 1999 by
Sapphire
an imprint of Virgin Publishing Ltd
Thames Wharf Studios,
Rainville Road, London W6 9HT

ISBN 0 352 33367 7

Cover Photograph by Steve Diet Goedde

Typeset by SetSystems Ltd, Saffron Walden, Essex
Printed and bound in Great Britain by Mackays of Chatham PLC

*For my sweet Simone,*
*with Xena-sized love and gratitude.*

*With special thanks to all the funky folks in Fiction — and to*
*Hélène and Carl, for the enthusiasm.*

There were once women in Denmark who dressed themselves to look like men and spent almost every minute cultivating soldiers' skills; they did not want the sinews of their valour to lose tautness and be infected by self-indulgence. Loathing a dainty style of living, they would harden body and mind with toil and endurance, rejecting the fickle pliancy of girls and compelling their womanish spirits to act with a virile ruthlessness. They courted military celebrity so earnestly that you would have guessed they had unsexed themselves. Those especially who had forceful personalities or were tall and elegant embarked on this way of life. As if they were forgetful of their true selves they put toughness before allure, aimed at conflicts instead of kisses, tasted blood, not lips, sought the clash of arms rather than the arm's embrace, fitted to weapons hands which should have been weaving, desired not the couch but the kill, and those they could have appeased with looks they attacked with lances.

*Saxo Grammaticus*, circa 1200
(*Saxo Grammaticus: History of the Danes I–II.*
Fisher, Peter and Davidson, Hilda Ellis (trans. and ed.).
Cambridge: DS Brewer, 1979–80.)

# ONE

There were no clouds in the evening sky, only a smeared rainbow of colours which made up the sweet twilight. Purples, oranges, reds, blues as bright as bird eggs – all melded together as smoothly as if a goddess had reached a finger out from Asgard and stirred them slowly, stirred them into the sheen particular to a rich and successful sunset.

This brilliant display was lost on most inhabitants of the village. Most were dozing or working too hard to notice the shifting colours in the sky above. But above the bay by which the village nestled, the colours twisted through the heavens and skimmed across the setting sun. The tiny settlement lay in the furthest finger of a chilly Nordic fjord, and the villagers who were awake thought as little of the autumn chill as they did of the gaudy sunset. They thought of the boats they polished and prepared with oil; they thought perhaps of those who had already crossed the ocean this autumn; they thought of the pounded iron they had to fashion into swords, knives, battle-axes and horseshoes. What they thought of, in short, was the war across the sea in Britain.

Around this preoccupied village wound a fence of wood and earth. It guarded the twenty longhouses in the settlement, each of which sat on its own fenced plot. It was here that people raised vegetables and the animals that sometimes took refuge in the low rectangular longhouses. As a thatched longhouse consisted of only one large room, cows and goats lived in the far end and the ripe smell was often overpowering. The walls of thick wood and straw kept the animal scent in, that was true – but the chill of fast-approaching winter would be kept out. This was much more important.

In one corner of the longhouse of the village's best ironsmith, Hans Leifsson, sat his disgruntled daughter Rika. The longhouse was empty, with the exception of several thralls pottering in the corner. Rika paid little attention to the white-clad, shaven-headed slaves; she was half contemplating examples of her father's weapon handicraft hung along the walls and half listening to a conversation her father was currently having with a visiting missionary.

The knives were beautiful. Glistening sharp iron, gilded hilts with encrusted gems, shiny new blades like mirrors. Virginal knives, innocent of pierced flesh, untouched by the blood of beasts or humans. She raised herself and ran a finger over one bright blade.

'Rika! Keep your hands off them!' her father bellowed from the doorway. As always, he was keeping one eye on his treasures as he spoke with the young eager Christian priest. Rika sat down again and then crept closer to the door so that she could better hear what was being said. It was unusual for her father to spend so much time talking to one of the men he called 'fish-believers' – on account of the crude little fish symbol they seemed to have carved or stitched on to all of their possessions.

She pressed herself against the half-open door and could see her father nodding in agreement with the foreigner. She caught one phrase: 'a lovely young woman, certainly ready to be married off quickly . . .'

She looked down at herself uncomfortably. It was true that she was considered an attractive girl. Her hair was long, blonde and straight, her breasts were full and high under the straining capture of the boyish shirt she wore, her waist was slim and her stomach gently rounded. Her eyes, framed with thick honey-coloured lashes, were a soft light blue and flecked with amber and her face was saved from sterile perfection by virtue of a sprinkling of freckles across her pert nose. But she had no wish to be quickly married off, and so she now listened with growing alarm. They were speaking more loudly, and she could make out their words only too clearly.

'It's true,' her father was saying, 'I've often thought that she should shed her breeches for a skirt and cover her hair with a shawl. She's nineteen, nearly twenty, and I know it's past the time when she would normally find a mate –'

'*Far* past the time,' the fish-priest interrupted.

'But, as you know,' her father continued, 'it has been our people's custom to let girls choose their own husbands once they pass the age of fifteen. And, truth be told, Rika has never been much interested in the idea. My wife's been dead five years now and I suppose I've let Rika run her own way . . .'

'But that is precisely what you must not do,' urged the missionary. 'That view is a throwback to the old heathen days. Now we know the truth: that a young woman has only two honourable destinies – that of a wife, or that of serving Christ. Women are placed on earth for these fates only.'

'Hmm,' said her father, as if he was considering the priest's words very seriously.

Rika was fuming. How dare her father talk about her as if he didn't know she was listening? How dare he view the priest's advice as anything other than a joke? She looked at the blades she had been scrutinising: the finest, sharpest knives in Scandinavia. She longed to plunge one straight into the neck of the meddling fish-priest. She reached her hand out again and –

'Rika, I mean it! Get away from them!' A knife grazed her arm and dived plumply into the wall beside her. Priest present or not, her father was still not about to let her touch his best blades.

Rika lowered her hand and peered out the door at the fish-priest again; he was looking visibly shaken at the momentary violence of the ironsmith.

'This is expressly what I'm talking about,' he said hurriedly. 'Women are not made for war or knives –'

'Well, I don't know about that,' her father interjected. 'There have been many warrior women amongst our people. Freydis, Sela . . .' He named a whole list of valiant heroines of the past.

'Exactly,' said the priest, glowing with religious fervour. 'That's exactly what I'm trying to say. In the old heathen days, that was acceptable. Now though, in a Christian country, women can fulfil their true destinies. Well, there's a young single man in the next village, a good Christian boy name of Mattias, and I told his family that I'd ask whether Rika . . .'

His voice faded as Rika at last drew away from the conversation, feeling slightly sick to her stomach and stunned. Curse the new religion, she thought. The old ways had been better. At least then it would have been her own choice to marry. *Fishmen*. She spat on the earthen floor. But panic was beginning to work its way through her body; she could be promised to young Mattias, whoever he was, within a week. And her father seemed disturbingly comfortable with the idea; the simple fact that he had let the missionary rattle on for so long made her worried.

She would be wrenched from this village to the next, forced to marry and bear children with a man she had never met. Worse, she thought, she would not be here when Ingrid returned, as she had promised.

For just an instant, she touched the rune-shaped scar on her left hand and remembered how Ingrid had held her thrilled and spellbound in her arms last spring before she left, and regaled her with tales of what a woman had the strength to do. Fight in battle, sail ships, bed both men and women without shame. It was the first time Rika had considered any option other than the dowry and the dull, capable suitors she was convinced her father would eventually assemble for her. Just remembering made Rika's body tremble. From that very moment, she had known that the life of the warrior, rather than that of the wedded

4

childbearer, was for her. And then the Viking season had come again and Ingrid had left.

She looked around the longhouse, at the banks of earth lining its walls, the smouldering, clay-covered hearthstone and the animal skins tacked to the inner walls as protection from rain and wind. Shortly she would have to say farewell to her home if she wanted to escape from an arranged marriage. A plan began to form in her mind, but she would have to obtain help from her best friend Lina in order for it to succeed.

She glanced at the jewel round her neck that Ingrid had given her, etched with a tiny rendition of the god Freyr. She had a bad habit of stroking it when she felt nervous, but the physical proof of Ingrid's love for her usually managed to make her feel more secure. The new ways could be crushed by Thor's own hammer for all she cared; a terrible new religion it was, one where she could be bartered off to a young swain from a neighbouring village. She thought of the old religion, with its exciting tale of the horrible bloodthirsty wolf that would come at the end of the world, and of gods and goddesses like the siblings Freyr and Freyja, who thought of nothing but pleasure and sex. Not at all what the fish-priests believed. She knew then that she was going to embrace the Old Ways: a faith where women could still be warriors.

Lina was surprisingly understanding. As she was also facing an imminent marriage to an unsuitable suitor, she vowed to run away as well, though she balked at joining Rika in the rest of her plan: the smith's daughter aimed to run away to join Ingrid's Crew, the terrifying select group of nine Viking women who bared their breasts in battle and fought in Britain with the strength of nine hundred men.

As she reviewed her plans for the hundredth time, Rika paused a moment to shod her feet with thick leather soles; aside from the clothes she wore, these shoes were all she was planning on taking with her at the moment. She hoped Lina would not forget the rest of her goods.

5

She knew that she had made the right decision; there had already been bad signs. In an unusual concession to Christian beliefs, her father had forced her to remove her Freyr pendant and had placed it in her dowry bag. Rika feared this was only the beginning. She had promised Ingrid that she would always wear it. Last night, as they made their plans for the next day, Lina had assured her that Ingrid would understand its temporary absence.

Lina had met Ingrid several times, and Rika had told her about their relationship. Shy Lina had been fascinated and often encouraged Rika to be more forthcoming with details. Rika had felt quite warm when recounting her exploits to Lina; she had been half in love with Lina since girlhood and relating such racy tales inevitably made her blush.

But Lina had been filled with trepidation when Rika detailed the entire plan of escape to her: Lina would steal a horse and provisions from her father's inn and Rika would meet her in the woods the next evening. They would return to capture Rika's dowry, race by horseback to where the ships set sail, and from there Rika would sail to Britain and Lina would ride on.

Did she need anything else? Rika looked around the long-house one last time and then – thinking prudently for once – grasped the hilt of the knife her father had thrown at her and in a single motion withdrew it from its nest in the wall. She tucked it into her belt before she took off for the woods and felt more secure for it. A girl could always use a good knife.

'Rika!' She heard her father shouting from the doorway where she had stood only moments earlier, but she put his voice out of her head as she concentrated on running as fast as she could. She hurdled the wooden fence surrounding the village and then tumbled to the ground. The rocks gouged into her feet even through the thick soles and she stumbled, swore and took up the pace again. She couldn't hear her father behind her, but that didn't mean a thing. The late twilight of the little bay was not much protection in the best of cases. Later, there would be many men more than willing to hand her over as bounty to her father. But for now, she was sure he would grumpily return to sleep –

as an ironsmith he rose early and subsequently was usually already snoring at a time when most villagers were beginning their evening drinking.

She guessed he would be even angrier when he discovered she had run off to join Ingrid. But by that time Rika would be long gone. At her hip she touched the knife she had finally succeeded in stealing from him, and she drew near to the clearing in the coastal forest – where Lina and the horse were supposed to be waiting.

She took a quick moment to absorb the fragrances and sounds around her: the sea-scent and the ripe soiled musk of rotting leaves and rich decaying trees working their way into her nose and mouth. She picked her way quickly through the brush, her feeling of urgency growing. When she pushed through the final branches, she saw Lina waiting with the horse by her side. Rika exhaled with relief. But she couldn't let herself relax. Not yet.

'Where have you been?' Lina's sweet voice was hushed and troubled. 'I was so worried, Rika. I waited and waited, and –'

Rika caught herself before she told Lina to shut up and get moving. 'I'm here now.' She couldn't be too harsh with the girl; she would not see her for a long time – possibly never again. Pretty Lina had a clear complexion and thick honey-blonde lashes fringed her slightly slanted green eyes. People had often remarked that they looked like sisters, if not twins. It was obviously too late now to do anything about the fact that Rika had always rather fancied her. But the girl would probably have not been willing. Rika dismissed all hesitations and misgivings: she had to do what was necessary to join Ingrid's Crew.

Rika made her face calm, but inwardly she was panicking. She squeezed Lina's hand. 'You're feeling better now?' Lina nodded. 'We've got to get going, then.' Rika looked around the clearing. 'Did you bring what I asked?'

Lina nodded again, her eyes shining with excitement and fright. 'I've brought you everything you told me to. Water, bread and cheese.' Rika briefly noted that the girl had copied her own custom of dress: instead of a dress and scarf, Lina wore a pair of blue breeches. She also wore a tight-fitting pale shirt that revealed the fine curves of her high breasts; Rika was almost sure she could see the outlines of Lina's nipples. Lina handed over the food, along with a hide satchel into which Rika placed the provisions. 'Everyone will be searching for us after tonight, Rika. Your father will be furious; he will kill when he finds us. He will sharpen his knives for it,' she added breathlessly. Rika thought of her father's collection of razor-sharp iron blades, but did not shudder.

She moved briskly to the horse and tied the satchel over its back, before helping Lina up. She then swung herself on to the dark mare. The colour was favourable: they would not be clearly seen in the fading light as they made their way back through the village to her house on one last important errand – and then on to the ship two miles away. Rika breathed in the scent of the forest and felt the coarse hair of the horse bristling at her thighs. She was going to be fine, she told herself; she felt confident.

She was just about ready to urge the mare on when Lina grasped her arm. 'I've got a gift for you before we go,' Lina said. For Freyja's sake, why was the girl delaying her?

'We don't have time for it right now,' Rika said abruptly. Her legs were tensed around the horse's body, ready to press the steed into action.

Lina quickly brought something small and round out from the depths of her pocket. She handed it to Rika. 'I brought you a gift, an odd fruit I found in the bags of the merchant Hrafn from whom I stole the horse. It was with his foodstuffs, so it should be safe.' Rika could see in the fading light that it was a red fruit with bruises on it. 'You must try it, Rika; I have only tried it once before myself and it is delicious.'

Rika noted how Lina's fingers shook as she gave the fruit to her. Rika pocketed the little round fruit and stifled an impulse to say: Is that all? Can we go now? She knew Lina could be very sentimental and she owed a debt for the girl's assistance. She could at least be courteous.

'Are you sure it's not poisoned?' It was only a half-joke. An uncle had died last month after drinking a honeyed venom of mushroom and mead. As ironsmiths who provided weapons to most voyaging warriors, her family had many enemies.

'No, of course it's not poisoned.' Lina seemed slightly shocked that Rika could ask the question.

Rika turned behind to Lina and took the girl's hand in a manner that belied her panic. 'Lina, we've got to hurry. We don't have much time to talk or worry about what happens after tonight.'

Lina looked up at Rika from underneath her eyelashes, her chest rising and falling as she listened. Rika felt her apprehension recede, just a little bit. She forced herself to smile at Lina and finally drove her heels into the dark mare. With Lina grasping tightly at her waist, she leant forward to coax the horse on through the treacherous bramble. The horse would have to stumble through a coagulation of moss and dead branches for a fair bit before they left the forest. And after the little visit at Rika's father's house, they would, she hoped, be able to race unimpeded to the ship.

Rika was uncomfortably aware of Lina's soft breasts pressing into her back but, as they reached the edge of the forest and the horizon opened up before them, she let herself enjoy the friction of the horse beneath her sex and a joy began to rise in her. She was going to be free and she was going to see Ingrid once again. She urged the horse on but, once they neared the village, she slowed the beast to a drawl of a trot.

'We should just ride straight to the ships. I don't know why you have to go back to your house, anyway,' Lina commented in her ear. The horse carried them calmly. They had passed the first of the houses quietly. They were going to be all right, Rika told herself.

'Yes, you do. It's because I want to take my jewel back,' Rika hissed through her teeth, 'and my dowry money, as well.' Now her teeth began to chatter, though she had been warm only moments before.

'Your father will never forgive you.'

'You already mentioned that,' Rika said, and then was silent.

Rika stopped the horse in front of her father's home, the cessation of the horse's steps seeming to echo in the night. Her throat turned dry and she swallowed hard: this was the most difficult part of the whole plan.

'Stay here,' she whispered to Lina and, swinging down, she left the other girl sitting uncomfortably on the horse. Adrenalin was pumping through her veins: if she were caught this time, her father surely *would* kill her, and not just throw a purposefully miscalculated knife above her head. Rika entered the longhouse silently and smelt the familiar mix of metal and musty tanned leather. She padded quietly through the large room to where her dowry bag was kept.

As she entered this part of the longhouse, her heart froze as she realised that the bag was by her father's head, safely beneath his outstretched palm. Several of his smithy thralls lay slumbering by him, too. She walked silently towards her snoring father and made a quick decision. She would have to grab the bag and then make a run for it. She observed the low-burning torches lining the walls and mentally measured the steps to the door: if she grabbed the bag, dashed out in a matter of seconds and then mounted the horse where it stood outside, she stood a fair chance of succeeding. She prayed to Loki, god of thieves, that Lina and the horse were still where she had left them. Nothing could be out of place, or she would be killed in the ensuing slaughter.

*Now.* She snatched her dowry bag from underneath her father's hand, raced quickly to the wall, wrestled down a torch and headed out of the doorway as she heard her father's shouts behind her in an odd repetition of her earlier departure. Yes, Lina was still there waiting, thank all the gods.

Rika paused just seconds to throw the flaming torch on the coarse and brittle piled straw outside her father's home, then dug her fingers into the bag to draw the chain of the jewelled pendant over her neck, shoved the bag in her waistband and swung herself once more upon the horse.

'Did you get the dowry?' Lina screamed as Rika kicked her heels hard into the mare. It danced out on to the dirt path, before she steered it towards the centre of the village.

Rika did not answer, for her father and his thralls were assembling behind her. His shouts had roused a crowd not too far in front of her, too – rough, drinking men who had already drawn their blades.

Rika's blonde hair streamed behind her as the horse raced through the settlement towards the beach, straight towards the growing crowd of armed and drunken Viking sailors. 'Close your eyes, Lina,' she advised, as she drove the horse straight into the midst of the throng. She drew her stolen blade out, its gleam shining in the reflection from the fire-torches of the crowd.

A man came at her with his dagger drawn; she slashed down at him and felt her knife enter deep within his arm, then wetly pulled the red-dripping blade out again. The men drew back some distance, but another soon came at her, and Rika heard not just the shouts of her own father, hell-bent on revenge for her treachery, but also the crackling fire of his burning house. It was my dowry, she reminded herself as she drove off a new pretender with a flat smack of her blade on his head, I had every right to it. The man stumbled behind her, and now there remained but two obstacles to the beach path. A pair of bald seven-foot giants with dirty, long-braided blond beards framed her escape, each holding a strange white cup of drink in one hand and each smiling a twisted grimace at her.

'The monster twins,' Lina said behind Rika, 'they can each tear a horse in half. We'll never get by.'

'Shut up and close your eyes, girl,' Rika hissed at Lina again, and then, holding her breath, Rika sheathed her blade, wrapped her fingers in the dark thick mane and rammed straight towards the giants, before quickly retreating. The giant twins seemed taken aback, as if they had not expected such a frontal assault.

'Hold on,' Rika said to the petrified Lina, who needed no encouragement as they smashed towards the brothers for the second time. Rika held the horse tightly with her thighs, then

11

snatched up both white goblets from the giant warriors. She realised she was triumphantly holding aloft two skulls filled with dark red liquor. Unconcerned, she swigged the wine from one gruesome vessel, feeling its bright burn rolling down her throat. Lina's soft breasts pressed into her back; she could faintly feel the girl's erect nipples, stiff from excitement. A thrill ran quickly up her spine. But not now, she admonished herself. She couldn't think about that now.

With pressure from her thighs, Rika instructed the horse to swivel round. Now she faced the horde and chaos. She took in the cries of the drunken sailors, her father and his men and, further back, the flames rising from her father's home. She could never return home.

The giant twins stood gaping at her and Rika took one more exultant quick drink from the ivory-smooth skulls – the liquid flaming in her mouth – and spat, before cracking the skulls down on the heads of the giants staring dumbfounded at her. The wine ran down their heads, and she was unsure where it mixed with their blood. She felt strangely jubilant. This is what war would feel like, she knew.

'Rika,' pleaded Lina, her fingers digging at Rika's waist, 'hurry!' Drunk with power, Rika finally circled the horse round and the mare made its run to the beach with no obstructions. Pressed hard against Rika's chest was the chain of her necklace, the pendant bobbing wildly with the motion of the horse. As the horse swung into a smooth race on the sand, she drew in progressively slower breaths. The worst was behind them.

'Lina?' She turned round briefly. Lina had her eyes screwed shut as the horse galloped on. 'You can open your eyes, now. They're not following us.'

'Really?' Lina raised her head and looked behind. It was true. For some reason, the pursuit had ceased. But Rika had no illusions; she felt sure it would soon resume. 'Rika, we can never go back now,' Lina said, voicing Rika's own thoughts.

Rika nodded grimly. But she dismissed that particular worry for the time being. They rode silently for some time, and then not so far ahead Rika could see the longboat and the women preparing to set off. Set off very soon, Rika hoped.

'You're sure my name is down as crew?' she asked Lina one more time.

'Yes, I told you, didn't I? I spoke with the captain yesterday at the inn when they were purchasing provisions for the trip. Her name is Pia; she's not just a sailor, either: she's fought in battle, too. I wouldn't worry anyway: they seemed happy to take you on.'

'What name did you give me?'

'Freydis,' answered Lina. Freydis was a female warrior whose exploits Rika had always enjoyed hearing. Daughter of the explorer Eirik the Red, Freydis had been a famous berserker – a Viking warrior who wore bear-shirts in battle and fought as if crazed. Rika approved of the choice.

But she had a right to be concerned. Her dowry would pay for the chance to temporarily join this company of women sailors; it was her ticket to see Ingrid again. Of course, Rika would not be revealed as thief and fugitive until long after they'd set sail, but she feared recognition of her family name, as no captain in her right mind would ever take on the daughter of the village ironsmith for fear of local repercussion.

Rika could see the longboat being pushed along the sand towards the water and, as she looked, she caught sight of their reflections in the glaze of seawater. Though reflections were deceptive in the twilight and in between the waves, they looked very similar astride the dark horse. Both had similar builds and she realised that what people said was true: they did look like twins. Though there were some differences – her eyes were blue while Lina's were green. Her own colour was also higher; she was more prone to flushing than Lina was.

And with a brave new name like Freydis, she already felt a stranger. Only the pendant and its weight on her breasts reminded her of who she had been and why she was doing this. Glancing down, she could make out the glow from its clear red stone. She slowed the horse to a trot and stretched out her finger until she touched the stone in its setting. The whole ornament was round and no larger than a walnut in diameter. Etched into its lower quadrant was a rune combination and a tiny rendition of the sex god Freyr, with his customary narrow eyes and erect phallus. The stone felt warm.

She tucked it into her shirt as they reached the longboat and the group of roughly forty women. The longboat was medium-sized; the wedge-shaped planks were stuffed with tar-covered animal hair and moss, ensuring a watertight voyage. There was a steering board at one end and, as the planks were not nailed directly to the ship's frame, the longboat could withstand tremendous waves without being splintered apart like kindling. Like most of the enormous open boats of their people, the vessel was set up with two lines of seats for the rowers and with an enormous dragon figurehead.

Rika's eyes moved up the curve of the oak boat as she and Lina swung off the horse in front of the group of silent women. She could sense the sailors staring at her, but she couldn't move her gaze from the side of the large vessel. It had always been her dream to travel on such a ship.

When eventually she raised her eyes, she squared her shoulders and readied herself to make her voice as deep and confident as possible. But it was one of the sailors who first broke the silence.

'Are you Freydis?' said the sailor, a tall woman. She had the bearing of a captain, strong arms bared by her sleeveless vest of orange-dyed wool and unbelievably blue eyes – widely set and with long dark lashes longer than Rika's own. The deep-blue colour was certainly a marked contrast to the woman's otherwise dark colouring and hair.

'Yes,' said Rika, 'here is my payment for passage and instruction.' She handed the captain the dowry bag. It was not yet pitch-black and, as they all carried torches, Rika could clearly make out the striking features of this woman. She was a strong woman, a formidable Viking woman, the type of woman who had brought their people pride in battle. Rika swallowed. The type of woman Ingrid had been.

The excitement of her escape had been arousing, and it was difficult to slow the pace of her heart. As the tall woman swiftly pocketed the dowry, her muscles rippling, Rika wondered if the captain's evident strength would be equal to other tasks; she stopped herself before she imagined the rough hands of this blue-eyed woman inside her breeches and against her skin, pushed inside her wet sex. There were more important things to consider at present. She took out her pendant and began to fiddle with it nervously.

'We're nearly ready to leave, Freydis –' The woman's speech halted as her attention fixed on Rika's pendant. Its unique craftsmanship attracted many looks. Before her father had appropriated it, Rika had usually worn the necklace proudly above her boyish shirt. But the captain didn't immediately break her gaze from the pendant balanced between Rika's breasts, and Rika grew aware of her nipples pushing hard against the thin material of her shirt. In fact, the longer the woman gazed, the more Rika's nipples pressed.

Rika cleared her throat, and at last the tall woman looked away.

'So,' she hurriedly continued in a low voice, 'if you'd like to say goodbye to your pretty little friend, we'll be setting off quite soon.' She added, unnecessarily, 'If that's all right with you?' The blue-eyed woman shifted her weight and Rika again sensed the movement of fine muscles beneath the rough-knitted shirt she wore.

'Yes,' Rika said to the tall woman, 'I'll be there. I've just got to finish some dealings with my . . . friend here. It won't take a moment.'

'Rika!' Lina hissed in Rika's ear. 'Towards which direction should I ride?'

'Take your time, within reason,' said the blue-eyed captain. 'We have twenty minutes before we set off.' She was observing Rika closely with what could be considered a smirk on the curve of her lips, then murmured something to her comrades, of which

15

Rika caught only the low sound and not the meaning. The sailors laughed and Rika's cheeks stung with embarrassment.

'Come on,' Rika said quickly, leading Lina up to the treeline. 'Ride west,' she said, once they had reached the relative privacy of the trees, 'until you come to a settlement. Continue until you've passed at least five such villages. Only then can you stop. Do you understand?'

The slim blonde woman looked up at Rika. She began to speak, but her voice was faint and lost in the sound of the waves; Rika could just barely make out the words of agreement.

She really was quite beautiful, Rika thought. She laid her hand against Lina's breast, against the light fabric of her garment through which she could feel Lina's heart beating strongly.

'Are you afraid?' she whispered. Lina stared at her with huge eyes. She nodded. Very beautiful. 'Of leaving,' asked Rika, 'or of my father's knives if he catches you?' Lina's only response was a finger at Rika's lips. In the exposed danger of the forest, Rika could feel the girl's heart pounding and pounding against her palm. 'Don't be frightened,' she told Lina. 'It will be all right. We've both done the right thing.'

She briefly touched the carving of the little Freyr on her necklace and felt all the lust that Ingrid had promised her the gem would bring. Lina's eyes were wide open. Rika was quite sure sweet Lina had never done anything intimate before. She was deliciously vulnerable, all soft skin and big eyes. Rika's groin grew wet with desire. She had always wanted to kiss Lina's lips and now it was almost too late. Lina would never know how Rika felt all those years. Rika helplessly brought the other girl's hand to her mouth and kissed it lightly. As the last twilight rays fled from the woods and left them in the warm dark shades of night, Rika kept her mouth open against the salt taste of Lina's fingers. They were as taut as a held string as her tongue explored their sensitive undersides.

'Do you like that?' Rika asked. Lina answered softly in the affirmative. Rika considered that she would have to hurry with her goodbye. But somewhere in her head was the little Freyr from the pendant, telling her that this was further than she had ever come with Lina previously and she would be a fool to miss her only chance.

And beneath Rika's fingers, Lina's nipples had hardened through the shirt. Lina moaned and Rika felt the points of her own nipples stiffen in response to the sound. Lina's eyes were closed, her curved full lips open. Rika grew convinced that she could smell the particular ripe scent of Lina's excitement in the air.

'They're waiting for you, Rika,' Lina said, her voice husky.

'I know.' But something was twisting in Rika; something churned up by her flight. She felt her sex momentarily tighten and release, as if someone had just briefly touched her clit and then just as quickly eased their finger's pressure. She needed some form of relief. She continued massaging Lina's nipple through her shirt and felt moist at the thought that underneath the fabric were Lina's soft and delectable breasts. There was that smoothness to Lina, the smoothness that Rika had always relished but never explored. 'You're very pretty,' she murmured.

She sucked gently at Lina's fingers and the girl gave a quiet moan in response. Rika's hand snaked down quickly to Lina's sex; underneath the garments she felt the honey deep within the girl's wet folds. This shy girl was more aroused than Rika would have ever suspected.

'We can't be too long,' she whispered. 'Where do you want me to touch you, Lina?' The girl hesitated under the hot pressure of Rika's hand, then pressed it down to the curve of her cunt. Excitement was churning Rika's insides. This is something I should be savouring, she thought, I should be going slowly. But the minutes were ticking away. And Lina had taken the initiative of tentatively rubbing her palm against Rika's mouth and lips so Rika could taste the salty flat of it again. *Only minutes left.*

'Touch me,' she whispered boldly to Lina. 'Run your hand beneath the band of my breeches.' The girl slid her trembling hand between Rika's thighs to the wetness there, and a sigh escaped from Rika's lips. She removed her hand and sucked

17

harder at Lina's fingers, running her full lips over their delicate ridges. Lina's elbow grazed her breasts as she slowly sucked and tasted, and Rika's concentration shifted from the tease of movement against her breasts to the wet sensations at the tip of her tongue to the excruciatingly pleasant feeling of Lina's hand slowly moving up over the curve of her thighs. Good girl, she thought – but hurry.

'Rika, I'll be all right, won't I? Once I leave, I mean, and go to the other villages?'

'Yes.' What was the girl talking about? Rika groaned as Lina fingered her thighs. Lina might be a virgin, but the manner in which she delicately held and stroked Rika's upper legs was driving her out of her mind. Inexperienced women could be clumsy, but Lina had intelligence and sensitivity; she seemed extremely aware of Rika's reactions and responses. When Rika involuntarily moved as the sensation of Lina cupping and stroking her thighs became too much to bear, the girl held on for several seconds more until Rika thought she would scream, except of course she knew she could not. Not here, not where she could be overheard. *Only minutes.*

'Just keep moving your hand and don't stop,' Rika muttered. She pressed her lips to Lina's mouth and was buzzing in an intense and slow kiss. She moved her hands under Lina's shirt and stroked the hard tips of her nipples again. Rika wanted badly to be fucked, but even Ingrid wouldn't have been able to train up a virgin with a time limit like this. 'Fuck me.'

'What?' Lina looked startled and Rika realised that she had gone too far. Her face was hot. If she didn't draw this to a close soon, she would not only miss the ship: her father would discover her. But Lina's fingers discovered Rika down under her breeches, finally plunging straight up through the slippery melting wetness of Rika's pussy.

'Move them,' Rika said against Lina's mouth. 'Move your fingers inside me.' Lina did as Rika told her, tentatively at first and irregularly. But as Lina gained confidence, Rika began to feel herself swept away by the feeling of her circling fingers; after

18

every fifth circle or so, Lina would repeat that first upward movement. Oh, Lina was gifted; there was no doubt about that.

Now Lina took off the pendant from around Rika's neck. Was the little minx stealing it?

'What are you doing?' Lina didn't answer and Rika was already too far gone. But only moments after Lina removed the pendant, Rika could feel the cold metal of the chain against the warm liquid of her cunt. There was pressure from the clear red gemstone against her clit, but it was a very precise tension with no undue force or discomfort.

'How does that feel to you?' Lina's voice was disingenuously innocent. Rika couldn't tell – had the girl been faking her earlier naivety or not? Lina rubbed the smooth carved surface of the gem over the dew-drenched folds of her sex, causing Rika to moan even more than if it had been a woman's purposeful hand. The girl knew damn well what she was doing.

It was the combination of flesh and metal; this distortion excited Rika and she knew she was close to the dangerous edge. She thought of her father's knives and of the Vikings who used them in battle. She thought of crimson blood on knives and the blood-coloured stone against her pussy, and rubbed herself against the pendant Lina held in her hand. The other girl's gold-tipped lashes were lowered, her face flushed with desire and concentration. Washes of sensation spread through Rika as she shuddered against the necklace. Her own desire was going to make her come, for Lina barely shifted the pendant.

Lina pushed the entire pendant up inside her, including the fine-linked chain on which it hung. Drowning in sensation, Rika panted and squirmed towards Lina; it would have made little difference what anyone would have done at this point. There were no thick distinctions; everything felt obscene and lushly dirty. So this is what she had been missing all those times she had denied herself the pleasure of fucking Lina. She cursed herself silently.

Lina was drawing the wet chain out of her, link by link in excruciating and near-torturous process. Rika crouched back

ASTRID FOX

against the tree-bark, smelling the sap of the birches and feeling hornier than she ever remembered feeling before. At last Lina drew out the gem itself, brought it up to Rika's lips, and gave it for her to taste and suck. She fucked Rika deeply with her hand, thrusting and by turns acutely touching and experimenting, and Rika began to let go, sucking at the clear ruby-red pendant. One of Lina's hands was deep inside her, the other at her nipples just lightly teasing and burning them with each touch. Rika's attention slipped from one thing to another, from her pussy-taste still on the pendant, to her wet sex, to the brushing of her nipples.

'What's feeling good now, Rika?' Lina whispered. 'Your pussy? My hand in your cunt?' Rika felt like she was going to come all over Ingrid's pendant. 'Or your own taste on the gem?' Then Rika did come, in a series of swells strung one to another like linked extensions on the wet chain dripping from her pussy. She clung to Lina and prayed she made no sound. Eventually the girl released her and she fell back against the tree.

Her breeches were soaking; she could feel Lina trembling beside her, her hips pressing into Rika. She slowly grew aware of her surroundings. How long had they been here? There was the sound of Lina's deep and quick breaths and, in the distance, a repeated drumming like a heartbeat. Caught for a moment in the sound, within a minute Rika's head cleared further and she finished her drift back to the present. She felt a warmth and tenderness she had not felt for months.

She moved to turn towards Lina, then stopped. There wasn't a thing she could do for Lina's pleasure; there simply wasn't time. She had to get down to the boat.

'Freydis!' Yes, they were already calling for her. She tried to ignore Lina's look of disappointment.

'Goodbye, Lina – remember, ride quickly past at least five villages, and –'

Lina gripped her shoulder and covered her mouth. 'Quiet. You need to hurry.' Rika, startled, stopped talking. Neither of them drew breath and Rika once more experienced the same sensation of intense listening. In the distance a repetitious sound

20

of what now seemed beyond doubt to be horses was echoing, although previously the drumming noise had reminded Rika only of a heartbeat.

'It's your father, Rika.' Lina quickly replaced the jewelled chain around Rika's neck. 'They're probably still a mile away but, for Freyja's sake, hurry, don't apologise.' Lina gave Rika a sweet smile, holding for a moment the pendant in her palm. 'Rika, I –' She did not seem able to continue. She leant forward and gave her a quick and sensuous kiss, the tip of her tongue smooth and wet in Rika's mouth. 'Remember me.'

They swiftly embraced and then raced down to the beach, whereupon Lina mounted the horse in a practised motion before riding speedily away.

'That goodbye took longer than I thought it would.' The captain's voice was sober, but her eyes twinkled.

Rika looked up quickly; had she guessed what had just transpired?

'Well – what are you looking for, girl? Help us to push out the boat.' Rika waded out with the other sailors into the cool, dark water to push the boat from the tide's edge. She could smell Lina's sex still on her fingers and, too dazed to think clearly, stumbled in the water. This is not a good beginning, Rika thought, dreaming of Lina's fingers deep within her.

Someone cleared their throat loudly. All forty women were staring at her. Something had been asked of her and they were waiting for a reply. One of the sailors repeated the comment: 'Yesterday your friend told us that you're eager to join Ingrid's Crew.' Rika reddened as a great, tattoo-covered woman grabbed and then released her upper arm muscles – quite solid for an ordinary woman, but relatively inadequate for a sailor. 'I'm not sure you'll even be strong enough to row, let alone fight in battle with Ingrid.'

The blue-eyed captain also took a step forward and grabbed Rika by the pendant. She observed it closely, turning it over in her hands and bringing it up near her face to examine it. Rika could feel her face burning when she thought of how recently intimate she had been with it; she could even see beads of moisture still caught in the chain. The woman held it up to her vivid cobalt eyes, drawing Rika's face closer to her by the chain. Her expression was unfathomable. Then she released it and gave Rika a wink.

'She wears the mark of Freyr himself, a hardworking god in some aspects. Maybe we could even learn some skills from her.' The company chuckled. 'We should welcome her here.' The captain directed this to the company at large in her singular low voice, then specifically addressed the tattooed woman who had questioned Rika's credentials. 'You know yourself we are in dire need of a good lookout since Ingela's untimely departure.' The captain made a face and rolled her eyes, evidently in reference to a recently demised sailor. 'It's not just stargazing, girl,' she added to Rika. 'You're expected to do your fair share of hard work as well. If you can pull an oar well, you'll fit in.'

Rika smarted from the implication that she wasn't strong enough for the task. Hadn't she just taken on her whole village? She was certainly strong enough to join Ingrid's Crew. But the company was waiting expectantly for her response. 'Yes,' she answered. 'Yes, I'll fit in. I'll pull as many oars as I'm asked to.'

The tall woman continued: 'What you lack in strength you might just make up in youthful endurance. Anyway, we'll see. Let's go.' Rika stepped gingerly into the bobbing boat, which was given its final heave and glided away from the shore. After they had passed the first breaking waves and made it out to the mere swells of water, Rika began to feel more relaxed. For it was none too soon – Rika could see her father's torches in the far distance. She turned around and looked seaward. That business was behind her.

'My name, by the way, is Pia. You're meant to go there, girl.' The tall captain pointed Rika towards the hull.

Freydis, Rika thought privately. She felt unsure of her duties. 'What exactly do I do?' she asked in a low tone. She didn't want to appear stupid; but then again she didn't want to appear lazy, either.

'It will be your duty to watch out through the night from the most sea-bound point of the ship, near the figurehead. It's a direct course and it's unlikely that we will see other vessels, let alone serpents or whales. I know it's night-time, but it just makes the crew feel better, really, to have someone looking out, even if there's nothing to see. It makes sense, since we've got our backs to whatever lies ahead of us. You'll be fine,' said Pia. 'The truth is, the reason you aren't beginning the first rowing stretch is because you're not as tall as most here. We want the full length of a tall woman's arms in the pull when we start out. You'll serve as relief when it is time for the others to rest.' Rika bristled: she had always been amongst the tallest of the village women. But there was something intriguing about the captain's stern tone.

The oarswomen were already in place in the longboat. As she began to make her way along the hull, Rika purposefully brushed her body against Pia as she passed by. The captain merely glanced up briefly before turning back to her duties. Rika knew she was flirting with danger, but she was pleased to note the slight smile that had escaped the corners of Pia's lips. She paused, marking the fine, straining sinews in Pia's arms as the captain continued to repair an oarlock. Eventually Pia raised her head and grinned. Evidently bemused by the younger woman's attention, she cleared her throat and pointed out a location in the heavy, still night sky for Rika.

'There is the Fenrir wolf – see his sharp teeth and the diamonds they drip. Below him you have the great ice-cow – watch the icicles curl beneath her teats. All the stars have meanings and stories, every one. And some help to guide our ships at night. These are skills that you will learn.' Rika gazed at the milky mass of stars. Something red flashed and moved in the sky.

'From which constellation does that come?' Rika asked the woman, excited and quickly pointing. The moon revealed the captain's expression as bittersweet.

'When the stars shoot fire,' she said, 'it is the Valkyrie maidens,

23

carrying with them another hero to feast forever at Valhalla in Asgard, the home of the gods. Another life has fallen for that glory.' Rika breathed slowly. Yes, she had heard of that before, but now she saw it clearly for what it was, a warrior maiden ripping across the constellations.

Once in place, Rika enjoyed the sensation of watching through the darkness, and repeated to herself steadily the names of the stars in the night. The longboat was named *Loki*, she had been told. The god of mischief and trouble, Rika thought, and she shivered in the cold air. She passed the time by thinking, the dark muskiness and the tide sounds of the clear salty water drifting in to envelop her and her thoughts. She hoped Lina would safely ride to freedom. For just a second she thought bitterly and enviously of whatever girl would next get the pleasure of experiencing the entirety of Lina's love, but put the thought from her mind. She was on to new adventure. The low chants of the rowing women added to the bewitchment of her surroundings and Rika felt the whole experience begin to take on the dreamy dimensions of a spell, an idyll in which she found it difficult to believe that sea-faring life could be so calm or so indolently relaxing.

That night huge waves rolled the ship from crest to crest, and the violet star-shot sky above the ship rained down hail on the forty women in the boat. The ice did not melt immediately; when dawn came the small and shiny frozen beads were dotted on the scant clothing of the women, tiny frosty ornaments that finally melted after an hour of morning sunlight. Only rowing kept the women warm, harsh labour bringing heat to their limbs and colour to their cheeks. On many necks where sweat had risen in the night, there were paper-thin glazes of ice, which also melted in the sun.

The women sailors snorted steam like fierce dragons into the cold air of the new day. Rika rubbed her freezing hands together desperately; she was eager now to row and warm herself. She noted the toned and muscled arms of the women, rhythmically pulling and releasing the oars, and something stirred in her. She pushed the feeling back down, but even when she closed her eyes the image of the twisting, tan arms of the women, sweaty and lusty, remained. She had slept only briefly and, when she had, her dreams had been full of similarly disconcerting images. As a result, she felt exhausted. A cheer rose behind in the boat – provisions were being distributed. She closed her eyes and pressed her hands against her stomach, feeling its low rumble.

'Freydis!' She raised her lids. Tall Pia was making her way towards her.

'Try some of this,' Pia said, as she plonked herself down and handed a small flask to Rika.

'Ale?' Rika asked hopefully.

'Even better,' Pia said. 'Mead.' Rika visibly brightened – she had always had a taste for good mead.

The liquor went down smoothly and warmth spread through Rika's body. Sea life wasn't so bad after all, she considered, as she watched the sun shimmering on the waves spread out in the endless grey water horizon.

'I want to ask you something,' Pia said, as she extracted a thick stick of dried jerky from her pocket and handed it to Rika.

'What's that?' The jerky was blissful in her mouth, dark and smoky.

Pia circled the carved rune-scar on the back of Rika's hand with a forefinger. 'How did this come about?'

'I don't know what you mean.' Rika swallowed a bite of jerky and looked away.

'It's a blood-oath, isn't it?' Pia's face was grave. Rika didn't answer. 'I'm wondering to whom you swore it – we don't tolerate conflicting allegiances once you've signed on board . . . Freydis.'

It could have been Rika's imagination, but Pia seemed to stumble on the false name she had been given. She could not tell the tall sailor to whom she had sworn the oath – Ingrid had made her promise not to. She had not forgotten the promise and, more importantly, Ingrid would have not forgotten her –

the young girl skilfully seduced over the last six months of Ingrid's extended homecoming. Why else would she have given Rika a bejewelled token with her family runic mark on it? Or have demanded a blood-oath from Rika?

'My loyalty is sound,' she told Pia.

'I don't doubt it.' Pia's tone was dry.

Rika closed her lids for a moment. She felt Pia's warm hand on her shoulder and she opened her eyes. Pia had a bright ring on which a small red dragon curled. 'I like that,' she told Pia.

'This?' Pia looked down at her hand. 'It's quite special; the ring design is unique to my family.' She paused, then gently said, 'I know blood-oaths are serious matters but if there's any doubt, it's a good thing to reveal their details. I've been bound to one before myself and my oath-sister was not honourable.' Pia glanced over Rika's shoulders to the backs of the pulling women, Rika following her gaze. The gap from which Pia had risen had been filled; there was no dissonance or break in the two rows. 'If you've been demanded silence as well as loyalty, you might well ask yourself what it is they're trying to keep quiet. Believe me, I know how hard it is to question a given oath.'

How could Pia know anything about it, or what drove Rika to find Ingrid again?

Pia reached over and touched the pendant round Rika's neck. 'And what about this?'

Rika's heart began beating quickly, though there was no real reason to be afraid. Indeed, she ought to feel safe back here with Pia, with the combination of rising sun and alcohol seeping warmly through her. The wood here in the hull was as smooth and as polished as the inside of a shell; the scent that emanated from the boards was rich, with just a hint of musk from the many sea-faring voyages.

'It was a gift from a friend,' she finally answered, forcing her manner to be steady.

'Indeed.' Pia raised one eyebrow. 'A friend, you say? Is she a close friend, "Freydis"?' Rika observed the rich blue eyes and dark skin and hair of the woman who was so persistently questioning her. Pia's deliberate gaze was causing her to feel slightly panicked.

'Very close.' Her eyes met Pia's in a challenge. She felt something akin to a threat – but not quite – and consciously noted the prickling of all the hairs on her body. She was very much attracted. She knew the signs; she had always reacted to Ingrid in the same way.

The tipped crests of the waves were caught by the sunlight as silvery crescents, which then disappeared in the following swells. The boat hummed on over the waters and over the next two or three minutes, Rika wondered at the brooding silence behind her and at her own disinclination to be forthcoming.

Something was making her uneasy: there was some truth to what this woman was saying – why had Ingrid insisted on absolute silence? 'If I told you who gave me the pendant, would you keep it a secret?'

Pia did not immediately answer, and the two women sat uncomfortably in the hull, listening to the chanting harmonies of the rowing women, who were now singing a bawdy melody about the joys of Norman whores, loudly and slightly off-key. The sun was now positively warm and had – along with the mead – obviously inspired the company to break out in song. Their backs were to them, which left Rika and Pia in relative privacy.

Pia was carrying out some type of mental reckoning. 'It's warm now,' she said, finally and evasively. 'That's the problem with these boats – the nights are frigid and the days are sweltering.' Rika heard, unmistakably, the sound of Pia unclasping her clothing. She casually looked behind her. Pia was stripped to the waist and her body was toned and muscled. The angles and contours made a rare beauty of her sun-darkened body. Her stomach was curved with muscles; the nipples on her small round breasts were plump and berry-red. The sunlight left shadows in the small hollows of her throat, her neckbone, her navel.

The beauty of the woman hit Rika with surprising force, deep down in the moistening twists of her sex. 'Would you keep the

27

secret if I told you?' she persisted. But Pia did not speak. Rika longed to touch the lovely, lightly rippling muscles of her tanned abdomen.

It was evident that Pia was marking Rika's appreciation. A smile grew on her lips. 'Perhaps I'd keep the secret,' she said, her voice teasing this time. 'And perhaps I would reveal it. Depends on how much I was paid.' It took a moment for Rika to realise she was joking. She wasn't sure if she appreciated the humour but, as Pia lay a friendly hand beneath Rika's loose shirt to her bare shoulder, she felt the urge she had had before on shore: the wish for Pia to stick her hands down her breeches right then and there, discovery or not, and rub open her wet sex, slide in her hand, easing through the heat.

'No, I wouldn't tell your secrets,' Pia said in a serious tone. 'I believe in more than fragile promises and it's clear that you do, too. It was wrong of me to tempt you.' On the word 'tempt', Rika felt Pia's hands on either side of her buttocks. The heat rose up through her belly and ribcage to a spot below her breasts. The moment seemed interminable; the moment before Pia slipped her hands under the waist of the garment and beneath the fabric.

She touched the smooth skin of Rika's buttocks, caressing Rika's skin as if it were the most precious and delicate silk, her hands sliding up under the curve of her buttocks to the cleft of her hot and beating wet sex.

'I knew you'd be wet for me, Rika. Ingrid's described you in some detail before, you know,' Pia said in her thick low voice, and Rika realised that the tall woman had already known the answers to her questions. But how on earth had she become privy to the details – not only of her name, the pendant and the blood-oath but the fact that Rika became, frequently and easily, wet? Because if that was what Ingrid was spreading around, it was hardly a respectful way to talk about a dear and longed-for lover.

# TWO

Rika groaned involuntarily and then willingly pushed her wet centre back against the sailor's skilful, probing hands. Pia withdrew her moistened fingers, unfastened and pushed down her own breeches, speaking while she moved. 'You're wearing Ingrid's pendant, so that means you must be Ulrika Hansdóttir, usually known as Rika. What's the name of the other girl, then? The one that helped you?'

Rika still wasn't sure if she was in danger of exposure. 'Inge . . . Ingeleth.'

For a moment, Pia lay one hand lightly across Rika's tensed buttocks. 'No.' Her voice was firm. 'Tell me her real name. I know it anyway.' The tips of Pia's fingers prodded Rika's arse.

'Kadlin. But we call her Lina. Kadlin Thorsdóttir is her full name,' she finally told Pia. She wanted the sailor to shift her hand, to slide her fingers inside her. But Rika knew she had no advantage with which to barter: Pia had pried important information from her, but she knew nothing of Pia. 'And your family name? Your father's name is –?' she asked Pia, trying to overcome her desire for the woman.

The ship moved suddenly over a swelling wave, and the two women fell into each other, their bodies shoved tightly together.

Pia easily detached herself, but kept stroking her hands leisurely over Rika's arse. But Rika wanted her to reach down slowly to her pussy, part her folds, fuck her slowly and deeply. For a moment neither breathed. The waves moved, battering underneath the planks of the longboat.

'Gunnar,' she said. 'I am Perþ Gunnarsdóttir, Pia for short. Now we're well acquainted. Some women might not think so, but I like knowing women's names before a certain level of intimacy, myself. Don't you agree?' Pia laid one finger gently on Rika's neck, under her ear and moved it back and forth, pressing slightly.

Rika didn't answer. How did she know her sensitivity there? She cursed Pia silently, but hot tremors were beginning to run through her body, even with her flesh still exposed to the night.

'Don't you agree?' Pia whispered again. Then she leant forward and put her mouth to Rika's ear. She slowly licked the tender lower flesh of it and Rika trembled as a feeling rose stinging up from between her legs, a sexual excitement that made her feel like a burst fruit, an opened sweetmeat for this strange woman. She *wanted* to open herself, too; lie on her back with her legs spread wide open to show the woman her red juicy pussy, creamy and ripe; wanted to hear what Pia would say then. She wanted Pia to push back all subtle manoeuvres and fuck her and grind her. But something about dark-haired Pia's manner made her think she was not going to get it all at once.

She hated having to be patient. Rika's hips twitched unintentionally and she swayed back. Pia spread her fingers on either side of Rika's pale cheeks, digging into her. When she groaned at Rika's ear, sharp arousal shot through Rika, from her cunt to everywhere else on her body.

Pia turned Rika round so that she was sitting facing her. The waves lapped threateningly at the hull; a large wave hit and the boat shivered in the grasp of the salty greedy water. Rika closed her eyes and waited for the swell to pass.

'Rika, the daughter of knives. I know your father. Is that one of his knives on your belt?'

30

Knives. Sharpness. Heavy probing blades. At the thought of shining edges, Rika suddenly didn't care if the other crew members saw, but even so she somehow knew that they would not turn around. Pia slowly slid her curled hand into Rika's wet pussy and gradually filled the whole of her burning, twisting sex. Pleasure hit Rika, as the captain's whole hand paused in the warm tight inner bowl of her cunt. Voluptuous sensations turned quickly into shivers that slammed through her blood. Her throat was tight and dry with arousal; she was deaf and blind, her cunt swelling around the pressure of Pia's stiff yet flexing fist. She groaned.

'You like those words, little Rika? You like sharpness? Battle? War? It's not as pretty as you think.'

Fine, thought Rika, just move your hand. A hot ache rose deep in her cunt, tight around Pia's curled fingers. Pia kept her fist still, yet Rika's cunt trembled around the welcome invasion. She stayed her contractions and fought to keep herself from sliding on to Pia's hand. But her self-control failed her and she began to move wetly and tightly. Sweat broke on her brow, but Pia pushed her down further, her buttocks flat on the wooden slats. Rika could see Pia rubbing at her clit with her other hand.

'Fuck me,' she pleaded, hoping Pia would be as obedient as Lina had been. 'Move your hand.' But Pia did nothing. She was going to burst on Pia's hand; be split open when she came. A minute passed. Eventually, straining with the effort to keep control, Rika relinquished the semblance of power and laid her head on the bottom of the boat, her blonde hair piled on the floorboards around her, her back chilled by the damp boards. There was no doubt as to her own arousal. She was now definitely out of control. The boards against her back were coated in salt and scent; a sheen of sweat covered her neck and chest. Why didn't Pia move her fist? Perspiration began to moisten all of Rika's body, dripping down her back, slick and hot. She felt like she was being fucked by Thor's velvet-covered hammer. Pia had to begin soon.

Her hand still up to its wrist in Rika's pussy, Pia stroked a
finger along the board near Rika's head and brought it to Rika's
lips. Rika flicked her tongue against Pia's finger and tasted
wetness and salt. Her patience was quickly fading. 'Please move
your hand,' she told Pia.

'Quiet.' Pia shifted her closed hand deeply inside Rika and
Rika bit her lip to keep silent, the blood like sweet and itching
iron in her mouth. For a moment she was filled by the whole
deep push of Pia's hand and then she was lost and empty again.
Pia began to move her fist thickly within her. She tightened on
Pia's hand; she became smooth like honey for Pia; she became
liquid for her; each rhythmic movement of Pia's knuckles pushed
her to the quick. Rika began to feel little climaxes each new
time Pia's fist shifted deep inside; she began to purr for the
sensation like a spoilt pet. Inside her Pia reached a sweet spot
with her movements, and this spot teased and fondled and
pushed and began to spill over within her. She was so wet. Was
Pia just as excited? She groaned, thinking of what the oarswoman's soft wet quim would feel like on her fingers.

'I said, keep quiet.'

Pia begin to speed up, bucking into a rhythm which Rika
eventually caught, as she put her fingers to her own clit and
rubbed it while Pia slowly fucked her. When her sighs grew too
loud, Pia clasped her hand over her mouth. In all her senses Rika
could only feel Pia; she was oblivious to anything else and this
was how she came for her: with the dark-haired sailor's hand
thick in her. Dizzy with pleasure, she ground on Pia's fingers
and her whole body tightened on the wood that supported her,
stayed tense and then finally released. As Pia carefully withdrew
her hand, Rika fell completely back on the weathered boards of
the ship. She exhaled deeply, her heart racing.

'Put your hands on me, Rika.' Pia spoke in her ear and leant
with her back on the rim of the boat, facing Rika. Rika placed
her hands on the other woman's wet bursting cunt, feeling Pia's
need as palpably as the dew that flowed over her fingers. Pia
came closer and Rika knelt and put her mouth upon the sailor

for just a second, tonguing the moisture, before drawing several inches away. Her heart was still beating frantically but she felt herself begin to melt in arousal all over again. 'Pia? Do you want me to –' Her voice was too loud, her words hoarse with arousal.

'Quietly, Rika,' the captain hissed. The admonishment made Rika blush with fury, but she contained herself. She placed her hands against the worn creases of the leather breeches already pushed down to Pia's knees, balancing herself against the other woman. The tip of her pink tongue tingled and her mouth watered. Supported by the boat frame, the huge red dragonhead rising up behind her, Pia fell back slightly, her legs wide open. Rika pushed her face up to Pia's sex again and felt the milky, sticky dew of the woman's pussy, the soft skin of her thighs. She wanted to take this cunt in her mouth and smother herself in it, bury herself in its rich, warm taste and in the pleasure of sucking and of moving her lips over a woman's wet sex. She ran her tongue over the folds of Pia's juicy inner lips, enjoying the sounds Pia made as she moved her mouth over her. She licked her deeply, tonguing and sucking at the captain's proud, stiff little clit. Pia groaned again and Rika felt it deep in the pit of her.

The boat glided on in the dawn. With Pia standing up above her, Rika tried again a slow and delicate moist lick at Pia's clit. Then open-mouthed, she explored and drank the sweet, sweet flow caught in her sex-lips. She had forgotten how she loved the taste of cunt; she had not tasted it since Ingrid left. She licked Pia like this purposefully, releasing at times the pressure of her mouth entirely so that Pia might feel the absence of pleasure and crave it all the more. When she worked this movement up, she slid her lips around the hard bead of Pia's clit and softly sucked in a slow rough rhythm, back and forth across her clit. Pia reacted by jerking and pushing her wet sex in Rika's face.

Rika surreptitiously ground the palm of one hand against her own mound. She stirred herself up this way, so that when her speed hastened on Pia's deliciously wet, tiny warm organ, she aroused herself in a complementary sweet drumming. When

Pia's whole cunt pulsed and trembled in Rika's mouth like a throat about to speak, Rika dissolved around her pussy, her mouth melting on to Pia as spasms began to grow intensely inside her and then, lingeringly, grew fainter as she continued to suck the woman. Rika's heart pounded and she came quickly. Pia's body rippled to savour every tiny movement, every variation of Rika's lips and every nuance of Rika's tongue against the sensitive swells of her honey-wet sex, until she was satisfied, too. Time slowed and Rika could smell the salt in the air again before they separated.

'Are you all right?' Pia asked.

But there were tears in Rika's eyes. Everything in her perception had swung round. Something hard within her had been broken for no discernible reason. Breathing in the fresh sea air as if for the first time, she didn't immediately notice that Pia had her arm across her face and had turned away from Rika. She looked at Pia and marked her wet eyes, too.

Pia brought Rika's hand to her mouth and kissed the wetness on it. Then, for the first time, she gently lifted Rika's chin up and kissed her lips, so that Rika tasted Pia's juices once again; rich as melted butter. These gestures of tenderness moved her but, worried that she would begin to cry in earnest, Rika gave the dark-haired woman a small smile and turned her head away. The rowers behind them moved as they had always done.

Nothing had changed but everything had shifted. Rika could make out the slender, narrow rays of the morning sun overhead and the tiny knotted twine in Pia's rough-knitted shirt when Pia slipped it over her broad shoulders. She glanced at Pia, who looked as if she wanted to tell Rika something but then hesitated. Perhaps she was just shy, Rika thought – though she had not fucked as if she were a shy woman. Rika didn't know what she should be saying to Pia, but she looked her back in the eyes. A moment passed. Their bodies were close to each other. Pia pulled up her breeches and Rika did the same. But before Pia finished buttoning her shirt, Rika laid a hand on Pia's still-bare chest. Her breasts were beautiful. Rika felt warm. They were both completely silent.

'Rotate!' A voice called out impatiently to them at this moment. Rika barely had time to straighten Pia's shirt as an unfamiliar young woman made her way up the centre of the boat towards them. Rika understood she was to take her place, which she did, struggling to seat herself in the lower right-hand side of the boat and collect her thoughts.

She was not looking forward to her stint at the oars, and the difficulty and the force needed to row did not surprise her. Rika found herself glancing behind at the carved and brightly painted dragon figurehead leading the boat, distracted by the thought that Pia might be enjoying identical pleasures with her replacement. She let her oar drift for a moment while she touched Ingrid's stone around her neck to remind herself why she was making this journey. She had no cause to be jealous over what the dark-haired sailor did. The rower behind Rika muttered pointedly, evidently irritated that she was letting others bear the burden for her. So she took the oar again with greater strength.

After several hours had passed, Rika ventured to ask the woman behind her when they would reach Britain. She had heard before that it took several days and nights to reach, but she was unsure if her sources had been correct. The woman behind her laughed quietly as she told Rika the truth of the matter.

'It'll be a long trip to Britain, girl,' she said. 'I reckon you don't know much about navigation. We're on the way to the Gaul colony first and only after that Britain.'

'What are you saying?' Rika was upset but attempted to be stoic, as a Viking sailor might be. 'I was told we were sailing to Britain.' Her arms ached; she wanted to rest from the endless rowing.

'Oh, we are, eventually,' the sailor assured her. 'But first we sail to the coast of Gaul.' She laughed again. 'We were desperate for a full boat; Pia's paid more that way. Maybe you didn't get the whole story.'

'No, I didn't,' Rika said, and then sullenly stopped speaking to the woman. Damn Lina, she should have paid more attention when she signed Rika up. It was too late to protest or to demand an explanation; she had heard terrible things about what happened to those that attempted arguments or questioned authority in the middle of the sea. She consoled herself with the thought that, after Gaul, they would be eventually be sailing to Britain and Ingrid.

But under her irritation, she was secretly excited: she had never been more than two days' journey from her home and now she was en route to faraway Gaul and after that Britain. Both of these lands were mysterious, exotic places she only had heard of in the sea-tales that the sailors brought home. Now she would see them for herself. Still, for several hours she nursed her spoiled dreams of immediately seeing Ingrid, before grudgingly admitting to herself that the extra wait would make their reunion even more poignant.

The rest of the journey to Gaul was uninspiring, broken only by the appearance of a ship of their people – returning warriors. The ships drew up alongside each other for a short period, Pia exchanging words with the leader.

There had been a great battle in Britain against Godwinsson, the leader of the Saxons, they said. When Pia asked how the great Norwegian king Hardradra had fared, they said that they had left early, but that they were sure he had fared well. The all-male crew looked sorely beaten, but after they drew away no more was said of them. In Rika's heart she wished them only good speed homeward, for they had a look of haggard exhaustion on them that made her feel guilty for objecting to fatigue from mere rowing. And to her disappointment, the episode with Pia was not repeated. In fact, Rika was made to work exceedingly hard over the two remaining days on the boat. She began to wonder if she had merely imagined the occasion in her head, but Pia's reticent manner reminded her that it had not been her imagination. Still, she was thankful that Pia had decided to hold her tongue regarding her identity even if there were no more occasions between them that indicated physical or emotional interest on either part. There was certainly nothing to indicate that shared moment of tearful intimacy after their coming-together. Yes, Rika decided, it was better that way.

On the third day and after what had been termed by all experienced sailors an abnormally peaceful crossing, they neared the rocky coasts of the Gaul colony. The morning sky was grey, with the pale-pink tinge of dawn. Rika's heart rose to see the shore, as she was tired of the monotony of sea. Although she had been complimented on her increasing navigational skills, by now she only wanted to step off the boat and wade towards the shore. As soon as the opportunity arose, she did so with several other first-time sailors who were overenthused to set foot on land. There was some sniggering behind her over her haste, but if the other sailors thought she was eager to be on land once more – well, they were right.

They were greeted by the distant cousins of their people, some of whom still spoke an oddly accented version of Rika's own tongue. For the most part, they spoke amongst themselves in the Gaul words. They had been there for generations and were becoming more like a separate people than true Norsepeo-ple, though they still called themselves by that name and the colony itself – Normandy – retained the name of the original settlers. Rika recognised her own family name amongst several of them and knew them to be cousins several times removed, but of course she could not reveal herself as to who she, in truth, was.

Rika was led to a bed consisting of little more than some hay spread in a one-woman tent and a horse-blanket; she later learnt that this was actually a privilege of sorts, since she had been placed in proximity to the tent of William the Dispossessed himself. Even Rika had heard the tales of how William had been cheated of his rightful title by the liar Saxon ruler Harold God-winsson. The truth was the stories had never much interested her, but now that she was to sleep in William's own camp she was slightly more intrigued. Or she would be after a full day's sleep, followed by another night to sleep as well. Still, she was glad of the bed: all other accommodation had already been filled by the other sea-women and her lodging was an afterthought.

She stripped off all of her clothes outside, giving little thought as to whether she was watched or not. She crawled in and covered herself with the rough blanket, pulled it over her naked body and fell asleep, using her crumpled clothing for a pillow.

She awoke first in what must have been early morning, since light was filtering through the tent; she had slept a day and a night. She stretched out and let the sieved sunlight flicker on her bare body. It felt wonderful to be off the boat. She didn't know exactly where the rest of the sailors were, but she was sure that she did not envy them. Perhaps they had forgotten to wake her; if this was the case, then it was fine with her. She could hear several birds and she knew that it would be chilly outside in the early autumnal dawn. Inside the tent, however, it was deliciously cosy. Light shone through, turning deep red and casting a warm diffused glow over the entire interior of her tiny shelter, and her skin drank in the sun.

She must have dozed off again, because when she next awoke the light had a different quality to it. She had no idea how long she had been asleep this time, but the tent had become quite warm; she was thankful that she had taken off her clothes. It had been an extravagant sensation to sleep nude and not feel the rocking of the boat, her necklace her only concession to clothing. The jewel on her pendant glowed in reflection of the sheer rosy walls. She fingered the little carving on it and then decided to get up. Unsure of what hour in the day it was, Rika now felt that it was best to dress and go immediately searching for the other crewwomen from the boat. It felt good to have slept for so long, but she didn't want to lose her place to Britain.

In the cramped tent, she knelt on the hay to pick up her clothes. She then dressed too quickly, her shirt catching on the gem around her neck. The pendant always got in the way. Rika removed the necklace, turning the pendant over in her hands.

Again she tried to make out the runic markings Ingrid had said were particular to her family. Several sticklike characters of the *futhark* runic alphabet, burnt into the glassy red surface of the gem. Rika traced the tiny letters – she did not recognise them from her limited studies – with the curve of her fingernail. She wished she had asked Ingrid what they meant at the time she received it.

But she still thought it beautiful and this was why she loved to touch it. The setting of the gem was silver. She lay back on the hay and lightly touched the metal curls, admiring their polish and sheen. Ingrid must have loved her greatly to give her a possession of such craftsmanship. She fell on her back and looked up at the joined peak of the tent ceiling, wondering when she would next see her Ingrid, then recalled that Pia seemed to have had knowledge of the gift, judging from her comments on the ship. She would seek out Pia, she decided, and find out more. She looked at the ceiling of the tent again, running her fingers over the pendant.

When she heard a small click from the pendant, she sat up abruptly, worried that she had broken the gift. But she had only pushed what seemed to be a small clasp on its setting; one of the silver curls seemed to act as a catch. It was strange that she had never noticed it before. She crawled closer to the tent-flap that threw shafts of light through the space; she wanted to look at it carefully and she needed more light. She peered at the pendant in her palm. It seemed to function as a locket; there was something inside its hollows, beneath the red gem. It was half-filled with ash, Rika saw as she held it up to the light, and she dipped into the grey ash with her smallest finger.

She rubbed the ash between her thumb and forefinger. She turned the pendant over and looked at the detailed engraving. Rika pressed and the pendant clicked shut without spilling a flake of ash. She then tried to loosen it again, but it was more difficult this time. It was stuck.

Well, she could not do anything about it now. It looked just the same as it had before, the little figure of Freyr shining in clear relief against the ruby-coloured stone. She briefly wondered why the gem might contain the burnt cinders, but she had no time to think about this; she had to find Pia and ask her some important questions. She braided her hair quickly, placed the necklace of ashes around her throat and went out in the hot afternoon sun. She saw a group of sailors some distance away and started walking towards them.

'Lina!'

Startled, Rika broke her stride and turned around, half-blinded by the intense sunrays shafting through the camp. Two women were walking towards her: blue-eyed Pia, looking confused; and a giant of a woman, a chiselled and tall blonde Viking, looking very angry indeed.

'Ingrid?' Rika couldn't believe whom she was seeing. 'Ingrid?' Then joy filled her and she began to run towards her, forgetting Pia at Ingrid's side. She reached Ingrid and threw her arms around her, but Ingrid snarled at her.

'You little bitch! What are you doing here?' Ingrid pushed Rika away from her so forcefully that Rika stumbled in the dirt.

'What?'

'I said, what are you doing here? Or have you lost your tongue, Lina?' Ingrid's whole massive body moved towards her; Rika shuddered as Ingrid grabbed her chin and dragged her up so she could see Rika's face. Rika was filled with horror; why was Ingrid saying this to her?

'Rika?' Both of Ingrid's great palms were straddling her face; she felt like a giant were holding her. An evil giant, a huge, crazy woman – what had become of her Ingrid? Ingrid's eyes flashed down at the pendant, and her face was cruel and arrogant. 'Is that you, Rika?'

Rika nodded, terrified. Her face was covered in dirt. Ingrid's terrible expression softened, but she still held her face just as tightly. Rika's eyes moved to Pia, but even she seemed helpless in the face of Ingrid's strength. This was a warrior-Ingrid she was seeing, and before she had only known the lover.

'What are you doing here, Rika? Why here in Gaul? Answer

me!' She shook Rika before releasing her face, and Rika fell forward. She could not bear to look at Ingrid. She had made a terrible mistake. 'Answer me, Rika!'

'I wanted to see you,' Rika said. 'So I tried to travel by boat to Britain.' Humiliated, she began to feel her own anger rising.

'And what about this?' Jerking her by its chain, Ingrid shoved her pendant in front of her face, then grabbed at Rika's left hand. 'I gave you this, Rika. We have a blood-oath between us, remember?'

'I know . . . I wanted to see you.' Why did she care about something so trivial anyway, when Rika herself was here? Rika stood up defiantly and brushed herself off. She avoided Pia's blue gaze; she didn't want her to see her so helpless before Ingrid. 'Why are *you* here, Ingrid? And why did you think I was Lina, and why in Freyja's name would you be so cruel to her, anyway? If you've found out about us, then it was my idea anyway –' She stopped herself. This couldn't be about jealousy. There was no way Ingrid could have known about Lina. Unless Pia had reported it to her?

'No.' Something shifted in Ingrid's eyes. 'No, Rika. You're right; you don't have to explain anything.' Her face melted into kindness. She looked only good and kind and noble, and as if she had always been so. 'I'm sorry, Rika. I thought you were someone else.'

'Lina? Lina from the village?'

'No, Rika, a different Lina. A Swede from Rusland.'

'But I look like Lina from my village. I'm sure that's why you mistook –'

'No.' Ingrid's voice was patient. 'Rika, Lina is no rare name, nor is there any scarcity of fair-haired girls with that name. It's just an odd coincidence, that's all. This woman, the Lina I knew from Rusland, owed me something – money – and now I see it wasn't her. I'm sorry that you had to bear my anger, Rika. Please accept my apologies.' Rika stared at Ingrid with a new-growing terror. This was much worse than her anger – why was she so formal and cold with her?

41

'Ingrid?' Rika pressed a hand to her strong forearm. The whole length of Ingrid's body was tanned and burnished by battle oil. She wore the short clothing of a female Viking berserker and the exposed blonde hair on her legs was also bleached by salt and sun. 'Ingrid? Are you angry with me for some reason?'

Pia averted her eyes and walked away. Rika watched her for a moment before turning back to Ingrid. Well, Pia couldn't expect Rika's loyalties to switch to her so quickly. She had sworn blood-oaths to Ingrid and nothing to Pia. And nothing had been promised Rika by Pia, either.

Ingrid's face darkened as she watched Pia's departure. She glanced down at the pendant she had given to Rika and it was obvious she had come to a decision. 'Let's walk by the sea,' she said to Rika in much warmer tones. 'There's something I wish to discuss with you.' She touched the nape of Rika's neck and stroked one calloused finger across her soft skin, rasping across the delicate hairs. Hard fingers. Fingers of thick, uneven iron.

Rika felt unbidden lust rush through her as her body remembered Ingrid's hands, their hot purpose when they had sought her out before, the way the lips of her plump sex had parted for Ingrid previously, hot and swollen against Ingrid's hard broad hands when she had dipped her fingers into Rika. She remembered how her own sex had looked and how Ingrid had showed it to her, made her lean down and look at it, wet and pink and tender against the back of Ingrid's tan hands. Ingrid had licked at her sex in the woods, had sucked Rika's dew from her fingers, had rammed her hands into Rika's pussy and mounted her on heat. Rika looked up into Ingrid's pale eyes and remembered the tastes and scents of that afternoon. The afternoon Ingrid had given her the pendant. She wanted the Ingrid of that afternoon back, hot and heavy against her.

'Let's walk to the cliffs together,' Ingrid repeated. She was looking at Rika with an expression of mixed lust and trepidation. Yes, Rika would get her Ingrid back. The lust in Ingrid always ran its course. However she had changed, Rika doubted she had changed that much.

They reached the cliffs, where Ingrid stopped to scan the sea. Rika leant back against the chalky stone. She couldn't help her attraction to Ingrid; Ingrid's animal sexuality probed far deeper in her than she cared to admit. When she looked at Ingrid, she tasted iron on her tongue; Ingrid reminded her of those days of coarse, heavy sex, of sex-flushes red on her throat and chest. She reminded Rika of iron. Yes, iron – with its salty flat bite against her skin. When she was a child, she would pick up the little chips of slag her father left behind and suck them to feel the metal mix with her saliva and bite her throat. The first time Ingrid had kissed her back home in the woods she had felt the same: the flow in her wet mouth had mixed with iron. Kissing Ingrid was like kissing something rich with blood; like the hot slaughter of animals, Ingrid had somehow got into Rika's blood and stayed there, too.

For a moment, she thought uncomfortably of Lina, whom she had left so abruptly. Kissing Lina had been the same as biting a little berry – sweet but ultimately unsatisfying, like a little taste of honey before a feast. But the first kiss with Ingrid had been biting something living, tasting the blood warm and delicious streaming through her teeth. Ingrid had showed her how rich and bright life could be. And even if she was wrong concerning Ingrid, how could she say goodbye to her so soon? Ingrid was the sole reason she had made this journey. How could she go out aimless in the world, with no goals? She would have to trust Ingrid. Ingrid's blood still flowed rich within her.

Ingrid leant over Rika, pressing her against the flat shale, her mass hulking and dwarfing Rika. She picked up Rika's left hand and turned it so she saw the back of it. She touched the narrow white scar on it. The blood-oath. It was always the same, always as if Ingrid could read her thoughts.

'Are you sure that you remember your promise, Rika?'

'Yes,' Rika answered. 'A blood-oath is exactly what it is – a blood-oath. And you know I would not break one, Ingrid. When you ask whatever it is you have to ask of me, at that time I will do it. I have worn your necklace ever since, as you can see.' She thought briefly of her father stealing it, and of Lina removing it and rubbing it on her, then put those thoughts from her mind.

'Good.' Ingrid strung out the sound till the word sounded like a slow question. Rika's face began to show heat; her thoughts were not where they should be.

'Very good,' Rika countered, reaching up and touching one finger to the pulse of Ingrid's throat. Iron. She was an iron woman. Ingrid looked as if she were gathering her strength for some mammoth task: she stood with both fists clenched, her light eyes squeezed tight. Was she not responding because Rika had lost her touch with her, or because she was fighting the temptation Rika presented? Rika had to find out. But why would she fight a temptation? She loved Rika, didn't she?

Rika stepped forward under Ingrid and rose on her toes to lick at her throat, the salt and sweat of her in Rika's mouth, the sweet musk of Ingrid entering her body. She wanted to eat Ingrid up. She ran her tongue under the blonde warrior's jaw. Her rough skin abraded Rika's lips. Iron in Rika's mouth, blood-metal in her mind. That's what she wanted.

Ingrid still didn't react.

Rika put her little finger on her pendant and glanced at the rune. She rubbed her scar against it, secretly. 'Promises,' she mouthed against Ingrid's skin, the nape of her neck. The sexual blonde fur of it. The flesh of Rika's chafing sex-lips moistened; her nipples grew hard. Iron.

'No,' she thought she heard Ingrid answer. She did not know if Ingrid had heard her invocation. Ingrid grabbed Rika's hands and cuffed them with her rough fingers, her rings digging into Rika's flesh. Ah, yes. Ingrid was finally returning to her. Her Ingrid, her lover.

'You'll pay for the games you play some day, Rika,' Ingrid hissed at her as she threw her back against the slate. Rika smiled inwardly; she knew she was joking. Rika easily unwrenched her wrists from Ingrid, whose fingers had become limp. Ingrid seemed helpless for a moment before her, but Rika knew that soon she would solidify again.

She gripped at Ingrid's fire-gold sheaths of hair and pulled her down to her, her fingers crinkling in the texture of Ingrid's salt-bleached strands. Yes. She wanted to smell the salt on her. Her Viking.

'You want to kiss me, don't you?' Rika snarled; Ingrid's mouth drew close to hers. How she loved this game. 'You want to kiss me.' It was an unequivocal statement this time.

With a sigh, as if she had indeed lost a game, Ingrid pressed her mouth to Rika's. Hot metal in Rika's mouth. She bit Ingrid's tongue and tasted blood. Her teeth were knives and they kissed and kissed while Ingrid's hand travelled down her body, running over the tight nipples of her breasts, rubbing against her crotch. Ingrid broke the kiss and Rika let her hands rest hot in Ingrid's hair, her salt-encrusted blondeness so coarse against Rika's soft palms. Rika's sex itched.

Then Ingrid kissed her again. This time Rika did not request it and she felt Ingrid's tongue probe her and she rubbed her hips against her. Iron. Metal. Blood. Ingrid took one hand and ripped her breeches apart. Rika grew wet as she heard the fabric tearing. Ingrid grasped both her wrists in one massive hand and pressed her hard against the slate rocks of the cliffs. Yes. Ingrid should plunge her other hand within Rika, now. That would be right. Hot and tight inside her. Her thick rough fingers smeared with Rika's liquid. Raw. Yes.

Ingrid grabbed her own crotch and showed herself to Rika before she thrust her hand into the younger woman, half-embarrassed, Ingrid's hard clit so thick and pulsing and drenched above her wet, salty cunt. Rika could see how much Ingrid needed her. Ingrid pushed inside her with one hand and kept Rika's hands pinioned in the other; Rika's cunt twisted to let in more of Ingrid. Hot iron. Rika was smelting inside herself; she was all the metals poured inside her pussy and she was slippery on Ingrid's hand. Her arms still fastened as Ingrid drove in her, her salt-hair falling between them. Rika moved her mouth and caught Ingrid's hair in it, tore at it.

Ingrid growled, the sound of a beast, and released Rika's hands to grab a breast and thrust deeper inside her. Bronze and iron, silver, gold; Ingrid seemed to melt in a thousand shiny colours before Rika's eyes. With no finesse at all, she rubbed a rough hand on Rika's clit, but it worked nevertheless. Rika felt the metal she had envisioned surging through her bloodstream; felt poisoned with Ingrid's heavy bloodlust and she screamed in delight as Ingrid pumped her, fucked her all the way over to the other side of the blade in Rika's mind.

Ingrid was hard thick metal; Rika squirmed on her after she came to keep her there inside her, but Ingrid was becoming once more flesh, soft and vulnerable. And did she love that in Ingrid, too?

Hidden behind a nearby rock, Pia watched the coupling between the two women. She was half-convinced that Ingrid's aim had been to murder Rika, but couldn't prove it and this sight hardly seemed good evidence. Though it would have been premature; Ingrid was sure to have future uses for the girl. Watching had left Pia dry-mouthed with an uneasy combination of envy and arousal. She slowly walked the cliff path back to camp, kicking at rocks as she went along, twisting her dark hair in consternation. She'd have to keep her eye on things. If there was one thing she knew for certain, it was that whoever wore Ingrid's gem was certainly in danger.

# THREE

Ingrid's temporary living area was far better placed than Pia's own – set right next to William's own encampment, where the grey-sheathed tents of those who held high rank stretched out in the rain-full Norman sky. It was still only sprinkling, but the luminous quality of the horizon made Pia suspect that they would all soon be drenched. Ingrid's quarters were higher up than the crew tents of the Loki and trenches had been dug which ensured a vast pool dripping down to where Pia and the rest were confined. Ingrid would remain high and dry. But then she always did, didn't she?

Curse the woman! Pia's head was pounding. She slammed her hand flat against her broadsword, which only resulted in that now her hand ached, too, as she walked up to the hall where the meeting had been called. She rubbed at her stinging fingers and at the nearly faded but still peculiar scar on the back of her left hand. She would be enduring far more pain than mere stings once they reached Britain – if she were lucky enough to survive the battle.

Less than half an hour ago, Rika and Ingrid had returned from the cliffs. Ingrid had looked somewhat grim, but Rika had been flushed and giggling. They had stayed on the cliffs for most of the afternoon by Pia's reckoning and she could feel jealousy biting at her. If only Ingrid had not sailed down to counsel William, Pia would have had a chance to tell Rika some of the truth about Ingrid, and maybe angle out a little information from Rika, as well. Discover how deep her loyalties to Ingrid lay. But no, once again Ingrid had pre-empted her, and she had to keep quiet, or else risk the taste of Ingrid's sharp sword – an act she was eager to avoid.

'Pia. I'm sorry our conversation was broken off earlier. I was . . . distracted.' Pia had been so preoccupied she hadn't seen Ingrid coming. With calculated affability, the blonde woman joined Pia's steps up to the meeting-hall.

'That's all right. Your business was obviously pressing.' She tried unsuccessfully to keep a bitter tone from entering her words.

'Oh, come now, Pia; don't be like that.' Ingrid halted for a moment, reaching out a conciliatory hand to Pia's shoulder. She brushed blonde hair-strands out of her face, a surprisingly girlish gesture. 'A lass is only a lass, but a friend's for ever, right?' She playfully punched Pia on the shoulder.

'Right,' Pia said tersely, wondering if Ingrid would have used the same words seven years ago. 'What have you decided, then? Are you sailing back up the east coast or the west?'

But they had reached the meeting-hall where William was to speak, and Ingrid had no chance to answer.

The hall was vast and the many torches glowing red in wall-niches sent out trembling streams of hot light into the cavern of the dark main room. The effect was odd shadows on all of the hundred or so professional fighters present, light flickering on faces, so what few expressions which could be seen were mutable; emotions could not be verified. It was not an environment that lent trust. Not that Pia trusted Ingrid anyway. Right from the beginning, Ingrid had hoped that Pia would die in the battles the Crew undertook – but Pia had hung on for seven years. And the blonde warrior could not merely kill her: it would be too obvious.

Ingrid lay a comradely arm around Pia's shoulders as they sat down on the oak benches near the front of the hall, before a table empty of drink. The roar of discussion made it difficult to hear Ingrid, but she made it clear to Pia that they were now the best of friends as far as she was concerned. Better drinking friends than drinking enemies, Pia thought, and then looked round for something with which to toast.

'Of course we've got to stick together, you and I,' Ingrid was saying in her ear, while simultaneously charming a serving-girl closer with a wink and a smile. 'We've got a bit of history, it's true; and I know you've let me down before. But it's hard to stand up to the men here, and my Crew has fought long and hard to gain respect as fighting women.' Pia knew this was true; this was one of the reasons she'd first joined the Crew herself. Of course, the other reason was that because of the scar on her left hand it had been impossible for her to stay in Norway.

A blushing young girl placed two frothing glass mugs full of spinning amber liquid before them. Pia bent over the beverage – it smelt like ale, but after an experimental sip she realised that the froth continued to swirl even in her mouth. She took a deep swallow, decided she liked it, and turned to share her observations with Ingrid. But Ingrid had already swallowed down the full mug and was bellowing for more.

Pia looked at her for several moments and something that felt like nostalgia passed through her. Ingrid's face was caught between a definition of handsome and beautiful, and even Pia could understand that it would be difficult to resist a woman with such a devilish sparkle in her eye – Ingrid with her beautifully high colouring; her flushed cheeks; the shine caught in the twists of the long glossy blonde braid that hung over her jerkin. And, what's more, as if further blessed by the gods, Ingrid's timing was always cocksure. It was hard to resist a confident woman and the current proof was the giggling of the serving-girl as Ingrid whispered in her ear. Ingrid's expression was serious and respectful as she looked the girl in the eyes, holding her hand sincerely and presenting flattering clichés as if they were heartfelt inspirations.

Pia watched the coal-glow catch the sparkle in Ingrid's eyes as she bewitched the dark-haired girl. Surprisingly, she felt a flicker of excitement deep down in her sex – she had thought she was far past that with Ingrid. She sighed and looked down at her empty mug, placing her hand round it and tilting the reflecting glass towards Ingrid and the laughing girl, then back towards herself. The images swerved until they blended together and Pia fought to keep back the tears swimming in her eyes.

Meanwhile, Rika sat in Ingrid's quarters, thankful that she had been allowed better shelter than her own meagre tent just as the rain began to fall. She felt giddy, almost deliriously happy. She stretched out her arms and lay back on the width of Ingrid's mattress. She didn't know how long the meeting that Ingrid was attending would last, but it did not matter. It was blissful to have some time to herself in such spacious surroundings.

The bed was enormous, low and cushioned on all sides, and it was luscious to feel the shimmery cool of wolf-fur against her flesh as she lay there. To her right stood a large upright mirror framed with carved and painted silver. Every time she moved her head, glitter and sparkle shot forth from the richly engraved border.

The temptation to look at herself was overpowering and at last Rika gave in. She crossed the room, briefly regarded herself in the mirror and then looked at the mirror itself. There were two carved and brightly painted figures depicted: one was female but for an enormous phallus that rose up from her; she/he sucked on the fingers of the other, who looked to be a sleeping female with no additional appendages. Both were vibrant with paint that detailed strange fusions of blue breasts, green torsos and red limbs. Their limbs were elongated and contorted in the customary Viking design, becoming trees and even other body parts. Rika tried to trace one figure's long leg through to its source, but it was too confusing. They were meant to be gods, she was sure, but she didn't know which gods. She couldn't think of even one male deity who had breasts – nor a goddess with a cock, for that matter.

She dropped her hand; there was a much more interesting object present. Near the mirror was a small metal box. Lying on top of it was a name-chain which she picked up, spelling out the rune characters. *Arje*. She said the word to herself, but the soft syllables slurred in her throat. She hung the chain on the back of the mirror and then picked up the box it had been resting on. Inside was a variety of little glass pots of fantastic colours and several thin-bristled brushes. Any colour she could imagine was there – blood-red, robin-egg blue, green and the glittering half-colours of metals: golds, silvers, bronzes, coppers.

She touched the lid of each in turn, before picking up a scarlet little pot that looked like it could be rouge. She wet her finger in her mouth, unscrewed its lid and touched the bright crimson colour to her bottom lip. She rubbed her lips together. Although both male and female Vikings frequently wore eye make-up, it was usually only the very wealthy who wore colour to shine their lips, and in the mirror she looked like a rich woman, powerful and seductively decadent. In the rain-dappled tent, Rika touched her lips softly and smudged the colour. Her cheeks flamed as bright as her mouth. She trembled and took a step back to look in the mirror, feeling only a little guilty for burrowing in Ingrid's belongings.

What she saw was a young woman, whose high colour in her cheeks matched the flush spread over her chest. There it was again, what Ingrid called a sex-flush. It was left over from the cliffs, she told herself. She heard a murmur of voices outside the tent and snapped shut the open box on the floor, replacing the name-chain as she had found it. Wiping her mouth on her sleeve, she hurried to the bed.

The tent door pushed open. Ingrid and Pia walked into the room. Both of their faces were taut with excitement and Rika wondered whether the meeting with William had been successful.

'Hello.' She greeted both women, rising from the bed.

'Hello, Rika.' Only Ingrid answered. Whether due to jealousy or not, Pia didn't meet her eyes. 'We're setting sail in the next several hours, little Rika. Are you going to miss me?' Ingrid strode towards Rika and confidently kissed her full on the lips. Rika noticed several long strands of dark hair on Ingrid's collar. Were they Pia's? 'Are you going to miss me or not?' Ingrid persisted.

Rika broke away from Ingrid's embrace, unsettled by the ludicrous thought of Pia and Ingrid as lovers. 'Aren't I setting sail, too?' She searched for Pia's reaction to the kiss, but Pia was gazing away at the mirror in the other corner of the room, seemingly preoccupied. Rika turned back to Ingrid, but Ingrid's handsome face had darkened. She had already turned from Rika and was busy with the removal of her boots.

'What've you got in that flask on that belt of yours, Pia?' Ignoring Rika, Ingrid addressed Pia across the room. 'Have you smuggled in some Turkish rum? Are you ready to share it?' Pia didn't respond, and when Rika looked over to see why, she marked that Pia's face was grim.

'Where did you get the mirror, Ingrid?' Pia asked softly.

Ingrid smiled. 'It was a gift from a Norman artisan, someone who had been all the way to Norway to see the rites and had such fond memories she carved it in remembrance. Why – do you like it, Pia? Are you regretting that you missed your chance?'

Rika's head bobbed between the two, bewildered by their strange references. They were discussing old battles, she decided. Sailors and warriors did that type of thing.

'And what's this?' Pia was striding towards Ingrid, in her palm the name-chain that Rika had hung over the mirror.

Bootless but formidable, Ingrid rose to face Pia. Rika stood in the centre of the room, unsure of where to look. By now she felt not only confused, but also angry. What was going on?

'An already answered question is a waste of breath.' Ingrid stared levelly at Pia.

A moment passed and then, with a curse, Pia walked quickly out of the tent, flinging the name-chain down on the floor. Rika felt tentatively at her own pendant around her neck.

There was a silence, which Ingrid broke with a forced laugh. She moved to Rika swiftly and placed a hand on Rika's hip. 'Well, to bed, then.' She put her lips against the fair hairs on the nape of Rika's neck and brushed her lips against Rika's skin, nuzzling back and forth.

Rika could feel the pressure of Ingrid's hand on the swell of her hip and it reminded her briefly of something. What was it? Ownership? Possession. Her father had showed her off with an equal amount of possession on the day that he had introduced her to the young fish-priest, before he asked her to let them speak privately together. Yet warmth was moving through Rika's body, as Ingrid's lips made her neck tingle.

'Ingrid?'

'Yes?' Ingrid murmured against Rika's neck.

'Whose name is that on the name-chain?'

'No one, really.' Ingrid slid her hands up to Rika's ribcage and then down again, rubbing over the slight indentation of the little pit of Rika's navel. The rough skin of her hands scratched over Rika's smooth flesh; the sensation was pleasant. But then she removed Ingrid's hands, regretfully, and turned to face her.

'Then what about Lina? You thought I was Lina, didn't you, Ingrid? Why didn't you recognise me?'

Ingrid smiled a lazy, slow-growing smile. 'Well, Rika. I had asked you to wait for me at home, so of course I knew it couldn't be you. Like I said, it was a simple mistake.'

'You've slept with her, haven't you?' Rika's bottom lip was trembling and she bit it, hard.

'I may have, Rika. I've slept with many maids named Lina.' Ingrid's eyes twinkled wickedly.

'You know precisely what I mean, Ingrid! Lina, from my village. The one who looks like me.'

'Oh, *that* Lina. The little inn-girl. No, Rika, I've not slept with her. A bit too demure for my tastes. Though it shouldn't bother you, really, if I had.'

'No, I suppose not.' Rika was gulping a little to keep from crying. But it would matter, she knew. 'You've not said *how* you know her.'

'Oh, I'm just teasing you, Rika. You're inordinately jealous of your friend, aren't you? Well, her father boarded my Crew last spring. I remember we had a couple of good chats last summer, that's all. You even introduced us, as I recall. You do look similar, it's true; and of course, as I assumed you would keep your promise to wait for me in Norway, she was the only logical alternative. Of course, once I got close to you, I realised who you were. You're so much prettier, you know. Very pretty. I think so, anyway; I've thought so ever since last spring. Remember?' Ingrid drew the chain of Rika's jewel up to her lips and flickered her tongue on its clear red-slated facets.

Rika realised she was holding her breath, just inches away from Ingrid's eyes – the colour of spring skies back home in the village.

'Don't you, Rika? Don't you remember?'

'Of course I remember, Ingrid.' Rika closed her eyes. Was Ingrid going to kiss her now? But even with closed eyes, she could feel the release of the pendant, could feel Ingrid withdrawing.

'Good. And I've got another favour to ask you from your blood-oath, Rika.' Ingrid picked up the name-chain Pia had flung on the ground and shoved it into a satchel she took from underneath the bedding. Her muscles rippled from the slight movement as she bent to her task.

'But what about us?' Rika stared with admiration at Ingrid, her blonde Viking and the justly ordained leader of Ingrid's Crew.

'*Us?*' Ingrid's face was incredulous. She stopped stowing odd belongings into the satchel and crossed the floor to where Rika stood watching. 'Us? There's a war going on, you stupid little girl. A *war*. Do you not understand that?' She grabbed a double-bladed battle-axe from underneath the bedding and swiped the spectacularly shining blade several inches in front of Rika's face, causing Rika to flinch and step back – though she still steadily kept Ingrid's gaze. 'Chances are good that I'll be rotting carrion in a field next week with one of these stuck deep in my skull. Food for dogs and a nesting-place for flies. *War*, Rika. Do you understand?'

Rika felt paralysed, unable to speak. Her tongue was a numb stump in her mouth. She was afraid now, but not of Ingrid's descriptions of war horrors. She was afraid of the mad look in Ingrid's eye as she advanced and then retreated on Rika, and once Ingrid mentioned war she became afraid *for* Ingrid: afraid of the likelihood of her death. She swallowed hard, then croaked the answer that she assumed the warrior wanted. 'I understand.'

'Good.' The mad flicker left the pale icy-blue of Ingrid's eyes. She moved forward and placed both hands on Rika's shoulders. 'Then you must not follow me to Britain, Rika. You return home to Norway and wait for me. As I asked you to do according to your blood-oath. As an additional promise, you must leave within two days.'

For a moment, Rika tried to remember what it was that Pia had told her about blood-oaths on the boat. Rika wished she knew the rules better, but it was the first blood-oath she had ever given and she couldn't remember if you were allowed to add on promises to the original oath, as Ingrid was now doing. But Ingrid had made blood-oaths before, so Rika was sure she knew the rules.

'Why do you want me to leave you?' She had to ask because she wanted to be with Ingrid, to fight in Ingrid's Crew, in battle with Hardradra and William against the Saxons. And because she wanted Ingrid to want her as much as she wanted Ingrid.

'Because –' Ingrid gave an exasperated sigh, and fingered a tendril of twisted hair that had unravelled from the latticework of Rika's golden braids. 'Because I want to keep you safe from the war itself, Rika.'

'I'm not a little girl. I can fight and hold a sword, Ingrid.'

'Yes, I know.' Ingrid chuckled, and Rika was sure that she was remembering more than one occasion last summer in which Rika had bested her at swordplay. 'I know, Rika. But I must ask this of you, regardless. Within two days.' She pressed lightly on Rika's rune-scar. 'I know you would not break a blood-oath, Rika.'

Rika was silent for several seconds. She could hear her heart beating. 'No, I wouldn't break a blood-oath,' she finally answered. She felt depression seeping into her and with it the fear for Ingrid's safety again, but when she looked up, Ingrid wore a merry expression; her face had crinkled into a wide smile.

'Good, Rika.' Ingrid laid a spontaneous kiss on Rika's cheek. 'Good.' She returned to her task of throwing odds and ends into her war-satchel. After several seconds, she suddenly looked up, with an idea that had apparently just struck her. She retrieved the name-chain, looked at it and pointed her finger to the runic letters. 'When you return home, Rika, you must contact a woman named Arje in the village of Tallby. She's a friend of mine; she'll take care of you until I return. Blood-oath, Rika. Remember.' Ingrid cheerfully replaced the name-chain and finished throwing in the last of her clothes in the satchel. Rika felt a wave of – no, it couldn't be – what almost felt like irritation.

'Right, then.' Ingrid stood before Rika, satchel in hand, cumbersome with a multitude of clanking weapons, eyes eager and glowing, her stature tall and warrior-worthy. She clapped Rika on the shoulder and then gave her a quick peck on the cheek.

'Who is . . .' Rika broke off her question, looking at Ingrid with growing trepidation. Was she going already? Was this her goodbye?

But now Ingrid had walked past Rika to the door of the tent.

'Remember, Rika: *Arje*. In Tallby. And don't forget to blow out
the candles here in the tent when you leave – they're rounding
up tonight and it wouldn't look good to have my tent
catching fire.' Ingrid paused for a moment and smiled to herself,
as if eagerly remembering something she had to do, before
continuing: 'We're sailing in the middle of the night, as you
know, but I've an appointment in the Great Hall with a serving ... man to William. A business appointment. Enjoy your
voyage home.' And with that, Ingrid departed out the folds of
the tent, leaving Rika dumbfounded in the middle of the grey
tent and transfixed with an odd fury. The candles were burning
low and beginning to flicker and splutter like grease dripped in
flame.

'And I wish you a nice trip all the way to the sharp jaws
of the Fenrir wolf!' she shouted out finally, but her words rang
strangely false in the quiet expanse of Ingrid's tent. If Ingrid
expected her to take that type of treatment, she was sorely
mistaken. She would die before she went straight back home to
Norway. And she would be cursed before she paid a visit to
'Arje' – surely just another of Ingrid's women, but one who'd
obviously entrusted Ingrid with her runic name-chain. It was
obviously a lover's gift; Rika didn't believe for a minute that
Ingrid was planning on returning it. She would be cursed before
she followed any of Ingrid's unreasonable requests.

She sat down on the wide bed and then began slowly to
devise a plan to be with Ingrid, but on her own terms. The
candles crackled out and went black, and still she sat there
thinking in the darkness. Eventually she rose, crossed the
room, picked up the metal box and exited the tent. It seemed a
shame to leave it behind and Ingrid had obviously forgotten it.

The sky was still dropping water, but when she looked up she
could see stars when the dark shadow-clouds of early night
shifted. She blinked away the rain and kept scanning for what
she eventually found: the shining, stellar journey of a Valkyrie,
tracing a flame trail of silver and hot scarlet all the way to

Valhalla. A fallen warrior, now with his or her reward. A courageous fighter. Like she was going to be. Then she wiped her face clear of the wet night and walked purposefully down the incline to Pia's tent.

'Rika.' Pia didn't seem too surprised when she drew open the entrance of her tent and saw Rika standing there; she ushered her quickly in from the rain. A dish of red coals was glowing inside Pia's tent and, though it warmed the space, the rain was sprinkling through in parts and the illusion of comfort was not complete.

It was nowhere near as fine as Ingrid's tent had been, though there were two large brown pelts spread across the dirt floor.

'Would you care for a drink?' Pia walked to a small table on which stood a jug, several glasses and a wooden plate piled with autumn fruits, and extracted a flask from her belt. That must have been the Turkish liquor that Ingrid had referred to.

'Yes . . .' Rika paused. Pia's manner was much friendlier than it had been earlier in the tent with Ingrid. Perhaps it had been Ingrid she was angry with. It would not hurt, then, to ask her help, would it? Rika spoke as she hesitantly accepted a filled wooden beaker. 'Pia . . .'

'There's water, if you prefer.' Pia nodded to the enormous clay jug, but Rika declined.

'Who is "Aardja"?' She was not sure if she was pronouncing it correctly.

'Aardja? I don't know.' Pia smiled. 'I don't think I've heard the name before.'

Rika was growing impatient. 'No, like this.' She set her drink down, dipped her finger in the clear wine and wrote out an approximation of the runes she had remembered from the name-chain on the cloth of the table.

'Gods!' Pia broke out in startled laughter. 'I think I know what you're trying to spell, but that's not even close. Who taught you runes, anyway?' It was Ingrid, but Rika decided not to answer. Pia dipped her own finger in the liquid, took Rika's palm, and fingered four runes in it:

'Is that the name you mean?'

Rika smarted. She didn't like being laughed at. And she had a mission here, too. 'That's right. Who is "Arje"?'

'She's a priestess back home in Norway. And not a Christian; she's a priestess of the Old Ways. And a very pretty one, so they say. Friend of Ingrid's, I believe. A close friend.'

Damn Ingrid. Rika should have known. She looked scrutinisingly at Pia. 'You know runes fairly well?'

'Fairly well? Yes, I suppose you could say that.'

'Then what does this rune mean? The one next to the figure of Freyr?' She thrust her pendant up to Pia's eye level.

Pia sucked in her breath; her smile was strained. 'That rune? That rune means . . .' She paused as if thinking hard. 'It's a bindrune made of three different symbols, which can mean several things. The outer one means change. That top one means, I am sorry to say, an ordeal, destruction or a lesson, and that last rune, below it, means a gift or offering – or even love. It means to be held to something or someone who has offered a gift, to be in thrall in something. It can be a positive thing, such as love, or it can mean something more . . . sinister. Which reminds me,' she added brightly, 'you were going to tell me about your blood-oath?'

Rika looked suspiciously at Pia. 'Ingrid has asked me not to speak of it. And she wants me to return to Norway.'

Pia's face fell and her voice was very, very quiet. Then: 'Are you sure you can't at least give me more of an idea of what Ingrid wants you to do?'

'No.' Rika was adamant.

Pia sighed. 'And what has Ingrid offered you in return?'
'What?'

'You're obviously under the silence of a blood-oath, but I'm just wondering whether Ingrid's given you something of equal value in return.'

'Oh . . .' Rika gripped the pendant and thought. She realised what the answer was and it pleased her. 'Ingrid has given me love.' Her face broke out in a smile. 'As you've correctly interpreted from the necklace.'

'One of several interpretations,' Pia muttered, but she shrugged and slung her beaker of alcohol down her throat. She turned her vessel upside down: empty. 'That went down quickly.'

'Let me get you some more.' Rika stood up abruptly, knocking the water-flask all over the dark-haired woman. None of this was going according to Rika's plan; she should have easily convinced Pia to take her with her by now.

Pia cursed. 'I'll have to change. We're sailing later tonight and I was planning on wearing this; and I still have to decide what I'm wearing for battle, as well.' Pia rummaged through a small pile of clothing that was heaped near her bedding, not checking to see whether Rika was watching. She pulled a dry woollen shirt over her shoulders and bound her calves with a leather strip. She tested the weight of her shield in her hands, before dropping it back on the pile. But Rika was indeed watching, unsure whether to speak. Pia seemed disproportionately angry over the spilled water and Rika had no wish to further upset the warrior. She had to ask a favour from her, and Pia was already noisily going through her weapon cache, no doubt picking out the best for battle as Ingrid had done.

'Are you angry with me?' she finally asked.

Pia eventually turned towards her; Rika was faintly shocked to see her face so tense and pale. 'With you? No, Rika, I'm not angry with you.'

'Good.' She sat down and watched Pia pick up an exceptionally sharp bright sword.

60

'What kind of blade do you carry?'

The question was abrupt and it startled Rika. 'I carry a knife that I stole from my father.'

'Here.' Pia carefully handed her the sword.

It was a beauty. Rika ran her hands along its double edges. It was the kind her father made only on commission; it was that expensive. 'Are you sure?'

'Of course I'm sure. I just want to make certain you're well protected for your journey back to Norway. Just in case.' Pia seemed embarrassed, and shoved another fine knife into Rika's hand. 'I can't take all this with me. Here, you can have this one too. It's a scramsasax knife, for fighting by hand.'

Rika was slightly put out. 'I know what it is. My father is an ironsmith, remember?' But then she realised that she ought to be more grateful, so she thanked Pia for her generosity.

Pia pulled on the last bit of military protection, a fine-linked chain-mail shirt and stood before her. 'What do you think?'

'You're missing your helmet,' Rika said. She was actually quite touched that Pia would care to ask. She didn't even know Rika that well, either. Rika felt her face blush. What had happened on the boat really didn't count.

'I prefer to fight without a helmet,' Pia said. 'But I'm no fool. I always put it on eventually.' She held up a plain Viking helmet, bell-shaped with a simple noseguard of metal.

'Pia.' Rika stepped so that she faced her directly, looking up into the taller woman's eyes. 'I need to ask a favour of you.'

Pia placed the helmet on her bedding. 'What would that be?'

'I need you to help me go to Britain.'

'Why?' Pia said calmly.

'Why? Because I need to be with Ingrid; to make sure she's all right.'

'You want to go to Britain,' Pia repeated slowly. 'You don't want to go back to Norway?'

'No.'

'Well, strange as it may seem, it might be safer for you to battle in Britain than to return home. "Even the handless can herd sheep, but a corpse is no good to anyone," ' Pia quoted enigmatically.

'What?'

'Nothing, it's just an old saying. I'll have to think about it, Rika. Ingrid would tan my skin for winter shoes if she found out.'

'You'd better think quickly. You said yourself that you leave tonight.'

'That's true.' Pia stared at her for a moment then said shortly, 'I need to get this gear off.'

It was rather a pity, since Pia looked so dashing in the battle-gear that she nearly rivalled Ingrid. And there was a curious tension in the air that hadn't been there before.

'Are you going to watch me strip this time, too?'

'Excuse me?' Until Pia said that, Rika hadn't realised that she was openly staring, waiting for Pia to undress. She remembered how Pia had confidently removed her shirt to reveal her breasts on board the ship, and it occurred to her that it was true – she *was* actually waiting to see the curves of Pia's breasts again, even if it was completely unconscious. She cleared her throat. 'Go ahead, don't mind me.'

She turned around, but now the only thing she could think of was Pia's dark red nipples, perfect for sucking. Then the thought of Pia's full thighs pushed its way into her head, thighs that she wanted to be squeezing, right now. She put her hands to her cheeks and her face was hot with embarrassment. She looked ahead at the dish of glowing coals, trying to think of something else. Think of Ingrid, she told herself. Think of the rain dripping through the holes in the tent. Don't turn round. But instead she thought of the lush sweet curves that Pia had revealed to her on the boat.

She turned round. The warrior's back was to her, as Pia bent over to take off the battle-breeches. There *were* fine curves there, curves into which she wanted to work her hand. Pia's haunches were beautifully muscled, the soft olive-toned flesh of her buttocks right before her eyes. Rika tried to resist looking, but she lost her fight; she could just see a glimpse of Pia's pussy and the thick dark hair that grew there. The warm sweet stickiness of her, the hot dew she would taste on Pia if her tongue were there, the wet . . . She glanced down for a moment and looked at her hands, nervously twisting together.

'I see you have indeed turned around to stare, Rika. Or are you planning on helping me undress?' Pia's tone was gentle.

'Maybe.' The woman stood magnificently naked. Rika took a deep breath and moved closer. Her hands circled Pia, but she felt like she couldn't touch this big, lithe animal before her; she could only skim the air around her with her inadequate hands. She couldn't touch all this lovely flesh being offered to her. It would be too easy. No, she had to draw it out, had to get what she needed from Pia.

'Is something wrong?' Pia's words were just a little too quick; Rika noticed that her breathing was rapid. It was exciting.

'Not at all.' How was she to begin? She found she couldn't think in an orderly fashion. 'Why don't you go and lie down over there?' In desperation, she pointed to a rain-sodden corner of the tent. 'I'll get your clothes. If you want me to help you dress,' she added. She cursed herself inwardly. It was the opposite of what she wanted to say.

'What's wrong with right here?' Pia caught Rika by the shoulder, pulled her in close and gestured down towards the soft elk fur that they stood on. Rika found she was trembling in such close proximity to Pia's small, soft breasts; Pia's naked body pressed against her own clothed limbs. Pia was so confident, too. As if she was in control. The way Ingrid had always been in control.

'Nothing's wrong with right here.' Rika stared into Pia's dark-blue eyes.

'I didn't think so.' Pia pressed her lips on to Rika's mouth, her hot salty tongue dipping past Rika's lips and into the erotic and wet curves of her mouth. Rika felt herself slipping in Pia's strong, naked embrace, her cunt close to melting in a pool of sex. She fought to keep control. It felt like her swollen pussy had doubled in size since the kiss began.

'Pia.' She pulled herself away from Pia's embrace. 'I need to know if you will help me go to Britain. You must help me. You have to.'

Pia looked bemused and let her arms fall back to her sides. 'I said that I would think about it.' It was amazing how she managed to look so proud, even when completely, vulnerably naked.

Could Pia tell she was not used to ordering someone else around? The only time she had previously been so insistent was with Lina in the woods. With Ingrid, she had always been submissive.

Pia sat down on the fur near the brazier, the light from it and from the surrounding candles setting her dark skin aglow. 'You look a bit chilled.' The woman winked at her. 'Why don't you move over here and warm up a bit?'

Rika watched her close her eyes; watched her lean half-smiling back towards the warmth of the coals, and wondered for a moment who it was Pia thought of when she smiled. Again Rika found her eyes skimming the woman's body, and she uncomfortably put her hands in her pockets. Something hard was there and she removed an oddly hard-skinned little fruit, rosy-pink and withered. Ah yes, the fruit that Lina had given her; she had forgotten. She glanced at Pia, still basking in the heat from the brazier, eyes shut. She wondered what would be inside the fruit. Sweet pulpy flesh, like a blueberry? Maybe she should feed Pia some. Or maybe there would be sections, like a Chinese apple Ingrid had once described to her. And what would be inside Pia, if she fucked and not just licked her? Would her cunt be soft and tight, or loose and wet and gently yearning?

With the fruit in her hand, she walked towards Pia. 'Keep your eyes closed.'

Pia stretched out on the rug and disobediently opened her eyes. 'I'd rather not.' She patted the place beside her on the fur.

64

'Why don't you have a seat?' She motioned to the table of fruits and wine. 'You can have a bite to eat. I'm not a bit hungry.'

I am, Rika thought, as she gazed at Pia's long warm body, its sexual secrets hidden by the growth of black curly hair on the mound of her sex. Rika again sensed that she was in the presence of a wild animal, someone who, like Ingrid, she would never easily tame. She frowned, wishing the thought of Ingrid had not come so easily to her mind.

She stood above Pia and handed her the little fruit. 'It's quite a special fruit, according to the friend that gave it to me. Do you want some?' she asked, anticipating the woman's pleasure.

'Where did you get that?' Pia said sharply; not at all the reaction Rika had been hoping for.

'From Lina.' This woman was so hard to figure out; Rika couldn't decipher her mood swings. Now she seemed angry again.

'Where did Lina get it from?'

Rika thought. 'I think she said she received it from a travelling merchant.'

Pia hissed in through her teeth and grabbed the fruit from Rika's hand, throwing it across the tent. It landed with a wet plop in a puddle in the far corner. 'If you're hungry, why don't you have one of these Chinese apples instead?'

Perturbed but not entirely put off by the aspect of tasting a fruit she had heard so much about, Rika reached to the table and picked up a fruit with an orange, puckered skin. 'Is this it?' Pia nodded and Rika tried to take a bite of it.

Pia laughed. 'You have to peel it first.'

Rika peeled the fruit, which was monstrously strange, with watery, clear orange sections amid waxy pockets. Her fingers shook as she bent down to put the pieces up to Pia's mouth.

At first Pia shook her head away playfully, but eventually she gave in to Rika's offer. Pia licked the juice on her lips. 'Not bad,' she said. 'It's much better than the other fruit would have been. Promise me, Rika, that you'll never try one of Lina's fruits. Believe me, they'll taste terrible.'

'Well, all right.' Rika was discomfited. At the same time curiosity made her want to taste the Chinese apple, too. She put a portion of the sunny fruit on her own tongue and then placed another fruit piece in Pia's mouth. She closed her eyes and lost herself in the tangy sensation, so tart her eyes watered but with a taste more clear and pure than even wild raspberries.

'Ingrid told me how good Chinese apples are. She's had them before in her travels. She was right, too.'

Pia's brow twisted slightly, but she kept her eyes closed. 'Give me your fingers.'

Shyly, Rika brought her hand up and Pia opened her lips fully, so Rika could first feel all the wetness of her mouth and then felt her tongue slowly licking all the remaining juice of the fruit. As Pia licked at her fingers, Rika could feel a tugging deep in her sex and the pounding of her heart. The picture carved on the mirror flashed before her; the intricate and brightly painted – if lewd – pictures. The image swelled until it sparked an idea.

'Stay there for a moment,' Rika told her. Pia was breathing hard.

Rika rose and went to fetch the metal box she had carried all the way from Ingrid's tent. When she returned, she stripped herself of her clothes. Pia's eyes glittered. 'Close your eyes,' she told Pia, 'but raise yourself so that you are kneeling, with your arms at your sides. And keep quiet.' And Pia made a beautiful sight once she had done so, her hard body trembling and strong, her lips still wet with juice, her breasts jutting girlishly high on her chest.

'It's called a pomegranate, by the way. The terrible fruit that Lina gave you. It tastes awful.'

'I said, keep quiet!' Rika answered in what she hoped was a harsh tone, but a smile quivered on the other woman's lips. She tried to remember back to her game-playing with Ingrid. Now she understood as well why Ingrid had become so irritated when she would burst into laughter. She opened the metal box and laid out before her on the pelt the brushes and the array of bright paints. There were around thirty distinct colours. She crossed the room and returned with the full glass of Turkish wine she had been offered earlier.

Pia's fine taut body was still trembling as she knelt, eyes closed and manner momentarily as supplicant as a caged animal. Rika reached out a warm hand to touch the dark-haired woman and a shiver rippled through Pia's body. It was anticipation then, not chill, that made Pia shake so.

Rika dipped one of the brushes into the wine and then opened a little pot of pearly-blue paint. She moistened the tip of the brush and smoothly plunged it into the bright-blue salve, stirring the liquor into an azure paste. The idea growing in her head was exciting: she wanted to paint Pia like the bright, strange-sexed characters carved upon the mirror. Her attention switched to the details of Pia's body: the tone and texture of her back, her smooth face and throat, her strong hands that had held so many oars and probably weapons, too. The fur beneath Rika tickled at her knees. Her mouth watered at the sight of Pia kneeling and naked before her, her breasts nearly touching Rika's navel.

She slowly painted the salve on to Pia's skin, tracing the peacock-blue fluid over the captain's clavicle. She dotted her throat with red and she stroked a green ribbon over the beginning of the swell of Pia's breasts. Eventually she touched the paint on Pia's skin with her own fingers instead of the brush and began to rub the colour deeply into her flesh.

'What are you stroking with, Rika? Water? Wine?' Pia asked, her eyes still shut. She grabbed Rika suddenly, sliding her fingers deep into Rika's hot cunt. 'Or from here?' She removed her hand and stroked her wet fingers against Rika's bare legs.

'Pia, you must not question me. And keep your hands to yourself, or I shall stop altogether.' There, much more forceful, and more like Ingrid than she had even intended. The blues and reds and greens dripped over Pia's muscular body, running off the tips of her breasts. Rika opened a jar of a silvery red-purple and again made a liquid with the wine. She painted it on to Pia's arms, raising each limb and scrawling rich curlicues of the

67

amethyst paint before it fell in rosy droplets on to Pia's blue breasts. She painted battle dragons, fighting with tongues of violent bloody red. She imagined her own sex growing red and wet as she stroked the colour over Pia's brown breasts, fingering Pia's firm nipples. She had half a mind to script a rune and invoke the power that came by writing it down in some fashion. She looked briefly at her rune-inscribed pendant and changed her mind, before coating the ruby-purple paint down Pia's torso. Another soft moan escaped from Pia's lips and Rika poured what remained of the liquor into a pot of buttery-smooth green paint. Then she threw her brush to the side, rubbing her fingers themselves into the fire-green glaze. Her hands travelled down Pia's body, her fingers heavy with the jade syrup. She began to feel and oil the outer folds of Pia's soft, ripening cunt.

'Ooh,' Pia moaned. Rika did not this time trouble herself with shushing Pia, but instead began opening the colour-pots at random. This time, just as Pia had accused her of doing, she used her own slick lubrication to wet the cosmetic. A silver gloss was sliding off the fingers of her left hand and there was bright sunny yellow on her right hand, smelling of her own juicy cunt. She expanded her strokes and slowly began to knead, oil and massage the colours into all parts of Pia's body, except for the inner folds of the dark-haired woman's sex.

Pia was beautiful with the spectrum of colours gliding over her skin. Rika ran a finger down a long scar on Pia's side. A sword-fight, apparently. In her enjoyment over the older woman's capitulation, she had forgotten the woman was an experienced sailor, who had probably experienced many sea-bound fights. She continued dipping into herself and rubbing her wetness into the warm, smooth coloured lacquers. She stroked Pia's calves and feet with emeralds and brilliant claret-reds. Pia revelled in the touch, unsuspecting of the kaleidoscopic vision playing over her body. She looked like an exotic beast; a painted dragon.

Rika withdrew for a moment and remained half sitting before Pia, breathless. Her hand neared Pia's cunt and she felt her responses lushly sway as she stroked the curves of exposed flesh on Pia's wet, rainbow-shimmering sex. She pushed down a finger and raised the paint, liquor and come to her lips. Her pink tongue licked lavishly at the erotic mixture. She tasted the proof of Pia's arousal and the traces of the orange fruit, and smeared her face with colour as she pressed her hand to her face and smelt the rich scent.

It was time to start fucking Pia properly, as Ingrid had taught her. 'Open your eyes,' she said softly to the oarswoman.

Pia's body was like a tight plump opal, shining with the alcohol-mixed paint, glistening with the still-wet turquoises, blues, ambers, tangerines. 'Just fuck me quickly, I don't care.'

Right before Rika plunged her hand into the delicious running syrup covering Pia's oiled pussy, she lingered over the inner folds, probing the woman's wet opening with flirtatious skill until she slid her hand to Pia's bud. She began to circle rhythmically, as thick honey poured out of Pia, mixing with blue and crimson and violet and silver. Rika's own thighs began to tremble. Her hand was soaked with come. She spelt out her own name in runes on Pia's abdomen, then smeared it quickly away.

Pia's eyes were screwed tight, her hands skimming the floor. Rika raised her fingers to her own lips, dipping and tasting the sailor's bright come. She repeatedly raised her hand from cunt to mouth and realised that Pia's flavouring shifted as her excitement grew. The taste was growing darker; and more sweet than salty.

'Don't stop,' Pia said, 'please don't stop.' But finally Rika pumped her fingers into Pia, watching the dark-haired woman's body rise up from the pleasurable shock. Oh god, the wonderful feeling of Pia's come running down her wrist. Ingrid had never come so much. Rivulets of smoke-blue ran over Pia's thighs, dissolving into indigos and marines as the liquid reached the flowing ruby and gold hues and the colours blended.

'Please don't stop,' Pia begged again, softly.

'What will you give me if I continue?' Rika asked.

'Anything. Touch me further down,' Pia whispered and Rika

pressed right in the edge of the upper wall, inside Pia's cunt. 'Perfect.'

As she pushed and fucked at this spot, Rika noticed Pia moaning even more, so she rubbed harder, pushing and pressing and just wanting to get further up in her, to fuck the oarswoman out of her head.

It was unusual that such a strong woman could make herself so vulnerable. Ingrid never would have allowed it. Rika remembered for a moment the secret spot Ingrid had once told her about that made women flood like fountains, the spot that only women knew in women. This was, Ingrid said, because women fucked with their hands and could reach more parts and places and so much deeper than a cock.

Perhaps, thought Rika, this was the secret spot that she now had found. Deep inside Pia's cunt, Rika whimsically traced the bindrune – ordeal, renewal and love. But it was another casting Pia would never see.

She pushed and rubbed and fucked her hard, and suddenly she felt a flood of liquid over her hand, drenching her to the elbow, and then another equal gush, and then another. The wet was mixing with the colours: green, silver, gilded orange and bright reds melting together in a delicious stream. Her own clit raging, Rika felt Pia's whole cunt expanding, and Pia's body exploded and bucked, forged on to Rika's colour-sprayed hand.

Pia squirted out come all over Rika's hand and grabbed at anything near her, as Rika's fingers moved like four stiff little probes inside the woman. Rika was entranced by the vision of Pia's wetly perfumed, writhing oiled body. Ecstasy was obviously flooding through every inch of Pia's body and surging once again when Rika rapturously kissed the come and colour off her dark, red-tipped breasts. She licked at Pia's nipples as Pia hung on, Rika's fingers digging deep into the sailor's wet cunt.

She paused. Pia opened her eyes. 'Don't stop!' Pia's voice was desperate.

'You said you'd give me anything if I kept on,' Rika pointed out, her own crotch wet and throbbing.

Pia moaned loudly. 'Anything.'

'Will you take me with you to Britain?' Rika paused once more with purpose and Pia groaned. Rika could smell only pussy and the tangy orange fruit.

Then, spurting out a glorious blend of colours, Pia flooded forth one final time and Rika's entire arm and neck were smeared with the coloured ejaculate, fluid as water but as vivid and as brilliant as a rainbow.

'Yes, oh yes,' screamed Pia. 'Oh, fuck, yes!'

Rika's clit felt painfully tight.

Pia looked at Rika and then down at herself, swimming in colour and musk, exhausted, her lurid torso tattooed and stained with the richness of sex. 'Yes,' she said. 'Yes, I will help you.'

# FOUR

The voyage across the thin-necked channel that separated Gaul from Britain was speedy, as two thousand ships ploughed through the water to the pale cliffs ahead. Overhead, the gulls pierced the ashen sky with their screams. An even uglier dissonance was introduced when a dark bird rose amongst them, croaking. The rowing Normans could accept angry gull screams, but the mournful scratchy call of the black bird sounded like resignation. And resignation was not an appropriate sentiment when a battle loomed before them in the too-near future.

But one of the Norsemen rowing near Rika smiled and named the bird: *hrafn*. The Raven. Rika frowned for a moment. *Hrafn*. The word reminded her of something, but for the life of her she could not remember what. She wrinkled her brow, trying to remember, and out of the corner of her eye saw that Pia was watching her. Ravens were battle-scavengers, but there was no need to become carrion if one was a good fighter. And the omen was surely a positive one, as the sailor had indicated: the standard of Hardradra himself was decorated with a huge black raven. It had long been a symbol for her people.

When the boats hit the grit of the shore and were pulled up, seven members of Ingrid's crew stood waiting for their leader.

Seven tall women: steely-eyed, proud and vicious. Their hanging braids were more lustrous and thick than the locks of men, but in all other aspects they were dressed the same as male Vikings, with long-sleeved, brightly dyed wool shirts with vests and belts, woollen leggings gathered with sinew at the ankle, softened leather boots and iron helmets, both simple and decorated with glittering ornate designs. Two or three were wearing additional armour.

From the boat, Rika observed them. They were handsome women and she found herself hoping that the legend that they fought bare-breasted was true. She looked from the first warrior in line – a tall, well-muscled woman with grey hair – to the last, a fighter with bright green eyes and such an angular jaw that she put most men to shame. Rika counted again, to make sure she'd got the number right. With Ingrid, they would number eight. But where was the ninth?

She looked speculatively behind her at Pia, who by odd coincidence was already gazing at her steadily. She always seemed to be watching, Rika thought. She had been observing her quietly ever since she sneaked her on to the ship back in Normandy. Then comprehension hit her, at last.

Why hadn't she realised? She swallowed. 'Are you a member of Ingrid's Crew?'

Pia gave a short nod. 'For the time being.' The meaning was unclear; surely members of Ingrid's Crew were members for life? But before Rika got a chance to ask, the dark-haired woman quickly moved away from her and stepped towards the front of the boat.

The other sailors on Rika's boat were preparing to disembark rapidly around her; other boats had landed and William's own had been pulled up on the sand near her. She crouched in the boat, shielding her eyes from the ocean spray so that she could see William more clearly as he stepped off the ship. He was a tall lanky man with dark hair and a sour expression. Rika felt vaguely disappointed, though she wasn't really sure what she had expected. She watched him tread the coastal sea-grass. He did not look how a king was supposed to look, she decided, as she and the rest of her ship disembarked. Not like Haarald Hardradra, her own ruler, all seven feet tall and fiery red hair. She trudged through the water, soaking her boots, and was cross for no good reason.

By now, the whole of Ingrid's Crew had assembled further up the shore, where the cliff-rocks began to jut dangerously forth. Rika's eyes ran along the line of nine women. There was the green-eyed woman with the angular jaw, the muscly grey-haired warrior, two fighters who looked like the female counterparts of the monster-twins from her home village, a heartbreakingly beautiful girl with light brown hair and huge pitch-black eyes, a short fierce freckly woman with an eye-patch and a tall slender sallow woman who looked too frail to hold a blade but whose stance was menacing. And there was Ingrid, armed but dressed in a sleeveless vest of bear-skin, standing in the cold morning sunlight. She was chatting to Pia, her arms open wide in description, then curving in and out again. No doubt bragging to Pia about the wave-heights en route, Rika thought, but she felt uneasy. Pia was not smiling and Rika wondered whether she was enjoying the conversation. These two stood flank-to-flank with the seven additional warrior-women, all battle-ready in manner.

Rika gazed up at this select group and something tightened in her chest. Still, she took her place back in the general throng of William's company where some other women were amassing, ones who had rowed over from Norway to Gaul when she herself had. No doubt they harboured similar ambitions to her own in regard to Ingrid's Crew. Up ahead of her, the Crew-members were still within eyesight. Ingrid had not yet realised that she was here and Rika ducked behind a fellow sailor whenever it seemed that the blonde warrior's gaze would shoot her way.

On through the morning the company marched, towards the flat area where they hoped to eventually meet Godwinsson. They progressed with authoritative struts, but Rika had an uncomfortable feeling that they would all look like ludicrous insects if viewed from slopes not too far away. Eventually the sun came out. There was a scent of heather in the air and just a tinge of the fragrance of juniper berries from overladen trees. Rika thought the entire landscape vaguely – if not exceptionally – pretty. It had none of the dramatic peaks or fjords or vast roaring waters of her own homeland, but she accepted that this land called Britain could be considered pleasant. Though she did find it difficult to understand why great men like William, Hardradra or even Godwinsson would fight to the death for it.

She was fighting for the good of Norway, she reminded herself sternly, and felt her thighs tremble with the exertion of continued, determined walking. For the glory of Ingrid's Crew, to which she secretly aspired. And some here marching beside her were fighting for eternal feasting in Valhalla. She gulped and kept hiking. She was not yet ready to die, she thought, not yet ready to blaze across the heavens in the arms of a gorgeous Valkyrie.

She kicked a pebble out of her way as she trudged on behind a line of grumbling men and women. Perhaps, she thought sadly, this was also why she would not be ready to join Ingrid's Crew, even if she were to be asked. She was not prepared to die. Not for Hardradra, not for love of Ingrid, not for anything. She flushed with humiliation at the realisation, keeping her pace steady as she advanced towards whatever fate awaited her.

After several hours, they stopped for water and food. Rika had just withdrawn her drinking-horn from her belt when she saw Pia making her way back to her, and her heart rose.

She handed Pia the horn full of volatile blackberry-mead, but first swigged at the alcohol herself. The mead was savoury-sweet and a wave of homesickness passed through Rika. Berry-mead was one of her village's specialities; she wondered if her father had concocted the pungent honey-liquor this autumn, mourning the loss of his daughter. Perhaps she would die before she next tasted village-stilled mead – no, she'd keep those thoughts locked away. She had left the village; she could never go back. And village life could never compare with the excitement of being along on such an important battle.

Pia seemed grateful for the mead and they passed it between the two of them. Rika's eyes drifted everywhere.

'There are so many different types of people here,' she said to Pia. 'Normans, traitorous Saxons, Vikings, Jutes, yellow-haired Franks . . .'

'Even Picts.' Pia nodded to a man nearby who was also fighting in William's army. He was far shorter than both women, with dark straight hair and shiny dark eyes and seemed, to Rika, quick-witted. He was watching them as well and flashed up a smile at them when Pia handed him the drinking horn. As he swallowed, Rika watched his face wrinkle up the two blue streaks slashed down his cheeks.

'Why the blue tattoos?' she asked Pia.

'He's a Pict and they sometimes paint their entire bodies blue.'

For a moment Rika remembered when she had painted Pia blue, back in Normandy, and her sex twitched at the memory. Then she thought of the question that hadn't been answered then: 'Where did Ingrid's paintbox come from, Pia? The one I – you know the one. The one I left behind in Gaul.' Rika had intentionally left it behind; it was cumbersome and seemed to have already served its – albeit pleasurable – purpose. 'Is it the paintbox of a . . . Pict?' She stumbled over the word.

Pia grinned, but her eyes flashed with a darker emotion. 'That paintbox has an entirely different source and goes all the way back to Norway.' So it was true. It did belong to Ingrid's friend 'Arje' after all. Rika shifted uncomfortably. They heard the command to commence the march again and Rika tucked the horn away in her belt.

'It came all the way from Norway?' Rika brought up the subject again as they marched along, Rika's new sword banging at her side. 'So then why did Ingrid have the paintbox with her? Was it a gift from a lover?'

Pia smiled and ignored the question. She ran her fingers up Rika's arm. 'Unmarked.'

76

'What?'

'Your skin is unmarked. No tattoos, no scars. Not like mine.' Pia pointed to the criss-crossing ridges up her own arms. 'It won't remain that way for long, Rika, won't remain so soft and so velvety smooth. Not if you're serious about joining us today.'

'No –' Rika's tongue quivered at her lips in hesitation. She privately liked the mixed textures on Pia's skin, the way the fresh scars faded from livid purples to mere bruises of colour, then finally became ornate spirals of chalky, fine lines. Now in the heat, for example, a film of sweat was forming on the curves of Pia's biceps, just beginning to run on to the old scars. She drew in her breath. Suddenly she had an urge to duck down her head and lick at the moisture, an urge to taste the salt and sweet of Pia's skin. Rika knew she was staring, but she couldn't help looking. Pia looked as strong as Ingrid. Ingrid had always been proud of her scars. Why shouldn't Pia be? Ingrid took pride in pointing them out: proof of her bravery, old and healed irregularities blending in with her many tattoos.

Pia placed a hand on Rika to halt her steps for a moment, and then gently took her hand in her own. 'I think you should –'

'Rika!' Far, far up in the company, there was Ingrid's unmistakable voice calling for her. What would she say? Would she care that Rika was here, instead of home safely in Norway?

'It's Ingrid!' Rika could not hide her excitement from Pia. 'I've got to talk to her, but –' she hesitated and looked at Pia's unfathomable expression – 'I'll be right back.' Pia's eyes flickered, but she released Rika's hand.

'I just have to talk to her.' Rika felt nearly apologetic as she searched Pia's face for some emotion, though she couldn't understand why.

'Well, you'd better hurry to Ingrid, then.' Pia's jaw was set, but there was no brusqueness to her voice.

'Yes, but I –' Rika jiggled from one foot to another. But Ingrid was waiting for her and Ingrid didn't like to be kept waiting, so she turned her back on Pia and ran on up ahead. For some reason, she felt oddly guilty and couldn't bring herself to look around behind her, where Pia was sure to still be standing.

'Rika.' Except for her hard, glittering eyes, Ingrid's face was expressionless once Rika – breathless and panting – caught up with her. 'I thought I told you to return to Norway.' People began to walk around them, leaving an island in the sea of marchers where they stood in weird, anonymous privacy.

Rika had no words, but just stared at the warrior. She was so glorious, like a shimmering goddess in the sun, her sensual lips just slightly parted. Her eyes ran over Ingrid's body, over the curves of her breasts and over her naked shoulders. Ingrid was licking her lips, seemingly in anticipation, though her eyes remained angry. But Rika felt herself growing wet at the mere sight of her; she couldn't help herself.

Ingrid grabbed at the crotch of Rika's breeches, running her fingers over the ridges of the material. 'It took a lot of courage to disobey my wishes once again, Rika.' Her fingers pressed slightly inwards and Rika felt a jolt to her sex. 'It just may have been the stupidest thing you've ever done.' Her voice was smooth, but vaguely threatening.

She raised her hand to the waist of Rika's breeches then shoved it rapidly down inside, skin on skin until she found the warm curls fringing Rika's sex. She thrust her longest finger further down, dipping into Rika's sex, stirring her up. She rubbed hard at her clitoris, which sent a spasm of pleasure running up the young girl's spine, then she withdrew the finger and smirked at Rika. 'As always, I can tell you're glad to see me,' she said in a dry voice.

Rika stared at her, flushed and humiliated, while Ingrid stuck her finger in her mouth and slowly licked off the sex-juices. The sight of the tall blonde warrior's tongue made her cunt tingle; she wished desperately that her heart would stop pounding so intensely. 'Yes,' she whispered.

'I thought I told you to return home.'

78

'Yes,' said Rika, even more softly. She looked down at her feet.

'Was it Pia who arranged the passage?'

Rika didn't answer.

'You've got a regrettably faulty memory.' With a lightning-quick movement, Ingrid grabbed at Rika's crotch again, holding tight outside the clothing. She twisted her hand, just slightly, increasing the hot pressure on Rika's mound. Her lips were still glazed with Rika's juice. 'Whatever Pia thinks, this is mine,' she said to Rika in a low voice. 'And that's one thing you won't forget.'

Rika felt as if Ingrid's fingers were burning through the material, melting through, right to the core of her crotch. 'I won't forget,' she whispered, looking down briefly at the red jewel hanging from her neck. 'I won't forget it, Ingrid. I don't forget important things.' She shut her eyes in pleasure as Ingrid stroked between her legs, pressing softly. Rika struggled not to rub her thighs together.

'Don't you?'

Rika opened her eyes. Ingrid's light hair caught the midday sunlight for a moment and a gold-red halo of beams framed her skull like a wreath. An inappropriate picture flashed before Rika's eyes: oranges, golds and blues swirling into the heavy sex-dew flowing over Pia's thighs; her own mouth kissing and licking Pia's nipples, red and hard and pert, and then her wet and sticky fingers slowly pumping inside the dark-haired warrior.

But Ingrid's gravelly voice brought her back to the present. 'You're enjoying this, aren't you, Rika?' Rika groaned as spasms began to invade her body, as Ingrid ground the heel of her hand hard into her groin. But then Ingrid removed her fingers. She moved closer and spoke in a low voice in Rika's ear. 'Do you know what this type of disobedience makes you, Rika?'

Rika shook her head, trying to catch her breath. Perhaps it made her a person who was stupidly besotted. Judging from Ingrid's reaction, it seemed like it had been a bad decision to come to Britain, after all.

'It makes you an *oath-breaker*.' Ingrid spat the word in Rika's ear, and Rika recoiled. It was the worst insult imaginable.

'But returning to Norway wasn't really part of the original blood-oath, was it, Ingrid? It was something you added later on,' Rika said in her defence. Ingrid was merely teasing her again, of course.

'Silence! How dare you argue the point? You're disgusting, worse than I could imagine, the lowest bog-swimmer, a vessel of Saxon pus. You'll have to pay the price that an oath-breaker pays.'

Rika looked at Ingrid. She was almost sure that Ingrid was wrong: Rika had followed all other points of the oath, had worn the jewel faithfully. She had broken none of her original oaths. Her eyes narrowed and, not for the first time on this adventure, she began to doubt the blonde warrior.

'Oath-breaker,' Ingrid snarled close to her face, so quietly that no one else could hear, her hot breath on Rika's face. This time the implication of the phrase truly hit Rika and her whole body froze: no one spoke to an oath-breaker, not even outcast members of Ingrid's Crew; they were worse than Saxon scum. But still, she was no oath-breaker.

'I'm not!' she cried, and tore away from Ingrid's grasp on her shoulder.

The blonde woman's face darkened, and she reached out a huge hand and swiftly pulled Rika back towards her. 'There's only one way out of it,' she hissed. 'You must do the favours I ask of you throughout the battle and afterwards, whenever I ask, or I'll make it known that you're an –' her voice broke off, then spewed the words out: 'an oath-breaker.'

Rika shuddered, seeing the contempt in Ingrid's eyes. She wanted dearly to join the Crew, but they would never vote her in if Ingrid told that. And if she went along with Ingrid's requests, she might convince Ingrid to put in a good word for her. *Favours.* She saw Ingrid looking her over, appraisingly, and she nearly sighed in relief and broke out in a smile, but instead simply nodded acquiescence. This was just another of Ingrid's complicated games. From experience, she knew what favours to Ingrid usually consisted of. And she had no problem with those at all.

For several days, Rika hung back, polishing her sword and helping the others prepare the fort where they were staying. She looked around for Pia more than once, but the dark-haired woman was nowhere to be found; neither was the rest of Ingrid's Crew. After six days a missive came from Ingrid, calling Rika over to the vicinity of William's tents immediately.

When Rika walked over to the nobleman's encampment, she saw all members of Ingrid's Crew training in hand-to-hand combat and realised why she hadn't seen Pia around. But she was strangely unsettled when, as she tried to catch Pia's eye as she approached, Pia didn't return her attention. Indeed – although Rika couldn't be sure – it looked as though Pia purposefully turned her back to continue fighting with the tall green-eyed woman.

'Pia!' she called out. She felt relief as this time Pia turned round and began to walk towards her. But at that moment she felt a rough tug on her hair. The motion was familiar and she knew immediately who it was that touched her so. Ingrid's hands relaxed on the strands and she caressed Rika's hair as if stroking a favourite pet. Then she removed her hands.

'Been waiting around for me long, have you, Rika?' Ingrid seemed amused and patted the long wooden handle of her battle-axe several times, as if enjoying a private joke.

Rika smiled back and then quickly looked over the blonde warrior's shoulder. But Pia had continued walking past and Rika realised that she had not been walking towards them at all, but towards the freckly Crewwoman. The red-haired woman was giggling up at Pia, making her laugh, too. Rika felt her stomach grow leaden. She pressed a hand up to her forehead, which had suddenly started aching.

'So you've found yourself a little friend,' Ingrid commented and Rika whirled round, suddenly remembering who had summoned her. Had Ingrid watched her watching Pia? 'But who would have thought that that little friend would be my swarthy-haired crewmate Perþ Gunnarsdóttir? Don't worry, Rika,' Ingrid reassured her, with a glint in her eye. 'I'm not angry. In fact, I believe in sharing, Rika. So much that I'm going to share the pleasant sight of you in a compromising situation with some of my Crewmates here, Pia especially. As a *favour*.' She emphasised the word.

Rika swallowed hard. She was – as always – enormously attracted to Ingrid, it was true, but the thought of being fucked before Pia and the rest of the Crewmates made her uncomfortable. How would they retain respect for her when she eventually joined the Crew as a full member? 'I don't think so,' she said, though she could already feel her sex growing rosy and wet, could already feel a steady throb between her legs.

'Don't you, my little oath-breaker? Remember, there's only one way you can redeem yourself. Through *favours*.' Rika noticed that Ingrid said this in a low voice, and glanced round almost as if she were nervous that someone might overhear. 'But I'm not going to tell you when, Rika, and it will be a surprise to us all. Particularly to Pia, I should imagine.'

To Rika's shame, she was already moist, just imagining the feel of Ingrid's hands on her body.

The day of the battle was overcast but dry. Rika felt nervous as she took her place in the lines. Others looked nervous, too; nearby there was a young woman her own age who was vomiting with fear. Her own gorge rose, but she kept her thoughts concentrated on William's standard. Still, she experienced a sickening lurch when she heard the call for helmets. The headpiece Pia had lent her felt like grey ice as she pulled it over her head and nose-bridge.

She put her hand behind the iron helmet and felt for the smith's groove. When her fingertips touched it, a tiny shock ran through her body. The smith, as she had faintly suspected, was her father. And perhaps she had seen him forging this very headpiece, the metal molten and red and alive. Not like this. Not like this dead metal.

There was a fumbling going on amongst the warriors ahead of her, but she couldn't see what was happening or if they were nearly ready to begin. Her mouth went dry and she wanted to jump, to scream, to run forward and slash at Harold the Saxon himself, anything to break the tension. She looked up the hill, above the bustle in the forward line, and saw how the skies stretched out, torrid, the wispy clouds dry as hanging calluses in the stagnant air. Something had to happen soon. She said a short prayer to the lightning god, Thor. *You can make it rain. I know you can.* She then fingered the little phallic Freyr round her neck for good measure. If it rained then they could all go away, go home, go somewhere else. But the sky remained heavy and dry.

Pia stepped back out of the lines up ahead and approached Rika. 'How are you feeling?' She laid a hand on Rika's arm.

Rika didn't answer. She was going to be throwing up soon herself, just like that young woman.

Pia bent down and whispered in Rika's ear: 'It's the same for everyone the first time.' Her eyes crinkled with a smile that didn't reach her lips.

'First positions!' shouted one of William's headmen, from further up ahead. The warriors moved into a position, but Rika noticed that Ingrid's Crew was not moving as quickly.

'It's so organised, isn't it?' she said to Pia in a low voice. 'William's people make our own warriors look clumsy.'

'Is that what you think?' Pia said sharply.

Rika looked up, startled. 'Well, look at them. We're strong and we look proud, I admit, but –'

'You don't know, do you?' Pia was looking at Rika with amazement.

'Know what?'

Pia threw her head back and let out a deep laugh. No one else around them was smiling; a male soldier from the row in front turned round and gave Pia a dirty look. Everyone was as nervous and grim as Rika herself felt.

'Second positions!'

'Listen,' Pia handed Rika a little leather pouch, 'I meant to hand this to you earlier. Here's our secret weapon. Here's why William's men will never be the warriors we are. Eat it quickly and pray fast to all the gods you can remember.' She reached for Rika's hand, touching it momentarily to her covered heart. Then she turned, looping through the lines.

She's in the front line, Rika thought, and her heart sank. She swallowed hard, one hand tightening on the leather pouch and the other on her sword.

The lines of Norman warriors and hired mercenaries spread out over the hills on which they stood like undulating, nervous liquid, ready to spill over the brim at the right word. The mass of fighters shimmered as they shifted, straining for commands, waiting for and yet dreading guidance. The air was hot. There was a scent of juniper in the air. Someone coughed; there was a mutter; someone else cleared their throat. The whole world was waiting.

Then a ripple of sound wound through the span of the troops, curving its way through the company like a wave. It was only when the wave hit Ingrid's Crew and the other fighting Vikings that its accompanying murmurs became shouts and then screams of disbelief.

Rika held her breath and laboured to hear what people were saying. One of the waiting warrior-women ahead had tears running down her face, as she angrily smashed the hilt of her sword against her hand, over and over again.

Just as a garbled roar at first, Rika began to make sense of what was being said amidst the screams and the gnashing of teeth: 'Hardradra is dead. Our Haarald is dead.' As she understood the words, her heart went cold. If they weren't fighting for Norway now, then for whom were they fighting? Surely not William? Her hands itched and she bit her lip until bright red blood ran down her chin. She tasted iron in her mouth and she hated it. But just then an enormous shout went up from Ingrid's Crew and rose, amongst the other Vikings, and amongst the rest of William's army. Despite these stirrings in the Viking ranks, they were commanded by William to hold their places for several minutes. This resulted in a feeling of tension that grew greater every minute.

Rika stepped out of line for several seconds and splashed dank water from a nearby puddle on her face, trying to scrub off at least some of the layers of grime with liquid only marginally less grimy. Two members of Ingrid's Crew fell out of line at the same moment and stood near her talking: the green-eyed one and the grey-haired one. They talked seriously and intensely and Rika heard them mention the name Ingrid.

She lingered on the spot on the pretence of scrubbing clean her hands, hoping to hear what was being said. The younger woman wore a pendant that looked like a bear-tooth. Rika knew what this meant: that the strength of the bear would enter the warrior and be transferred to her in battle. Her heart beat rapidly while she considered this; it felt as though she had swallowed dust. The shouts around the three of them were growing, becoming vicious and reverberating.

'She knew all along,' the tall green-eyed woman was saying, shaking her head.

'Watch your words, Sela,' the grey-haired woman answered in a fierce tone. 'She didn't know of Hardradra's death any sooner than we.'

'Did she not? Not even when she's so close to William and all his spies?'

'And speaking of spies . . .' The grey-haired woman cleared her throat. Sela spun round, saw Rika, and clamped her mouth shut.

Rika pretended that she had finished rubbing clean her hands, but did not immediately rush away, taking the time to dry them on her rough breeches. Her face was hot and she could feel her ears burning. When she walked back to her position with measured steps, a voice shouted after her, even louder than the cries around her: 'Hey, girl!' It was the green-eyed woman, Sela.

'You breathe a word of this and I vouch Ingrid will have to find a new pet!'

'Quiet!' Rika heard the older woman hiss at Sela. 'Do you want to stir things more than you already have?' The two women turned back to each other, bickering in low voices that were lost amidst the general rumble.

Rika paused and stood quite still, her hands wet and clammy from the foul water. Ingrid had said that hers was the most loyal crew there ever was, but Rika was beginning to doubt the assertion. She was already starting to feel sick with fright and hadn't yet managed to summon up the battle-fury over Hardradra's death that the others had.

As she took her place back in the fighting line, she noticed that the murmuring had become worse, though she could still only make out what those next to her were saying. It was being suggested Hardradra had been dead for days, that William had suppressed the news merely to make the Vikings fight better in their anger at the Saxons. If this was his plan, it seemed to be working: already there was a buzzing of rage amongst the Viking troops. Rika had an odd, detached feeling that this was all going to get much, much worse.

The noise, in fact, was growing painful to her ears; the noise was rising; she was tasting blood; her heart was pounding and sweat was dripping down her faceguard and running down to her neck. Salt and blood. The bastard Saxons had killed Hardradra. The shout was still rising in volume and now it sounded like rage; it was the universal sound of hatred. Hatred! The Saxons had killed the Viking king. And now they'd pay. Though she'd been detached up to this moment, now the infectious fury hit Rika, too, hard in her stomach. She would lop off a hundred Saxon heads with her brilliant blade if she only had the chance. Her hand went down to her bright sword and raised it up, just slightly, and it felt as light as dandelion fur, as light as an eyelash. It was buoyant and she was worthy to swing the sharp and quicksilver blade.

'Start moving!' someone shouted from Ingrid's Crew and

everyone moved, nearly ran forward. Rika was filled with a pure rage; she knew instinctively that everyone around her was feeling it, too. She barely thought as she mimicked the motion of those up ahead of her and opened the compact little pouch that Pia had handed to her earlier. Seeing that it was small fragments of leathery-looking mushrooms, she rapidly chewed the greyish remnants, as the others in front of her did.

The fungus tasted rich and musty, reminded her of home and the forest there. She chewed it all and swallowed it down, feeling a steely calmness settle itself on her. She looked around her as she continued to move forward with the rest of the company. Everything seemed clear and she felt her hatred disappearing. It was dreamlike as they gained ground, but she still was thankful that they were only moving, not fighting yet.

The sun above was burning down its beams in a curious geometry; the warriors squinted in the sun, but no matter how they shielded their eyes, the rays crept in and half-blinded them. The juniper scent was still present, but it had turned foetid when mixed with the scent of sweat and fear. The strange food was doing something to her, Rika thought, but surely not anything that would help her fight.

She watched Ingrid up ahead as they all marched forward and shivered as she saw her beauty: her blazing spread of flaxen hair, bare arms solid and muscles lustrous with fighting oil. Rika watched Ingrid's breasts rise as the berserker Crew leader raised a sword in the air with a jubilant cry. Rika bit her lip again and the blood turned sweet in her mouth. The sky was flickering; there rose a haze above her comrades' heads as they advanced which left patterns in the air through which they moved. It felt like the battle-smoke was blowing straight into her mouth and she was filled with a hunger for violence she had never known before.

This queer combination of fear and fungus: only minutes ago she'd wanted to go home, then seconds later she had suffered anguish over Hardradra's death. Now she moved forward as if in a reverie, towards something over which she would have no control, admiring both women and the smoke of war in this abnormal vision. Then she knew the secret of the dried fungus. It took away the fear. That can only be a good thing, Rika thought, as the haze lifted. Reaching a swell of a hill, they were commanded to halt. She felt the residue of the mushroom in her mouth and moved her tongue in the taste.

Everything was growing bright, even the tiny glimpse she caught of Pia's dark hair up ahead. Rika shook her head to clear the apparition. Her nipples were stiffening and she shuddered with growing arousal. Her mouth grew moist and wet and loose-lipped. She righted her father's helmet, placed her hand on her new, bright sword.

She stood tensely in place for a moment; she just couldn't believe that Haarald Hardradra was dead. So many times she'd imagined him standing there in battle, seven feet tall, his long red-gold hair floating like jagged fire behind him, his arms raised high, his battle cry, his breasts jutting full and proud – with some embarrassment, Rika acknowledged to herself that she had always substituted an image of Ingrid in for Hardradra.

Now, her mind and body buzzed with the drug; she felt eager, sex-ready; even thirsty for the war to begin. Up ahead she again saw Ingrid raising high her blade, her blonde hair sun-glossed and blowing, screaming out a cry – but she wasn't charging; what was going on? Rika stretched her neck, but Ingrid disappeared from sight. And then the company moved forth, a surging wave of metal, flesh and spirit on the hill, and the battle began.

The details of the battle were unclear; there were anomalies such as dark-haired Saxons merging and fighting with blond, fair-skinned Picts. Blades sliced the air and screams that began as agonised and vital dwindled to death-cries. Above, the heavens still held back the rain and the tension of the skies was felt below.

Warriors fought out unsuppressed and deadly, bloody fights, but for individual soldiers it was difficult to tell if their own side was succeeding. As is common in battle, this was a privilege retained by the commanders themselves. Though after several hours of combat in which she fought, but never drew blood, Rika could see that Godwinsson's troops were clearly gaining. Even the drug she had ingested could not fight off the fear that made her throat grow dry and hollow as she tried to mimic the battle cry of Ingrid's Crew. A Saxon near her threw a torch and it quickly singed the fine hairs along her arm as it missed her, passed her by. But after that, she couldn't clear her head of the acrid, burning scent, and when she raised her arms to drive off those who came too near, the smoky, offensive perfume reached her only too clearly.

Then she saw Pia some distance away, standing atop a flat rock on a smallish slope and fighting off pretenders to the ground she had staked. Rika gave a final slamming thud on the helmet of a Celt who had strayed too close, and then she half ran, half pushed her way towards the hill where Pia stood. She shoved her way through the anonymous, twitching and bleeding mass of people, which heaved and trembled its gleaming swords like a malevolent, spiny but cowardly animal. Somehow, the beast did not touch her and she was ignored as she made her way up to Pia.

Pia nodded grimly when Rika joined her. Sweat was rolling down between her shoulder blades like little lustrous fluid pearls, as the dark-haired woman shifted to let Rika fight beside her on the hill.

The late-afternoon weather turned prematurely dark as warriors gasped and choked in the fumes of smoke. Trees near where Ingrid stood and waited were burning. Some who had lost their weapons had the wits to be resourceful and cracked off the burning tree-limbs to use the flaming sticks as weapons, often twirling the branches so quickly in their hands that the fires seemed to spin in circles. It was an effective illusion, as it often caused already war-addled opponents to gaze slack-jawed in wonder and horror at the sight – too late to stop the fire-wheels from being shoved straight and blinding into their faces.

Ingrid snickered at the painful but comical sight and looked at the glow of sun behind the mask of clouds. She had held herself back from actual combat and now stood safely on a hill, observing. There were several hours left till twilight, but only an hour or so before the chaos she and Hrafn had devised would start its course, beginning with the death of Godwinsson – and perhaps later William's, if the dual spy-work she had done had appropriately chaotic repercussions. It didn't really matter – she had been paid well in slaves in return for information she had supplied. The sale of the thralls would jingle nicely in her money-pouch.

And in the meantime . . . She looked around and saw the little slut of a smith's daughter fighting shoulder-to-shoulder with her own Crewmate, Pia. Ingrid felt her sex trembling and her hands gripped her blade more tightly. Battle always made her randy and the passions stirred up by holding herself apart and just observing were no less for it: all the blood and fury, sweat and passion. It never failed to make her horny. A thought came to her: she could have the little slut right now if she wanted to, battle or not. She owed Ingrid a lot.

Ingrid watched Pia and Rika fight for several seconds more, her pulse beginning to race. The younger girl was doing admirably, really. Though it was a bit pointless: Rika wasn't long for this world. Still, she was a feisty little shag. Not a mark yet on her pretty skin. There's just enough time, thought Ingrid, just enough time to redeem some pleasure before she was due to meet Hrafn. But for a moment she contented herself with safely watching the two women battle off opponents, their bodies swerving and curving with well-judged movements and a strong sense of preservation. Watching Pia alone made her feel irritated and strangely jealous; it was Rika she preferred to look at, remembering for a moment the younger woman's tender, eager virginity in the wet and mossy glens of Norway's forests. It was Rika's young firm body she wanted, Rika whose sex she inexplicably craved, right now. Rika whose pussy she wanted to grab and take and conquer with her able, rough hands. But she had had both women before. The thought reminded her of her prowess, and at the thought of her own virility she smiled. The scent of juniper and blood was close to overwhelming.

They were fighting back to back and whenever Pia's shoulders slammed against her, Rika could feel how slick with sweat the other woman was. But she soon grew aware only of the sword she swung, fighting off the men as she pressed against Pia, comforted by her presence. The hill below them was rampant with blood and gore and mayhem, and Rika saw a group of blue-painted Picts battling down below – against the Saxons or for, she couldn't tell. For a moment she remembered Pia mentioning Picts to her when they had first reached this land. It seemed so long ago. And Pia had taken her hand then, her body strong and comforting and close to Rika; she had wanted to tell Rika something. Just as she had wanted to tell her something after the occurrence on the boat.

'Rika, look out!'

Rika took a deep breath as she drove off a man with matted red hair. She saw the orange tattoo circling his mouth in the shape of the sun as he lunged to loop her throat with a knotted, stinking rope, but she drove into his shield and he fell back. Pia paused and pressed Rika's lips close to hers. They kissed softly in this moment of respite. As she felt Pia's warm body against hers, a enormous shiver ran through Rika and all the hairs on her body rose.

She nearly trembled with relief when another man advanced – grateful for the distraction from the inappropriate sensations Pia brought up in her – and she exploded in violence, slashing out, carving a cobbled red oblong that dripped blood as she drew her blade away from the remaining stump of the red-haired man's arm. He screamed and fell back as just another casualty amongst the twisting throng. She felt something die in her for just a moment as his screams continued, something important. But she had to make herself numb. As numb as the man had to have been himself, to have wanted to kill her. She hoped he would survive.

'Now.'

Rika quivered and caught her breath as she heard Ingrid's voice behind her. Surely not now, not in the middle of battle, not in front of Pia? 'Hello, Ingrid.' Even to her own ears, her voice sounded full of resignation.

Five men had advanced on them in the course of the short conversation, but with a quick and needle-sharp attack Ingrid gracefully dispatched them with a few well-chosen thrusts, leaving their lifeless bodies sliding down the slope. Others who had aspired to attack quickly changed their minds. Suddenly the hill which Pia and Rika had been defending was strangely devoid of battle-sound as they were left alone and the tide of combat moved away from them.

Ingrid indecorously wiped the blood off her blade and then turned casually to Pia. 'So, do you want to watch?'

Pia looked from Ingrid, then back at Rika. 'Watch what?' She was breathing heavily.

'Rika owes me a little favour, don't you, Rika?' Ingrid gripped the smooth skin of the younger woman's neck like a soft small kitten. 'She promised me she'd keep it, no matter when, no matter where I choose. I choose now. Here. And Rika's not the type to break a promise, are you, Rika?'

Rage was flowing quickly through Rika's veins, but so was an inexplicable and altogether unsuitable surge of lust. The thought of Pia watching made her tremble. Though there was no fear of that as Pia glanced down briefly at the rune-scar on Rika's hand, cursed under her breath, glared at Ingrid and spat in her direction.

'No thanks,' she said to Ingrid, then bent down to whisper something very odd to Rika: 'She's a good fighter. At least you'll be safe from battle up here with her.' Then she shoved her blade in its scabbard and rushed quickly down to the heart of the battle several hundred feet away.

And Ingrid was already urgent, it seemed, pushing Rika down on her stomach on the flat smooth rock and tearing off her clothes so that Rika lay naked and exposed in the middle of the battle. Ingrid fumbled with the small food pouch on her belt and brought out a leather packet oozing honey. Rika could smell its lazy sugary aroma even through the masking scents of war.

Ingrid rubbed the wild honey on Rika's arsehole, just nudging her fingers past the tight ring to moisten Rika inside, too. Rika could feel it warming her, the sweet ooze running between her thighs and she told herself to relax. The sun was heavy and hot on her skin; she could smell her arousal being mixed in with the syrup, as Ingrid rubbed it in between the lips of her pussy for good measure, hot and sticky.

'You should loosen up, Rika,' Ingrid told her. 'You knew you had a bit of punishment coming after you disobeyed me by coming first to Gaul and then to Britain. I thought I had taught you better than that.' Just within her eyesight she could see Ingrid's arms, muscles flexing as she efficiently prepared her smooth, sticky arsehole. Rika could see the beetle tattoo on Ingrid's arm, the one Ingrid had told her was from Egypt, a land far away to which Ingrid had once travelled. At least that's what Ingrid said. She could see all this, and it was fine and good, but she could also hear the sounds of the nearby battle, shouts and clanging metal. She could feel the viscous golden liquid running and running down her legs, and it was true – she did find it difficult to relax.

The flat of Ingrid's hand pressed against the whole of Rika's wet, sticky sex and moved up and down over it, from the throbbing bead of her clit to the wet centre. Ingrid's hand splayed flat her moist inner lips, her inner wrist on the little bridge of sensitive flesh between Rika's arsehole and her cunt. A shiver ran through Rika and she thought she would choke on the scent of battle smoke. Still, something held her captive there. And it wasn't only Ingrid's talented hand, Rika thought. As if in a dream she watched the tall blonde Viking woman withdraw and take out her battle-axe.

Lying on her stomach with her head turned towards Ingrid, Rika couldn't even manage a scream, but she whimpered at the sight of Ingrid's great flashing blade, held high in the sky, its long wooden handle arced and gripped by her strong right arm.

Ingrid gave out a harsh laugh when she saw Rika flinch and brought the double-edged blade down deep into a nearby tree-stump with a war-whoop, then pulled it out nearly as swiftly. Rika caught her breath: she could hear only a roar in her ears; even the battle sounds were quiet. The sun burnt slowly up above her.

'You think I meant the axe for you?' Again Ingrid let out an unkind laugh, then with her free hand gripped at Rika's naked shoulder. A tremor ran through Rika's whole body. Worse, she could feel the itch between her legs growing even stronger and throbbing like a powerful second heart. The honey was still dripping over her arsehole. She held her breath and nodded.

'You stupid little girl,' Ingrid said, and for a moment anger flashed through Rika, but to her shame the pull between her legs and over her whole taut body was stronger, and there was an edge to it with the danger in the air. Her nipples were stiffening into hard little beads, two tight points on her chest. She couldn't let herself hope that Ingrid would soothe them with a wet and suckling kiss.

'Girl,' Ingrid said again, and again Rika saw the silver blade flashing past her eyes and smelt the scent of battle-smoke, 'this is what I'm going to do.' And Rika felt the pain of Ingrid plunging the unbladed, smooth dowel-end of the axe deep into Rika's honey-drenched arse. Rika yelled out, but within seconds she was squirming on the round and polished stick, as it became a pleasure within the soft, tight circle of her anus. Ingrid was not holding the blade of the axe directly. Rika realised this when she felt Ingrid tickling the curves of her arse with her other hand, while driving the smoothly wooden stem into her arse with the flat sharp blade pressed safely against her strong arm. Back and forth, powerfully and slowly.

The pain had almost gone, and Rika screwed her eyes shut and let Ingrid fuck her with her arse in the air. She moved one hand between her legs and then, unmindful of Ingrid, she

was masturbating freely. The dowel was making the honey-coated walls of her arse shudder, and she was stroking herself towards such a dirty raw climax, she thought, rubbing hard on her clit as Ingrid pushed the polished stem deep, deep into her arse.

A warmth was gathering in the lower half of Rika's body. Ingrid removed the handle and thrust in four fingers, rasping them together in the dark, concentrated, honey-filled crevice of Rika's arse. As Rika came, the hot sweet stickiness was so thick in her that she wanted to taste it. She was full and sticky in her pussy, too, where she was creamy from excitement.

She looked up in the sky, where hot droplets of the rain she had prayed for were just starting to pool together and fall. The sky was no longer grey, though; it was a dirty orange colour and spirals of gritty smoke were rising up to it. It was lucky, though, because from where she lay on the hill, looking straight up, she could see none of the carnage or death below.

The warm raindrops hit her eyelashes, falling and mixing in her eyes, blinding her for mere seconds. She raised a hand, rubbed away the weirdly hot water and looked at Ingrid, still standing over her with a self-satisfied look on her face. What in Odin's name was she doing up here, being fucked, while people died below?

But her thoughts never ran their course, because at the moment all other eight members of the Crew came tearing towards the hill. 'Ingrid,' they called, 'we've got to assemble.' The grey-haired woman's voice rose above the others: 'Ingrid! We need you!'

'Damn,' muttered Ingrid, shoving the sticky shaft of her battleaxe back in her belt. Rika looked up, shocked: surely Ingrid should relish the opportunity to assemble with her Crew and fight?

The eight women rushed and stumbled to the bottom of the battle-hill, desperate to secure their leader. Rika stepped into her breeches as quickly as she could, but none of them gave any notice to her nudity. Maybe it's happened before, she thought cynically. Maybe this is another one of Ingrid's favourite games. The thought made her instantly feel somewhat sickened, that she had gone along with pleasure and indulgence while below warriors fought not only for their lives, but also for their peoples.

'We'll speak again.' Ingrid patted her on the shoulder and rushed off, though she was heading down the hill in the opposite direction from where the Crew stood.

'Ingrid,' she called, 'you're going the wrong way!' But there was no answer.

'Come on, Rika,' Pia yelled from the bottom of the slope, 'we need you.'

For a moment Rika hesitated, looking at the Crew, then wildly scanned the battlefield for Ingrid. 'Ingrid! Come back!'

'Rika!' Pia's voice was desperate, as the Crew began to fight off a horde of ambitious Saxons.

'Ingrid?' But she could no longer hesitate; the Crew needed her. Rika whooped as the others had done and tore off the jerkin stained with the dark arterial blood of the red-haired man. Her naked breasts felt liberated and powerful, and a surge of vigour hit her. Now she was a berserker, too. She roared, gripped her sword and took it out, and then ran down bare-breasted into the mêlée, to fight as a temporary member of Ingrid's Crew.

She slashed away, and after several resounding hits she fought with confidence. This is what a berserker feels like, thought Rika, and she could sense the fury from the mushroom drug still spinning through her veins. She cut a long crimson line down one man's face and was rewarded with a terrible stinging in her upper left arm. She didn't dare to stop and look, and instead kept slashing and cutting and lunging. The metal taste was on her lips again, and she tried to remember why she had always loved it so much before.

The blood was pouring from her upper arm, but finally she saw Ingrid, standing outside the battle-area, fairly close to where the Crew was fighting, perhaps the span of several longboats away. She was speaking to what looked like a sour-faced Saxon head soldier and an old man dressed in an aqua-coloured shroud.

'Ingrid!' she shouted, but there was no response. 'Wait a moment,' Rika screamed to Pia and, after lunging at a fresh attacker, her breasts gleaming with sweat and scarlet blood and her pendant shining against her bare skin, she shoved her sword back into her belt and headed towards Ingrid.

'What are you *doing*?' roared Pia, but it was too late; Rika had already left Pia and the rest of the Crew fighting behind her.

'Ingrid?' Rika cried as she rushed up to the group of three, feeling an inexplicable anger.

Ingrid didn't even turn her head. 'Get out of here, you little bitch.'

The reaction from the old man was different, however. Surprisingly relaxed, considering the mayhem around him, he reached out to touch Rika's jewel; he fingered it slowly while she stood there gaping at the blonde warrior, before turning back and murmuring something to Ingrid. And the third man, the grimy Saxon, just stood silently glancing at all three of them. 'You've got a pretty one this time.' The old man directed this comment to Ingrid. He was Norse and spoke a dialect not too dissimilar to her own.

'What?' Rika was flabbergasted, but pursued her case: 'They need your help, Ingrid. They need your fighting skills.'

Ingrid laughed. Considering the circumstances, it was a chilling sound.

The old man looked from Rika to Ingrid. 'Does she know?'

'Know *what*?' Rika cried in frustration. 'Come on, Ingrid, we've got to hurry.'

'She knows nothing – yet.' Ingrid still kept her eyes from meeting Rika's. The screams of the Crew nearby grew louder. Rika knew she had to convince Ingrid to come and fight with them in a matter of a minute – perhaps seconds.

The Saxon stepped up to Ingrid now, filthy and demanding. He spoke a guttural, broad tongue, just barely distinguishable to Rika's ears. 'I don't care what anybody knows, but I happen to know this, Ingrid. You promised me payment for at least thirty sacrificial thralls and I've yet to see a piece of coin.'

Rika shot him a quick glance, trying to work out exactly what he meant. He didn't look like a turncoat Saxon, but they weren't even loyal to their own people – it had happened before.

'Shut up,' said Ingrid with a malevolent smile. She looked slightly amused and in her panic Rika found this unnerving. Her wound was throbbing now and she clasped a hand to its searing bright heat.

The Saxon was insistent. 'I won't shut up. You made promises to me, Viking woman; I've paid out a sum of shining gold for transferring the thralls to Norway for your abominable heathen "rites". In exchange, you promised William dead by noon, and look – there he still stands, healthier than ever.' The Saxon pointed to a hill where the Norman stood.

Alarmed, Rika looked quickly from William to Ingrid, then back to Ingrid again. 'You mean that you sold out William –' She couldn't finish the question. The battle sensations began to press in on her again: a hot thick salty taste in her mouth and a roaring in her ears. That Ingrid was buying and selling slaves for sacrifice was seedy enough, but if part of the bargain meant allowing the Saxons to win – well, that was unimaginable. She gripped her sword nervously, like a newly bladed drummer-boy. The roar increased.

'That's right, Rika.' Ingrid smirked. 'Does that shock you?' Ingrid stepped closer. 'I wouldn't let it worry you. You're not just any thrall, I assure you. You're reserved for something special.' She tugged at the pendant, then back-handed a club-wielding Celt who had sneaked up behind her without once looking back. 'You've got a far greater destiny than this, Rika. Don't fight it.'

Rika swallowed as a new thought hit her. 'And Hardradra. They say you must have known of his death far before . . .' Her voice trailed off. The blood was streaming to her fingers now.

The old man moved in to the three of them, almost gently. 'May I call you by your first name, Rika?' Rika merely glared at him in mute horror. 'Our dear friend Ingrid has done all Norsepeople a great service today by warning Godwinsson of the bastard William's strategies. By doing so, she has received enough foreign thralls to keep our ancient religion continuing to spread to distant areas for years to come ... places where they only have access to the worship of a dead, already-murdered man can witness the miracle of what a true blood sacrifice means.'

Rika screwed her eyes shut in consternation. Both religions were starting to sound as bloody as each other.

Hrafn turned away from the Saxon and said privately to Rika, 'As indeed she did for William, when she told him he would find Godwinsson exhausted from his battle with Hardradra and could easily attack him. Our friend Ingrid is many players in one huge game, Rika.'

Rika shook her head: did this mean that not only had Ingrid helped William, but that she was helping Godwinsson as well? And why? So she would be paid in sacrifices? It didn't make sense – unless Ingrid was a far more devoted follower of the Old Ways than she had ever suspected.

The old man glanced down at Rika's hand, which was gripping her blade, still wet with hot blood. 'Ingrid tells me that you're bound to her yourself.' Rika looked down too; she could still see the rune-scar of her blood-oath through the viscous crimson sap. 'You've a great destiny to fulfil in the plot of things, my dear, when the rites begin –'

'Shut up, Hrafn.' Ingrid's voice broke in, violently.

Hrafn, Rika thought; there it was, that name again. She glanced desperately over at the Crew, fighting for their lives, and she saw the grey-haired woman take a blade, fall and then lie still. Rika held her breath waiting for winged maidens to carry her to glory, but bitterness filled her when it did not happen. A horrible suspicion began to dawn; perhaps it had merely been a myth told to encourage battle-risk. And for whose benefit? She looked over at Ingrid, who had been treacherous in every way imaginable. She was playing games of business, bartering human lives while others fought for the honour of Ingrid's Crew – an honour that now seemed false. The betrayal was incomprehensible. A great sorrow churned out of her and she screamed at Ingrid: '*No!*'

It was if her fingers moved of their own volition, as they raised high the sword in both hands high over Ingrid's head and then drove it down, as quick as –

'Bitch!' There was a great cracking sound. Rika knew the blade must have struck its mark, though at the same time a searing pain ran from her skull down to her toes. She felt a darkness spidering into her vision, which eventually became as impenetrable and dark as a wall of thick, black tar, and she saw no more at all.

When she woke, the clinking and clashing sounds of the battle had ceased and thin dogs were roaming the field, partaking in a gruesome feast. Bodies lay in puddles of blood and rain and Rika screwed her eyes shut, willing out the terrible sights spread before her. The scent she had relished so before, the scent of iron, had become an overriding stench. All she could smell now was blood and metal and cinders. She realised, as she stroked the pendant round her neck, that the appeal of the odour had lost its charm for her. And the faint fragrance of the juniper trees had entirely disappeared.

'Are you all right?' A worried voice wormed its way past her thoughts, when all she wanted to do was just lie there and watch the camp robbers take gold and weapons from the slain, lie there and die.

Her head was pounding, and in the faint grisly light of nearby fires she could make out great reddish puddles of dirt and blood near her. The rain had done its work, she thought; the battle was complete, but her head ached too much even to contemplate the fact. She tried to rise and stumbled. Her arm was stinging, too, and when the owner of the voice that had enquired after her reached out to help her to her feet, she yelped in pain as fingers cracked through the drying wound.

'I've been looking for you, Rika.' The voice meant something to her and she tried to crawl her way back to the present. The arms which gently lifted her, the soft deep voice which spoke . . .

Pia. A robe or cloak or something similar was slung over her shoulders. 'Shh, don't worry now; I'll take you somewhere warm.' Rika realised she was shivering uncontrollably, but when she tried again to think and reason, her head ached with the effort.

'Who . . . who won?'

'Hush, Rika.' Pia's arms were warm and comforting as she directed Rika towards a hearth a good distance from the battle-field. 'We did. But don't think about it at the moment.'

After her wound was cleaned and dressed, mead and roasted boar went easily down her throat. And with her whole body warmed by the elk-fur Pia had thrown around her, Rika found it easier to adjust to the company in which she found herself: six sober-faced members of Ingrid's Crew, including Pia.

Pia stood behind her, relaxing and soothing her neck with her strong hands, and Rika found herself asking the question no one had yet dared to answer: 'Where are the missing Crewmembers?' By implication, one of these was Ingrid. Out of respect, she did not refer directly to the grey-haired woman she had seen bravely falling in the battle.

'Asa and Sigridr have fallen.' It was the green-eyed warrior, Sela, who spoke solemnly. Rika's eyes went across the company: yes, both the grey-haired woman and the short freckly woman were gone. 'And your friend Ingrid is nowhere to be found.' The tone was menacing and, startled, Rika instinctively drew back from the woman's rage.

'Take care, Sela!' Pia's voice was sharp and full of warning. 'You saw yourself how Rika fought for the Crew.' As Pia's hands massaged her shoulders to alleviate her aching, tired muscles, Rika wondered if Pia had also seen the last thing that she remembered herself: her own desperate lunge at Ingrid after her betrayal.

'That's true,' Sela grudgingly admitted and shoved a bit more of the smoky roast into her mouth. 'But now we have no leader, and whatever trouble Ingrid has stirred up here, she's bound to have done back home as well.'

'Rika!' Pia was suddenly urgent. 'Do you remember anything important Ingrid said to you today?'

Rika hesitated before answering, unsure if, in the midst of a blood-oath, she should switch allegiances so quickly. But Ingrid was a traitor, she reminded herself, and she answered with assurance: 'There was a man with her, a man from home, a priest of the Old Ways called Hrafn. There was something about spying and chaos, I think, and something about the slaves for the rites.'

'I knew it!' Pia vehemently slammed her sword into the wet earth nearby. 'Did they say anything else to you?'

'They said I had a destiny . . .' Rika's voice trailed off, the memory of Ingrid's treachery too fresh and painful.

'A destiny? Where?' All six women were straining forward now, listening eagerly.

'Well, I'm not sure. But Ingrid had told me once to go to Tallby, and seek out a woman, name of Arje.'

'Arje again.' Pia breathed out the words in a sigh, but the others did not seem to recognise the name. Pia leant in. 'Rika, do you want to help our people and the Crew?'

'Yes . . .' Rika felt flustered: hurried promises made her think of how easily Ingrid had manipulated her.

'Don't worry – you don't need to promise anything. Just go to Tallby and find out what business Ingrid had with Arje. Don't go anywhere with her, though, especially not to an event called the rites, nor should you go anywhere else she suggests. Just find out, and then come back and tell us what all of this means.'

'How can I trust you, though?' She looked at Pia's eyes glowing in the campfire. She felt it was a fair and genuine question.

'How can we trust *you*?' green-eyed Sela broke in, nastily.

'Quiet!' Pia told her. She leant close to Rika and spoke so that no one else could hear. 'Rika, I know I can trust you because I know you tried hard to keep your promises to Ingrid. I know this, because I've made promises to her myself, before.' She revealed the rune-scar of a blood-oath on her hand to Rika.

Rika drew her breath in sharply – she'd seen the mark before, of course, but never suspected it had been linked with Ingrid.

'And you know you can trust me,' Pia continued in a lower voice, 'because I've never once betrayed you, and I've always kept a close eye on you to make sure Ingrid didn't, either.' That was true, and memories of Pia's careful observance now came flooding through to Rika. Her eyes pooled with tears; she turned away from the fire so that the other Crewmembers would not see her weeping.

'Just try,' Pia pressed. 'That's all we're asking. To find out Ingrid's plans, and to stop needless bloodshed and betrayal. There's a strange religious justification to her trading with thralls – or perhaps it's just a monetary justification. I don't like it. I'm no Christian, but I don't like either her or Hrafn's interpretations of the Old Ways – they're zealots, and those who examine every facet of a faith too carefully in order to find the "right" reading are always dangerous. Look at our stories – our gods are a fun-loving lot, not obsessed with sacrifice, as its followers often are, nor sin, as the Christian god is. Blood sacrifice is no necessity, in my mind, to being a good believer in the Old Ways. We believe that Ingrid sells the thralls to sacrificial groups, new rabid ones combating the strangling grip of the fish-believers, and the thralls die painfully. At least that's what we think. We aren't sure.'

Briefly, Rika wondered how it came that Pia seemed to know so many of these details. She looked up into the blue of the warrior's warm eyes. 'All right,' she sniffled, 'I'll do it. I'll go to Tallby.'

A great cheer went up amongst the Crewmembers. Most went over to clap her on her back and offer her the full drinking-horns of mead in toasts, even Sela.

But Rika was still shivering and feeling overwhelmed, though she tried to grin and boast with the others. She thought of the man whose arm she had severed from his body and a weird grief swept over her. A single tear ran down her cheek, but quickly Pia spoke: 'I think Rika's a bit overcome with it all right now. We're going for a little walk.'

'Well, you'd better take the laying-rug!' Someone cackled lewdly and threw the bronze-furred spread in their direction.

They sat on the warm elk-fur together, facing away from the waste of battle wreckage below. From where they sat, Rika saw the trees spread peacefully below and she was nearly able to shut out the whole terrible day. Though she had aspired to be a Crewmember, she was nearly convinced that a life of violence was not for her. Though neither, she admitted to herself, was a life in her own small village. She would have to consider this further, later.

Pia held her hand tightly. 'Are you feeling better now?'

'Do Valkyries truly exist, Pia? Do they truly carry off only the brave?' The stars were flickering and dancing. She knew full well what befell those who died safely at home and not in battle – banned to eternity in the Cold World, sailing to the icy, misty land on a ship made of toenail clippings. Horrible.

'Well, now.' Pia's voice was measured as she considered the question. 'I've seen many brave fighters fall and I've never seen these warrior-virgins people make so much of. But I think the warriors go to Valhalla anyway, leaving their bodies behind. Just as when souls rise from a normal death of fire and the bodies are no more.'

The answer made Rika feel better and she snuggled in slightly closer to Pia. 'Will you miss me when I return to Norway?'

'Of course I'll miss you!' Pia was outraged. 'How could you ask such a question?'

Their lips met lightly and a gentle pulse began to reverberate inside Rika, as Pia pulled her close and their tongues touched and melted into each other. Rika kissed Pia's face carefully, the little dimples on her cheeks, the dip of the bridge of her nose, her closed, long-lashed eyes. The stars continued to glitter above them.

'That's nice, Rika. I remember your kisses very well,' Pia murmured, leaning back on the soft elk fur. She held the exhausted Rika gently in her great strong arms for a long time, and did not attempt to caress the girl further.

From a higher hill nearby a tall figure stood watching their barely discernible shapes. Her reaction was initially one of worry and resentment, but then a smile curled on the lips of the tall figure, then disappeared. Knuckles tightened on a sword, and then relaxed. She's a pretty girl, thought Ingrid, but unbelievably stupid.

# FIVE

There had been snow during the night, and the straw Rika had stuffed into her goat-leather shoes was not enough to keep her feet warm.

It had taken her three weeks to find a longboat captain willing to let her row back to the Norwegian coast for free passage. But once on board, the journey went rapidly, three days only, and she had landed safely. Now here she stood in the coastal forests, on her way towards Tallby. There was a light frosting of snow on the ground – just enough to make it feel stiff and crunchy as she walked over the earth and crisp leaves, but not enough for her feet to sink into. Her skin was chilled; early winter winds were whistling and she thought that in the distance she could hear the mournful howl of a wolf.

She trudged through the trees. She knew vaguely where she was and thus was careful to avoid all paths that led back to her own village. Something preyed on her mind. She would have thought that Pia would have been utmost in her thoughts, or perhaps Ingrid's betrayal, maybe even the possibility that if her mission was successful she could now join the Crew. But no, what was bothering her was Lina. Guilt rose from Rika's gut and for a moment she felt warmed by shame. She had ruthlessly taken advantage of the girl, treating Lina nearly as badly as Ingrid would have done. It was funny how she hadn't really thought of her since she had left. But now that she was home she was thinking of such things, the things she'd left behind. She even found herself wondering how her father was faring.

The forest was quiet. Once she looked up and gazed at the infinite branches of a birch, naked and stark and twisting against the sky. Her stomach rumbled, so she tore off a bit of pale bark and chewed on it to keep the taste within her mouth. It wouldn't satisfy, but it would keep her stomach occupied with juices. As she walked on, she began to notice signs that she was nearing a village: small paths, the spoor of domestic animals. She remembered how, when she and Lina had parted, she had urged Lina to ride on to the fifth village past their own. Now she followed the same route, but she had no horse, as Lina had had, and her feet were aching from walking on the frost-imbedded earth. But she would seek lodging in this village and news of a girl who looked like her.

Rika wondered if they still looked so similar. She had a strange feeling that she was different, that somehow her face and body had registered the wondrous and terrible events of her adventures and that she had irrevocably changed. She had a scar now, anyway. The wound to her left arm had started to heal, but she would always bear the evidence that she had fought bravely for the Crew. It made her feel proud, but she suspected that she could never again capture the look of innocence that Lina wore so well and which she had once shared.

But now she had reached the outskirts of the settlement. She crawled over the wall of a village even smaller than her own. It was not long after dawn, and only smiths and farmers would be up at this early hour. She felt again a twinge of some weird, lost emotion for her ironsmith father, then she steeled herself. After all, he shouldn't have been forcing a marriage on her in the first place.

A cheerful, grubby child – why were children such early risers? – ran up to her. Its mother had obviously padded it out in winter-wear so that it would not get cold, then gone straight back to sleep.

'Hello,' Rika greeted the small being who was gaping at her with a slack mouth. She didn't feel particularly friendly.

The child only stared at her.

She might as well get some information out of the brat. 'Where is the boarding-inn?'

The warmly wrapped child – of indistinguishable sex – stuck its gloved hand in its mouth for a second, covering it in slobber. It was about seven or so years old, reckoned Rika, surely old enough to answer the question. 'Well?' she prodded.

'There's a place where you can sleep.'

'Far away?'

'No.' The child kept staring, but Rika's irritation disappeared when it added. 'There's a lady who looks like you, too. Another stranger.' Rika's heart leapt – another stranger who looked like herself. It could only be Lina.

'Where?' she said quickly, her breath coming out in short frozen cloud-puffs in the air. She tried to appear patient. 'Where did you see this lady?'

'Don't know. She's not a thrall like you, though.'

'Not a thrall – what do you mean?' Idiotic child.

'She doesn't have the slave mark on her hand, like you do.'

Rika glanced down at the rune-scar on her left hand, the remnant of her blood-oath with Ingrid. 'That's not . . . Oh, never mind.' The child wouldn't understand the complexity of a blood-oath.

The child lost interest, shrugged and turned to play with a frisky wolfish-looking puppy several paces away. She gave up. There was no use pressing someone so young for information. She headed off in the general direction that it had pointed to.

The wind crooned past her ears in a low persistent whistle, and snowflakes began falling on her cheeks and melting immediately from her body heat. They wouldn't melt indefinitely. Her cheeks would turn stiff and waxen and cold as stone if she didn't find a warm place to board for the night. She looked down.

With her fingers ashen with the first pale stages of frostbite, the rune-scar shone in sharp relief on her hands. Her hands were stiff and she put them inside her jacket and kept walking.

But there ahead was the inn, with a light that looked welcoming even for so early in the cold morning. Rika's head was covered with the light flakes, and she looked up at their source, at a sky grey and so full of falling snow it looked like the soft breast-down of a white duck. She quickly put her head down so that she was not blinded by the soft crystals, and looked behind her. Even the child and the puppy had gone inside. It was snowing in earnest, and so she knocked.

She heard footsteps as someone came to the door and her face cracked into a cold smile. Please let me in, she thought.

'Yes?' An old woman held the door open just a crack and her face was suspicious. She peered out in order to see Rika's face. 'You again!' She slammed the door shut.

Rika's toes were stinging with cold. She wondered if it was her warrior garb that the woman was objecting to. 'I'm here for board, if that's all right.'

'Here for board!' The crone opened the door again. 'And after the problems you caused last time. There's not a person here who will open their doors to you, no matter how sweet your ways and pretty your face. Though your clothes are nothing much to speak of,' the old woman conceded, looking at the muddy blood-stained garments Rika wore.

Though chill was making her teeth ache, the comments boded well for Lina having been there. 'What do you mean?'

'What do I mean? When those types that seemed to know you so well ran into town, causing the worst rumpus we've ever seen yet?'

Rika told herself to go slowly despite her suspicions, so she said through chattering teeth, 'You mean me . . . and my horse?' It was the only way she'd know for sure that it was Lina.

'Of course I mean you and your horse! Though your horse ran away a long while ago, girl. We found it dead later in the woods, the result of a sacrifice, no doubt. And I'm not paying you for it, no. You should be paying me for its board, while I fed it and brushed it and waited for you to return. And that's all I aim to say to you at all. Causing a good Christian village to be disgraced by those types of people! You should be ashamed!' The woman slammed the door in her face again and Rika blinked, startled.

'But where shall I go?' she shouted in desperation, stomping from one foot to another for warmth.

'Why don't you visit your friend?' the woman muttered behind the closed door. 'The trampy-looking one with all the grey hair. The one who seemed so fond of you when they ran over our nice, quiet town. It isn't natural that she should look so young, anyway,' she added in a surly tone.

'But I'm cold!' Rika protested. She rapped on the door with her knuckles, but her hands were going numb.

'So walk the extra miles to the hills they came out of and keep yourself warm in the bargain,' said the pitiless old woman. Rika heard her walk away, and with a sinking heart she realised that she would get no more out of her.

She rubbed her hands together briskly to warm them and walked quickly away. She couldn't waste time arguing, or else she would freeze to death. Up to the hills, the woman had said. She would find the grey-haired woman and find out what had happened to Lina.

Rika guiltily hoped that Lina hadn't come to any harm for her sake. She had half a day's walk ahead of her to the hills, she thought, but she knew she would have to do it. And at least she had heard some news of Lina. And later, after she had made sure that all was right with her friend and had warmed up a bit, she would chase up the woman Arje and find out the extent of Ingrid's treachery. Fortunately, the way to Tallby was the same direction, as she recalled, so she was not making any unnecessary detours.

The sky was still full of snow, and the gentle flakes piled up on her clothes in thin white fragile layers as she walked on, melting with the heat of her exertion. One thing had been true of what the old woman had said, anyway. At least the long walk was warming her up.

She made her way to the coastal hills, avoiding all routes that headed back to her own home. At the first large town in the heart of the fjords she asked for directions to the home of the grey-haired woman. It seemed that the woman was popular – or infamous – for everyone she asked pointed her in the same direction. And when she asked whether a blonde-haired girl had been in her company, they had all answered yes.

Now here she stood, knuckles poised to rap on the huge oak door of the small longhouse. She should knock and make it known that she was here. Around her, the tips of the tall spruces swayed in the wind and the wind curled in wickedly and swept around her ankles. Her teeth chattered as she raised her hand up to the smooth cold wood of the door. She released the tight fist she'd made and stroked it for a minute, wondering what secrets lay behind it. Would she find Lina warm, chatty and happy – or worse? The wind blew furiously on her body and she shivered, not only from the cold.

Before she had a chance to knock, the door opened. It was dark inside and Rika couldn't see who had invited her in. She walked to the frame and peered into the dwelling. A strong hand grabbed her by the neck, pulled her in and slammed the door shut, before Rika had a chance to look at the abductor or reach for her blade. She flailed and tried to kick out.

She found herself lying flat on her back. A torch was lit in the darkness; she focused on her attacker's face above her.

A woman.

A beautiful woman.

A woman with silver hair twirled up on her head in a twist, but with a young, unlined face. Dark skin. A soft, red, full-lipped mouth. A pair of violet eyes, fringed with gold and silver lashes. She was gorgeously voluptuous, and wore only a necklace and a vest that was far too small for her, from which spilled a pair of extremely large breasts and which even revealed the large,

111

dusky-red nipples on the huge soft mounds. Silver threads of pubic hair grew lushly over her sex, the soft metallic tendrils intertwining like the finest silverwork she had ever seen. The necklace was a wolf-tooth pendant – and looked to Rika just like the polished enamel totem Sela Beartooth had worn before the battle.

A nearly naked woman. A vicious, nearly naked woman.

Rika shut her eyes for a moment. This surely couldn't be Lina's abductor. Then she opened them immediately, judging wisely that it was best to keep aware of things while she was laid out so vulnerably. The interior of the woman's home was quite bare, except for shelves piled with assorted flasks and bunches of musty-smelling, faded-green herbs; a bed of furs, the hearth and stacks of wooden bowls in the middle of the room. There was one container on the fur-strewn ground that looked made of a more disturbing source than wood. Polished white, it was the cranium of a wolf. Holes had been drilled in a circle around its base, and in these abscesses sharp white shards of wolf teeth had been pushed, so that the bowl stood upright with the support of the curving, snow-white canines. She wondered if she would receive an indication as to why the woman had kept company with Lina. She held her breath, waiting for the woman to speak.

She didn't have to wait long, however, because her assailant spoke to her nearly at once.

'You've made the acquaintance of Ingrid,' the beautiful grey-haired woman commented, then just as matter-of-factly helped Rika to her feet again. The lush globes of her breasts gently brushed Rika's face and Rika shivered. She had an odd craving to touch them, to slide her hand into that delicious, pliant cleavage. Rika was rather dazed, but she noticed the woman's piercing violet glance had fixed on her pendant, and something clicked. It all seemed to revolve around the jewel given to her by Ingrid, and people's reactions were always strong. Perhaps she ought to have removed the little locket, with its secret cache of ashes.

'Yes, I know Ingrid.' She wasn't sure if that was a good thing to admit or not.

'Well, when you next see her, tell her she owes me my favourite paintbox back. She stole it away for a little fun of her own and thought I wouldn't notice. It had my favourite name-chain inside it, too. She knows very well that I have to use the box for decorating the bodies of particular participants.'

Rika cleared her throat and tried to retain some dignity, brushing the earth dirt of the floor off her. She would be polite and ignore the woman's singularly unpleasant greeting. After all, she was here to find out what was going on. And now with the mention of the paintbox, she had more than an inkling of who the woman was.

'Are you Arje?' When she exhaled, a cloud of mist hung in the air for several seconds.

The woman laughed. 'Of course I am.'

Well, that was two missions accomplished at once.

Arje set down a large bowl of liquid and an array of bottles from the shelves. 'You're just in time for the rune-casting.'

'Listen,' Rika said, and swallowed nervously. Her finger flickered momentarily at the gem around her throat. 'I've been told that you can let me know where Lina is.' She would try to get some information for Pia and the Crew about these rites, as well.

'Lina?' The silver-haired woman's forehead crinkled for just a moment as she attempted to remember – but to Rika it looked suspiciously like a mockery of memory.

'Where is she?' For the first time she rose and addressed Arje with something that approached aggression. But she moved with some caution – worried that the woman's formidable strength would lay her flat on her back again.

'Does she look like you, by any chance?' The woman's violet eyes twinkled merrily, and her round, deeply tanned breasts shook with pleasure.

'Stop laughing,' Rika snapped. 'Yes, she does, and I know you've got something to do with her disappearance.'

'Oh, do you?' Arje bustled over to the hearth and stirred a pot

113

that was cooking there, her full bare bottom momentarily distracting Rika.

'I do, and if you don't tell me where you've taken her, I'll . . . I'll . . .' Rika's voice faltered as she grew unsure whether she could carry off any threats. She stepped back.

The grey-haired woman's face softened somewhat when she realised the extent of Rika's distress. 'Girl' – she reached out and took the younger woman's hands in her own – 'Lina was not taken anywhere she did not already want to go. She was taken quite happily to the rites; she was sleeping like a baby at the time, after the administration of certain soporifics, of course.'

'Lina? At the rites?' Those were the only words Rika heard. Her tongue thickened in her mouth. Ingrid's friend Hrafn had mentioned the rites. And Pia had specifically warned her off them.

'That's right.' Arje's face was beaming with relief that Rika understood what she was talking about. 'And naturally your friend Ingrid arranged it all, of course.'

'Ingrid?' Now Rika's ears felt as if they were bursting out of her skull.

'Well, of course.' Arje's voice was gentle and she confusedly searched Rika's face for clues as to why she sounded so excited. 'But of course you already know why Ingrid had decided that.'

'Of course,' Rika echoed. Lina and Ingrid. That was why Ingrid had mistaken her for Lina in Normandy. Her blood was boiling with anger – and a fair bit of lust for the priestess, if she were honest – but she realised that she could not let on that, as yet, she knew nothing of the rites, nor of Ingrid's plans – not if she hoped to discover the meaning of the mysterious rites and report back to the Crew on Ingrid's involvement.

Arje walked over to the hearth and ladled out a mug of warm root-and-herb soup for Rika. 'Take this, you poor thing; you look cold. And there I was going to ask you if you wanted to rehearse a bit of the rites with me after I cast the runes for it. We'll do it after you warm up a bit, before you head off to the

Great Thing tomorrow.' Rika could have sworn that the woman gave her a lascivious wink. 'What's your name, anyway?'

Rika told her, swallowed down the last warm sip of the broth and stared at silver-haired Arje. Surely she didn't mean the great Viking political assembly? Rika had never before heard of any rites being performed there. The caucus was a judicial and political meeting of old warriors and old men – not for silver-haired madwomen, no matter how beautiful and lush they were, Rika thought, averting her eyes from the plump valley of cleavage caused by Arje's inadequate vest. Her nipples were just ripe for sucking, plump and luscious. Unless women had a very special cause to champion, they didn't usually speak at the Thing. And she couldn't understand what Lina would be doing there, either. The Thing was certainly not for meek, shy women the likes of Lina. It took a courageous and inspired woman to state her case at the Thing.

At the Thing, as always, women were mostly secondary – unless their men were dead or unless they were divorced. Of course women ran the farms and such when all the men were at sea, but when the men returned, well, it was back to being under thumb again. She guessed that this was one of the reasons she had always aspired to Ingrid's Crew – because of the slim hope that as a warrior she would be playing a different game and could control her own destiny.

'And Ingrid's told you, of course, what Lina's role will be?'

Rika considered the question. After a pause, Arje cleared her throat pointedly.

Rika's head jerked up as she realised the woman was waiting for a response. 'Yes,' she muttered darkly. She was fuming inwardly: she could distinctly remember Ingrid promising that she had never touched Lina. She obviously bedded the girl before Rika had herself.

'I thought so. It's a brave choice you've made, your own role in the rites; I'm not sure that I'd do it myself.'

What choice? But she'd have to play along. 'Yes. It took me a long time to decide.' Silver-haired Arje was bustling around in the dimly lit cabin interior, her body shining with firelight. The hearth was crackling; Rika could smell the burning of fresh green wood, with its peculiarly sharp, verdant scent.

She drew in her breath. If Arje wanted to 'practise' the rites, well, that wasn't really the same as attending, which she had promised Pia she wouldn't do. Surely this occasion could develop into something she could report back to Pia. Wasn't that what the Crew wanted to find out?

Near the fire, Arje busied herself with the pouring of various bottles into a basin and blending them. A thick steam began to arise from the bowl. Then she looked up at Rika, smiling. 'You're lost for something to do, aren't you?' She cackled. 'You can undo my vest, if you want to be of any help. I can't be wearing clothes for the rites, for Freyja's sake. Not even for a practice run. That would never do.' Her matter-of-fact tone was not unkind.

Rika's hands trembled, as she was so close to the woman's voluptuous curves and she could smell the scent of her body. Slowly, she undid the vest, extremely conscious that all she had to do was move her hand around the sides of the woman's soft back and her hands would be resting on the huge, smooth breasts, fingering her nipples . . .

'Put it there,' said Arje, pointing to a neat pile of folded clothing to one side of the bed.

Rika went over to look at the pile of furs and various pieces of clothing. On top of the pile, cleaned and oiled and lying neatly coiled, she found a tan leather band. The softened leather was like touching the underside of her forearm; it was so soft and smooth. She picked it up and stroked it, but put it down quickly when she saw the avid look in Arje's eye.

The young-old woman smiled widely. 'I'll bet you know what to do with that, eh, if you've been chosen for the rites. Hand it here.' An image of the strip being drawn moistly between the legs of young virgins filled Rika's brain. The woman, however, only used the flat strip of leather to smooth what looked like bear-grease over her huge breasts and narrow

116

waist. Rika felt embarrassed for some reason, compelled to look away.

Eventually Arje came over and raised Rika's face so that she could look her straight in the eyes. The woman's breasts brushed softly against Rika's bare arm; Rika bit her lip in embarrassment as her cheeks went red-hot. 'You've got a good name, Rika. Short, easy to remember. We don't want complications, do we? There are so many girls in the rites that it's hard to keep them straight all the time, eh?'

Now the image of virgins became a room full of nubile young women, sighing and stroking each other. Rika shook her head to shake free such thoughts. She wasn't exactly sure what the woman meant, but she nodded. 'Will I be meeting them, then? Tomorrow at the rites?' She figured she'd better ask, even if she had no intention of attending.

The woman chortled. 'Will you be meeting them! Of course you will, you little sparrow! What a question. As if you didn't know and you wearing Ingrid's pendant and all!'

That was another thing accomplished, anyway; at least she was in the right place to explain the meaning of her pendant. Rika's face was on fire and her palms were itching with nervousness. Arje seemed to notice she was uneasy and stepped closer. Again Rika became aware of the woman's nakedness and tried desperately not to think of the woman's huge, lovely tits pressing into her as Arje put an arm around her.

'You've done the rites before, haven't you? You've been a minor acolyte before, at least?'

Rika shook her head in denial.

'Loki's armpits!' swore the woman. 'No wonder you look so nervous. I assumed that as you're wearing the jewel . . .' Her voice trailed off, then she looked at Rika sharply. 'You know the story behind the rites, at least? You know why we're doing them?'

Rika admitted that she did not know the specific details.

'But you know Ingrid . . .' The woman grabbed for Rika's

hand and scoured it carefully. She pressed so firmly on the rune-scar that Rika yelped and tore her hand away.

The woman broke out in laughter again, gaily brushing back the silver currents of the hair that flowed over her face. 'At least I know you're genuine, Rika. No one could fake Ingrid's mark quite that well, I'm sure. Although it puzzles me that she'd pick you, as you're obviously a novice. You know nothing of what awaits you.' The woman mused over her last statement. 'Ah well, more fun for you. We do like to initiate new devotees.'

'I made a blood-oath.' Rika's voice was unwavering. She got the feeling that something important was being kept from her.

The woman stopped laughing. 'As long as you're able to accept what it entails.'

'I'm sure.' Rika's voice was equally solemn.

'And you know nothing of the rites?'

'Nothing.'

'Well then, you'd better get changed if you want to get some explanations from me. I trust you know the story of the world's creation?'

'Of course.' Rika was insulted.

'Good. The imagery of the rites is heavily based on it: Loki's child – the Fenrir Wolf – who will eat the world one day; those lecherous twins Freyr and Freyja. You'll see. We'll begin by casting runes – the runes you choose will actually determine what rites take place tomorrow. Now step out of your clothing for a little practice session for the rites.'

Rika's eye caught again the towered heap of clothing and luxuriant furs. She walked over to the clothes, her bare feet padding on the thick furs laid out in abundance over the earthen floor, strewn strangely with fresh green spruce needles that prickled her feet. The garments were decorative and extravagant, the like of which she had never seen before. She gingerly reached out one hand to pluck at a piece of red fabric from the pile.

'You realise, of course, that we must *both* be naked for the rites. Not just me.' Arje was rubbing her whole body with the grease now, so that her breasts and abdomen glistened wet in

118

the firelight. Rika tried not to look, but she started to feel a familiar warmth growing in the pit of her stomach.

She shook out the fabric she held and a shimmer of gossamer-like material unfolded out to her ankles. It was a sleeveless dress, if one would call something so insubstantial and delicate a dress, and tiny rows of perfect, small blood-red gems were stitched across the straps which held the lovely and translucent scarlet garment to the shoulders. There was an especially low bodice to this wine-red dress, embroidered with both gold and silver thread, and this was made of stronger material than the rest of the dress in order to cup and push forth the breasts.

She peeked over at Arje, but the woman was engrossed in stroking the warm tallow into her body and didn't look up. Rika watched her for a full minute, watched her breasts swaying full and plump and glistening as the woman bent over. She turned away, feeling ashamed. How could her allegiances change so quickly? First Ingrid, then Lina, then Pia, and now . . . Arje?

'Hurry up,' the woman said to Rika, breaking the spell somewhat. So Rika replaced the dress reluctantly in the pile, but not before holding it up to her body. It was gorgeous, extremely taut and figure-hugging. Rika noticed with some surprise that the bodice wasn't intended to cover the nipples at all; it was meant merely to lift up the breasts and support them. She glanced down at herself, thought of the rosiness of her erect nipples underneath the sheath and imagined the curves of her pressed-up breasts within the red dress. The resulting cleavage would be amazing. The tawniness of her summer skin and the lovely ruby of the fabric would be a nice contrast.

'We're ready now to cast the runes, Rika,' Arje said in a low voice. Rika's heart was beating violently; she was recklessly excited from having absolutely no idea what the future held. She removed her clothing quickly; her whole body was tense with anticipation.

She approached Arje and sat down cross-legged in front of the priestess, shutting her eyes. She hugged her knees towards her, kept her eyes closed and listened for movements and breathing, but heard nothing in particular.

'Closer,' said Arje, slowly. 'Bend closer to me.'

Rika leant lazily forward on her hands in the heat of the cabin, her eyes still closed. The woman placed a butter-coloured woollen cloth across Rika's lap, embroidered with green snakes with flashing yellow eyes and red-tipped scales. Rika knew she was ready for whatever had been prepared. The room was now very warm. The two women looked very different within its smoke-browned log walls, yet an observer would have been forgiven for noticing a similarity between the two: both were intent on second purposes and both were hiding their intentions under a now mutually acknowledged mask of desire.

Arje picked up the tooth-bowl and placed this vessel before Rika, along with another, larger wooden bowl pierced with many holes along its wooden circumference, followed by various glass bottles from the shelves. 'Now, Rika. Now we begin.'

In her hand Arje clutched something and she released it over the bone bowl. Little chips of bone clattered to the bottom of the bowl, each with a rune inscribed upon it. Arje turned them so that they were all blank and then asked Rika to turn over nine of them. Once Rika had done so, Arje ordered them into a line.

ᚢᚦᚠᛁᛟᛒᛏᛒᚷ

The priestess smiled with pleasure. 'That's wonderful, Rika.'

'It doesn't matter that one of the runes came up twice?'

'Not at all. We couldn't have a better reading for the rites.' She pointed to each rune in turn. 'We start with an example of instinctual sexuality, which is followed by a painful event – or the clearing out of a bad situation. This, in turn, is followed by bliss, or success after a hard endeavour. Then we experience the primal powers of ice and fertility of the land, then purification. My favourite follows – the wolf rite – and then purification again. Finally – *perp*.'

With a start, Rika recognised Pia's full name.

'It means vulva, sexuality, fertility. And this is our last rite. It couldn't be more perfect.' Rika was uneasily pleased to see the woman so ecstatic, even if she still had no clue of what the rites would actually consist.

A heavy perfume of steam rose from the bowl of bone and in the warmth of the hearth-red room, Arje began to intone a chant in a low voice. After droning for several moments, she got up quietly. Rika felt herself beginning to relax but, just as drowsiness lowered her heavy lids, a blast of frozen air hit her as Arje exited the cabin, leaving the door wide open. The priestess quickly returned, slamming shut the door of the hut. In her hands was the wooden bowl, filled with the mush of pure, fluff-topped white snow.

Arje placed it down with ceremony, then went and touched Rika on her neck; the heat from her hands transmitted directly to Rika's flesh. It felt like the woman was on fire, and Rika knew this was wrong, since she had just been outside gathering snow.

'We will begin our practice, Rika.' She bent towards Rika and then pressed her warm fingers on the younger girl's lips. It was a light caress, but it still made Rika's stomach turn over in desire. Arje's thick grey hair hung in loose curls from its twisted bun and she moved her hand on Rika's cool pale face, then offered her lush, velvety lips to Rika. Rika returned the kiss, gripping Arje's bare hot shoulders with her hands, lost in a dreamy wetness and kissing her deeper still. She could feel the wolf-tooth totem pressing hard between their breasts and the woman's tits pressing softly into her own. A raging desire to lower her head and suck overcame her; her hand reached out and touched the soft flesh, the ripe fruits of Arje's breasts.

Arje broke off the kiss and thrust Rika away. She intoned the chant even more vigorously and, thus reprimanded, Rika tried instead to listen to the music. But the low sound from Arje's throat sounded like a song of lust, the gravelly timbres hitting with a force on all twists of Rika's folding, moist pussy so that she itched to stroke herself. She found herself waiting for the next notes of Arje's dark, syrupy voice. The music shook her to her hollows and she longed to touch herself lightly and obscenely. Even better, she wanted Arje to touch her, but she didn't move or breathe. There was something that made her want to keep on listening to the edgy rumbling grit of the woman's strange song.

The shaman seemed to read her mind. 'You can touch yourself if you want to . . .' Arje nodded down to Rika. Stirred by such thoughts, Rika put a finger down towards her sex and pressed against the fabric of the yellow cloth Arje had laid across her knees. The act gave her a fantastic thrill: she was kneeling before this silver-haired goddess of woman, behaving as obscenely as an animal. She touched herself on her clit and lower, felt her wetness dampen her fingers through the heavy woollen material. She put her hand against the coarse wet cloth and rubbed downwards. She looked up at the pendulous, smooth globes of Arje's breasts. The sight stirred her and caused her to groan loudly enough that Arje turned towards her for a moment and then went back to the steady chanting of her song.

Rika slowly slipped her hand below the cloth, masturbating, and Arje took no notice. Rika came softly and sweetly, gazing at Arje's velvety, plump breasts and the rest of her smooth curvy body. She exhaled deeply afterwards and at last she began to listen to the words of the chant itself.

'In the beginning . . .' Arje rhythmically sang. Rika settled herself down comfortably, the fur soft against her nakedness, her cunt still twitching, finally eager to hear a good story. She told herself that this was the best way to go about it, secretly finding out as much as she could in order to save Lina and in order to let Pia know what was going on. Despite her previous distraction, she resolved to now listen carefully to the words of the peculiar, silver-haired woman.

'. . . there was only the Abyss. And north of this was the Cold World, and south of the Abyss burnt the Hot World. In the Cold World there was a well, though none knew whether it flowed or whether it only spouted forth cracking ice-towers of frozen water.' Rika's eyes grew wide as Arje related the familiar tale; despite having heard it so many times as a child it never failed to affect her and she suppressed a shiver.

Arje stood up and undulated her hands and body, her eyes dazzling and glazed, her pupils dilated. As if in a trance, she walked to the shelves and returned with a long white spoon and presented it to Rika.

'It's carved of reindeer antler,' she murmured to the younger woman. Rika ran her fingers over its cool, silky texture. It seemed more delicate and more unearthly than mere bone. A flash of coal-sparks shot forth from the hearth and settled in the older woman's grey hair for a moment like a hail of lightning. Rika gasped; the effect was violent and immediate, and the woman's sudden electric beauty was frightening. But Arje swung in place unflinching, gently crooning, before beginning with a new tonal song. She seemed to have forgotten that she had begun a story.

Rika gripped the long spoon Arje handed her, spellbound by the sight of the priestess's softly swaying breasts. She watched Arje's curving abdomen grow glossy with sweat as she danced. 'What happened next? What happened with the cold well?' she prodded in a whisper, uneasy that she would break the spell that Arje was weaving.

'From this well flowed a thick ice, which choked the huge Abyss. But remember, there was also the place of burning heat.' Arje swayed to the hearth, took up a stick and danced with it, its coal-red point dotting through the air like a lazy and insane comet. As her hands moved the torch, her lower body continued to writhe slowly and erotically, and the implication seemed voluptuously lewd.

'The flames of this place licked at the icicles which grew like waxen frozen forests from the Abyss, and the two mixed, hot and cold together.' In emphasis to the story, Arje plunged the burning stick into the wooden bowl of snow. A great hiss sizzled in the vessel, then the water began dripping through the pores drilled within the bowl. 'Hot and cold together,' she repeated. She danced still lower, her hips and buttocks gyrating slowly, and crouched before the bowl. She caught the droplets that poured from its holes on her tongue, swallowing down the melted snow. Her bright pink tongue greedily sought out the cold moisture.

'From this blend, Rika, came all life.' It was the first time since she started the dance that she had spoken Rika's name and it startled the younger woman. Through her veins Rika felt both the chill and the heat flow, just as in the story, and she leant forward eagerly.

Arje picked up a bear fur lying before the hearth and ran it leisurely over her limbs. The fur had been oiled more than once and left spiralling designs of warm bear-grease on Arje's body as she stroked the fur over her fire-flushed breasts and between her legs. Arje trembled as if she were feverish, or in a fit. Then she sighed and began to speak again.

'From the ice and heat were formed a giant and a great cow of ice –'

'An *ice cow*?' Rika interrupted. 'I thought there was a garden, with a man and a woman and a snake.'

Arje gave her a disparaging look. 'Yes, well, that shows you how much progress those celibate book-thumpers have made when tearing apart the beliefs of our own people.'

Rika held her opinions to herself. It was true that she must have remembered some of the tales that the bossy, fervent male foreigners had spread, but she had really never thought much of the stories themselves. The only positive thing she'd ever heard was that the son of their lonely god had turned water into wine. Before they recently started making progress with their missionary work, with fools such as her father, they had been notoriously unpopular. Once, about ten years ago, one of their priests had ventured into her village. He had been tied to a tree with a sliced-open stomach and been forced to walk in circles, twisting his own entrails around the oak. Officially, of course, they were all supposed to be practising the myths of the fish-men since her grandfather's time, back in the days of Olaf. Privately, though, most of the villagers had ignored the edict and she had personally never been friendly with a fish-believer.

Her eyes ran over Arje for a second, as the woman ground her hips in an unheard rhythm. She wasn't altogether sure that the grey-haired woman's fundamentalist faith in the Old Ways was the way to go, either.

'. . . and the giant suckled at the cow with all of his four mouths and the ice-cow licked at the white frost nearby, until these sheets of scaled ice congealed and, while the giant sucked, where the cow licked, the first of the gods came forth.' Arje broke off her chant for a moment and whispered, 'You must remember these details, Rika. They are important.'

But then Arje dropped the fur and squatted on it, running her hands over her oil-softened body, pinching her nipples until they looked like raspberries after the first frost, red and glistening and icy and perfect. Arje ran her hands over her face, smearing it with grease, so that it too was lustrous flesh before the light of the blood-red fire. She came close to where Rika sat and thrust her huge breasts into Rika's face, lifting them up with both hands.

Rika lowered her head to gently suckle at one rosy nipple; and the ice-cold tip of the nub was melting water in her mouth, liquid running over her tongue. She withdrew, ice-water running down her chin and Arje was ice and only ice, her whole hard body melting into the bear-fur, until at last Rika sat there wondering, her legs pressing into the bed of wet, soft green needles strewn over the earthen floor.

'The warm breath of an ice-beast created all we have today,' Arje said, and she stepped in close to Rika and breathed deep and hot into her ear, her tongue dipping deep in for just a second. In that moment Rika had a flash of perception of why flesh and heat and breath made life. But quickly the moment of understanding left her and she retreated back to role of observer rather than participant. Her hands were cold and frigid, but her blood rushed hot through her veins again, pounding in her temple, her stomach tightening deep in the pit of her. She was feverishly aroused again. She laughed nervously, but Arje didn't seem to notice.

'The cow brought forth a god, but it was the giant who became the earth we know today –'

'The *giant*?' said Rika in mock astonishment, wanting to give Arje some feedback.

'Yes, a giant, as I said before,' said Arje, annoyed that her dance and story had been interrupted for a second time. 'I thought you said you knew the story. Now pay attention and keep quiet.

'The giant was also a master of creation. From his arms and feet and toes came forth both monsters and the fates, but among the children of those licked forth by the ice-cow was the god Odin, who did smite down the giant, and from the giant's body was created our whole world. His thick white skull became the sky-dome that stretches over us and his writhing brain its clouds. His hard bones became the mountains, his blood the liquid sea, and when pulverised all his tissues our own dirt and earth.'

Rika smiled. She liked these details of the familiar story and, when gazing at the horizon, had always felt safe and secure within the giant's skull.

'And you know as well as I that this new middle-earth was covered by the roots of the great tree of life.'

Rika nodded; Arje was driving towards a conclusion, an explanation of the rites and her own future role. The room began to swell with heat and, as Rika's hands and toes began to thaw, the hot tingling as blood rushed into her extremities was painful. She rubbed at her aching hands, felt the chill that had come with Arje's icy kiss leaving her body; her whole flesh went feverish as her body tried to adjust to the too-hot room. There seemed to be no way she could escape the suffocating warmth; it was as if every inch of her skin was licked by a fire from which she couldn't shift away. Sweat began to trickle down her neck.

She felt hot and sticky and strangely juicy in the over-warm hut. The perspiration began to run freely over all the places of her body which had been near frozen before.

'Do you know which well fed the roots of the tree of life?' Arje was crouching confidently before her. 'Do you, Rika?' Slowly, Arje opened the lips of her sex, exposing it to Rika's view. The silken lips of the shaman's pussy were already wet and droplets of her dew were caught in the tight-curled tendrils of her silvery pubic hair.

'There were three wells there and one of the wells was the well of wisdom.' Rika's mouth went dry and her own cunt began to pulse. Arje motioned that Rika should move the long spoon – which Rika had completely forgotten – slowly between Arje's legs. It suddenly seemed less ritual to Rika and more of an immediate sex act. When faced with carnality this raw – with the earthy musk, the deep, dark, wet centre of Arje's cunt, it was less about the detachment offered by the spoon and the ritual, and much more about the lust Rika again felt rising inside her.

With her tongue physically aching to touch and lick Arje and her hands yearning to smear her face with Arje's liquid, Rika forgot that she was practising for a performance she had been warned against. She felt a sudden urge for Arje to sit on her, with her ripe, wet earthy cunt smashed on to her face, near smothering her. If she did, Rika could move her fingers on herself, could masturbate again to Arje's scent.

'Move the spoon slowly inside my pussy,' Arje commanded. Rika moved the long, long spoon into the tight depths that Arje held splayed open before her, her clit beginning to twitch. There were little circuits of excitement shooting off like sparks in her quim.

Were the rites equally sexual, she wondered; did they involve licking and rubbing faces into women like heat-driven animals; longing to be smothered and dripped on and engulfed by musky, dripping pussies? If so, maybe it was a good idea that she investigate them first-hand after all. Right now, she was kept from acting on her desires by the detachment of the spoon, but she could not shake her mind clear of an image of slowly sucking Arje's clit.

Rika circled the spoon inside the tight curves of the priestess's pussy. Arje lay back in her naked brown magnificence, moaning and surging with movement as the ivory spoon tickled her depths. She moved shamelessly on it, evidently lost to all other sensations. She pumped out rivulets of liquid around the long stem of the smooth-polished ivory spoon, a utensil of frailty and slenderness. Rika was amazed at the amount of come. It occurred to her that this could have been where Pia had learnt the singular technique of coming in rivers – the technique she had been so impressed by back in Normandy. She wanted to ask Arje if she knew Pia, but it might be unwise. It was not the right time to ask, whatever the case.

Arje squirmed and moaned, her hands pinching hard at her own stiff nipples. Rika felt powerful and smiled for a moment, then drew open the silken lips of Arje's sex, so that the lush little pearl of her clit was visible, shining and pink and lustrous. Slowly, ever so slowly, Rika pulled out the sticky spoon, but not before dipping its little curving bowl amid the woman's pooling lips to fill it.

She raised the spoon full of the warm liquid to her mouth, but hesitated. She knelt trembling, the long spoon in her right hand cupped full of the milky-white honey of Arje's arousal. Arje was panting, her huge breasts heaving above the inward curve of her brown waist. Her legs were spread wide open on the fur, and there was the beginning of dampness where she lay and where her juices ran down her legs. The torches lit the bear-fur with a fiery light and the air Rika breathed was full of Arje's earthy and sensuous fragrance. Oh Freyja, Rika could smell the woman's cunt, the musk rising up through her nostrils to her brain. She could smell her and the thought that she was not able to directly touch this ripe woman was almost too much to bear. But she could taste her. She raised the spoon to her lips, thirsty for the savoury taste of pussy.

The taste of a sweet sea, a musk more powerful and beautiful than anything else, the strongest flavour in the world, filled Rika's mouth and her tongue curled in this taste of pure sex, which she greedily swallowed down. She fought an instinct to thrust her whole face into the woman's rich, warm cunt. But she now understood that this 'practice' session involved a test – she could lap and drink from the woman with this detached, impersonal spoon until she was told to stop, but there could be no climax for her, only just this licked droplet.

It was torture, Rika decided, as again she pushed in the long-handled utensil; again heard Arje moan; again felt her own desperate need and longing, and again tasted the musk-residue left on her tongue and, when she licked them, her lips. Arje tossed back and forth, her beautiful silver hair tousled, its colour blending into the wolf pelts on which she lay.

Rika drank and drank Arje's sensuous fluid from the spoon and eventually it began to quench her and, though her clit was still tingling, buzzing, near-bursting, she drank down Arje's hot honey with concentration. Her whole body began to ache for it; she could not get enough of the taste. Not if she drank it for days, she realised. She repeatedly raised the spoon to her lips.

Arje, with her full, dark, heavy-breasted body, now squatted rudely in front of blonde Rika; Rika's face was flushed and eager, her lips feeding from the juices caught in the delicate long spoon, the carved bone reaching Rika's come-covered lips again and again. It was an obscene and beautiful picture. The older woman's silver hair glittered into muted sunset shades in the reflection of the burning logs. And in the hazy, smoky room, Rika felt more debauched than she ever had before.

Her entire body was hot and flushed, and in the hypnotism of the moment all she could feel was her need, and all she could hear through the roaring in her ears was her own animal-like slurping sounds, drinking down the other woman's dew. Her throat and belly were full of sex, her belly rounded out with the heat of the liquid, tight as a little drum. Her clit was so tight she thought she would burst, and the flames of the hearth flashed patterns on her closed eyes like little suns. She was desperate and aroused, and still Arje flowed and still Rika lapped from the long ivory spoon. It was a splendid, wonderful torture.

'Stop!' commanded the priestess. Rika looked up like a feeding beast, Arje's sticky fluid slipping over her lips and throat. Her body trembled. Her face was just inches away from Arje's luscious, dripping curves and her hand was dangerously close to fondling her own sex. She could smell more than ever the rich elixir pooling between Arje's legs: the smell of the green forest, of pine and flesh, of orgasms and ash. But if she touched either Arje or herself, she had a feeling she would fail the undefined test that she was undergoing.

She drew back, the spoon still in her hand. She continued to flush and tremble. There was a sheen of slick sweat over Arje's body. Rika closed her eyes and could feel the blood roaring in her veins.

'This was the well,' Arje explained to Rika, fingering her pussy slowly as the thudding in Rika's breast grew more steady and regular. 'It is this well that nourishes the world-tree, the sacred tree of life. From this well is wisdom, which causes both thirst and fulfilment. It is a hard lesson to learn. And it is hard to drink from this well without also wanting to drown in it. It is said that Odin once gave an eye to drink from it.'

Rika's pussy was still pounding. She could well understand why a god would pay this price. Even now, she felt she could taste sap in her mouth, the ash-taste of the tree swirling like thick sexual smoke amongst her teeth, and even now her hands craved to caress Arje's slick, lush body. She took a deep breath. She had passed this test of sexual control and it flashed through her brain that she would indeed be able to withstand the rites. Despite what Pia had said, there didn't seem to be any way round it if she wanted to find Lina. She would be careful. Arje opened her arms to Rika and Rika came into them, exhausted and grateful.

'Why are you worried about Lina, anyway?' Arje asked several hours later. It was only afternoon, already growing dark, and they lay warmly cuddled into each other's arms. Rika pulled herself up to look Arje directly in the face.

'What do you mean, why am I worried?'

The woman shrugged and smiled.

Rika thought for a moment. She answered the question honestly. 'I'm worried because I left Lina in a situation where, like me, she could never go home, yet I haven't thought about her for weeks. I'm worried because Lina gave up a lot and risked a lot for me – her life, her home and her family, and I never got a chance to thank her. I'm mostly worried, though, because she seems to be linked to –' Rika almost said Ingrid's name, but then snapped her mouth shut – 'to potentially bad situations.' Deep inside, she realised there was another, more selfish reason why she was worried: she wanted to know if Lina had indeed been susceptible to Ingrid's undeniable charms.

Arje frowned for several seconds, taking in Rika's long-winded explanation, but then burst out into merry peals of laughter.

Rika blinked; the woman's mood changes seemed to be very rapid.

'Oh, I'm sorry,' the older woman said, with tears running down her face. 'I really should have made it more clear from the start.'

'Made what more clear?'

'That your friend Lina really didn't go willingly. You see, my dear, I thought I told you that she was given a sleeping drug before she was taken to the arena. But it was officially arranged and without concealment.' The woman was so convulsed by laughter that she could not continue speaking.

Rika stared at her. 'Which arena?'

'The arena for the rites accompanying the Great Thing, you little ninny. For Ragnarök. There are rumours that Hrafn intends to set it off this year. Me, I'm just concerned that the rites reach new heights of sexual magnificence. Haven't you been listening?'

*Ragnarök, the last day of the world?* Familiar names and fears were ringing in Rika's ears, but she couldn't consider them right now. It was too much. She knew she would have to tread very, very carefully with her next words. 'The same rites I'm to participate in?'

The woman was gripping the dark fur on which she lay, shrieking. 'Of course! You and Lina, what a beautiful sight. In the beginning, anyway, while you fuck her senseless before all those delicious girls who will be watching you. Again, it's not a choice I'd make myself – well, you know how it is going to end.' Her laughter turned into girlish giggles.

Rika forced a smile on to her face. She had a chilling feeling she would find out.

After they slept and made love for another hour or so, Arje suggested that they go outside for refreshment. When Rika moved to put on her clothes and shoes, Arje stopped her.

'Barefoot,' she said. 'You'll do it barefoot and naked. Get used to it – you'll experience far worse during the rites. In any case, it's good for you.'

Rika stepped gingerly outside, sceptical of the beneficial qualities of freezing snow. Her suspicions were confirmed when her bare feet hit the layer of snow and the cold stung on the sensitive pads of her toes.

Arje's voice was right behind her and hot in her ear. 'Perfect. This is the type of thing I love about the rites, Rika. We revel in contrasts and, as in the Creation story, one of our favourite juxtapositions is that of chill and heat.'

She withdrew and then walked round so that she was standing straight in front of Rika and could peer directly in her eyes. She did not so much as flinch from the icy bite of the snow beneath her naked feet. Her face was almost serious, then she cackled again. 'Do you think you'll be able to bear these types of rites, Rika? Do you think you'll be able to stand tests of contrasts far more extreme than these?'

Rika took in a deep breath, and the chillingly cold air stung her lungs. It was jolting and it stimulated her. As she looked up at the moon faintly glowing in the dark-blue evening sky – a harbinger that dusk came rapidly in the winter months – and then lowered her eyes to the snow-dipped, heavily laden trees, she realised that the sting in her feet was becoming tolerable. She thought of when she had last watched the stars with Pia after the battle, and resolve strengthened her. Although Pia had warned her, she was reasonably certain she could withstand the rites.

'I'll be able to handle anything that comes my way,' she told the charismatic grey-haired woman. As if in refutation to her confident words, she immediately felt the cold pain on her soles grow close to unbearable. 'Though I think we ought to go inside for the moment, so that I can save my energy for tomorrow.'

Arje, seemingly unflustered by the fact that she was standing barefoot on three inches of snow, nodded and opened the door again to the inviting interior of the fire-warmed hot room. Rika wondered if she could convince Arje to give her feet a hot bath. If she was lucky, maybe it was already part of the enjoyable aspects of the rites. Rika had enjoyed the sexual acts so explicitly illustrated, but she was not sure about the tests of tolerance that obviously awaited her.

Arje did not rub her feet, but she told her tales for several more hours into the night, often accompanied by graceful and strange dances as a demonstration of what awaited Rika at the rites.

By the time Arje had finished her last lewd dance and latest strange rendition of the Creation story, Rika's head was spinning, full of disconcerting and disturbing images: snow, dwarves, weird licking cows of ice, wells that mixed with flame, eight-legged horses, dead gods, one-eyed gods. There was something of a nightmarish quality to the Old Ways, Rika had always felt, but yet there was a strangely erotic undertone to all the tales, too, and the effect left the listener's sentiments pulled in different directions. Perhaps that was the intent of the stories, Rika suddenly thought, remembering how Arje commented on a love of contrasts. She had no idea what would come her way tomorrow at the rites. She felt exactly the same way she had after ingesting the battle fungus-drug – terrified and still aroused.

# SIX

It was morning and, though the winter sun was finally rising, she still held a torch in her hand. Through the bare branches was the annual meeting place, but the boughs divided the vision of the famous political assembly into triple, distorted visions. By a frozen lake she could see a huge circle of planks laid on the stumps of trees, an enormous longhouse near it and what looked like a wide clearing behind both, above which a large stage had been set up on tall upright poles. She could just make out that there was a shiny backdrop where the back of the stage met a sloping hill – perhaps ice, or snow? But above and beyond this stage there was only the tree-dotted hill. Large numbers of people were already gathering everywhere she looked. Her hand curled round an aspen tree as she leant forward to peer at the distant wooden stump-circle within which most discussions of political note would take place. William's great hall in Normandy had been more superficially impressive, but this seemed more ominous, resonant and real, with none of the Norman fripperies and decoration. It was in her own land and she had heard tales of it since she was a child.

Arje had told her to walk boldly up and enter the ring, but now Rika questioned the validity of the advice and stood in the wood, looking over the scene of the Great Thing. She clarified her motives for putting herself in what Pia had insisted was a dangerous situation: she would find Lina. And she would also discover the meanings that Arje, Ingrid, Hrafn and Pia had insinuated to her since she met them. She had been sheltered from the truth. Yes, but no more.

She pressed her hands harder into the brown living wood of the aspen that hid her and was more than a little surprised to feel a little groove in it. It reminded her of when she felt her own father's groove on the war-helmet and she bent down with the torch to further examine it. A little rune showed up on the green inner flesh of the tree; a rune that had been carved out not more than a day previous; it had not even started to heal into a tree scar. It was the same rune as the last that Arje had cast: *perþ*. Meaning vulva. And meaning Pia, too, she thought hurriedly.

It was always like this: secrets upon secrets, things doubled up and hidden from view. She sighed and looked at the carving more closely, wondering about its meaning and pondering the significance that it would be carved on a tree. She realised that it looked exactly like the little chalky scar on Pia's fingers, the one Pia had admitted had been related to a long-ago blood-oath to Ingrid. She knew that people often carved runic symbols as spells, to connect with the magic associated with a particular rune. She was struck suddenly with the idea that perhaps Pia had been here, invoking power from her name-rune. With a rush, she decided to interpret this as a good sign.

She raised the torch and looked again at the Great Thing, wondering how its own mysteries would be revealed and exposed to her, knowing that she would soon find out. She squared her shoulders, held the torch in front of her to light her way in the snow and pressed forward, treading lightly on the frosty firm drifts. She walked so rapidly that she made only slight indentations on the crisp top layer of the snow; if someone were following her, it would be difficult to read her prints.

It was a silly fancy, that someone might be trailing her. But more than once she had had the sensation that she was being followed, only to find upon turning that there was no one there. She hoped vaguely that it might be Pia. It made no difference now; if someone were close behind, they could still easily follow her torch in the late dawn of winter. The sky was still a dark purple, turning slowly to lavender. A spot of coal-red light floated above the ground as she headed towards the stump circle she had seen from the woods.

She approached along the side of a lake, where eager morning skaters whizzed by on cattle shinbones, cutting deft patterns into the first thin layers of the thick winter ice. A glint in the earth caught her eye and she bent to pick up a simple gold ring. She tucked it into her pocket, reminding herself to look at it later.

Rika tried to bolster up her courage. Still, it seemed that most people's attention was fixed not on the stump circle but on a clearing near it, where a duel was being played out. A man and a woman fought bare to the waist, both equally fierce. The man's long black hair was sweat-logged and lashed wildly like dark snakes as he charged at the berserker woman, who confidently waited his attack with open, tensed hands, gnashing her teeth as she squatted with her legs wide apart. Though duelling was officially forbidden, people were cheering both to fight to the death, as everyone knew that if one were to die, then all acquired riches would go to the survivor. Such stakes made the duel all the more exciting.

Rika walked past the duellers towards the huge circle, where throngs of people were milling about. People ignored her as she walked past them, but she stepped inside the circumference of the benches, stood proudly with her hand on the belt supporting her blade, eyes flashing, and then swept back her cape in a proud movement and revealed her neck. A silence fell over the participants of the Great Thing. Yes, as she suspected, again it was the power of the pendant round her throat.

For several seconds, the silence held. Then a figure rose from amongst those sitting round the circle and walked towards Rika. For a moment, she could not place the hooded eyes, nor the wrinkled, leathery skin; the clawlike hands reaching out to

136

embrace her evoked no memories. But from the recesses of her battle-memories, recognition stirred.

Hrafn.

He wrapped his arms around her as if she were a beloved friend. Rika dropped her sword in shock and a clanking sound echoed across the circle as it hit a stone. The crowd around her continued to stare. Smirking, Hrafn collected the sword and handed it smoothly to Rika. There was a disturbing dignity to the man, but all Rika could think of was how he had encouraged Ingrid with her treachery. He was not a person she could trust.

'So you've come.' He grinned slowly, his smile an odd combination of putrid gaps and finely chiselled, sharp-ended teeth. 'As Ingrid said you would.'

The pain of the blonde warrior-woman's betrayal ached in Rika's mind. She pushed it back and then the more accessible emotion of anger flashed through her. She controlled herself, gripping tightly on the recovered blade. It was tucked safely in her belt once again, but she patted her single-edged scramsasax knife as a warning to Hrafn, reserved for hand-to-hand fighting. She looked behind her. Even the duellers had stopped and were watching with gaping expressions.

'Why are you here?' Rika snapped, hand still gingerly afloat on her scramsasax. 'Where is Ingrid?'

The old man coughed violently, as if to draw attention away from her words. At first it looked as if he would answer her questions, but after glancing at her sharp and ready weapons, he shook his head and stepped back into his circle of cronies, a group of old men who were oblivious to all but their serious board-game of *hnefatafl*, ignoring the excitement around them and remaining intent on putting the dowels in all the right places.

Rika cleared her throat. Women did not often speak and when they did it was usually to demand a divorce or some household trifle. But to save Lina and help Pia, she had to impose herself and gain their attention; Arje had promised her that they would listen. She thought for a moment of the jewel that, once again, had swayed people's reactions. She was beginning to have

137

an uneasy feeling about her little pendant, not only because it was treacherous Ingrid who had procured her oath to wear it. It was a more sinister feeling, as if it were a weight around her neck, heavy as a stone used to drown unwanted infants in the lakes. Her hand quavered at her throat. Once again she threw back the red cape she wore. 'I swear by this pendant, that my questions will be answered.'

The effect was predictably magical. People stopped talking and fighting – even the old men ceased their game-playing this time. Hrafn's attention was once again fully on her; his face pale and his eyes narrow. There was power in the jewel, whether she liked it or not.

She removed it from her neck, wrapped the chain several times around her fingers and swung it in the air – mainly to just hear the gasps and sighs of her spellbound audience. She was nearly enjoying herself. She would ask the questions she wanted to – she had nothing to lose, after all, and this jewel seemed her only coin with which to buy information.

'Where is Lina?' There was a murmur around her, but none of the whispering voices answered her openly. Her voice rose in pitch: 'What is the meaning of this jewel?' Again, no answer. She took a deep breath. 'What does the warrior-woman Ingrid have to do with any of this?'

People began to hiss and several near her spat. But still, the company kept their tongues. She was very frustrated; perhaps the pendant could not buy as many answers as she had hoped. She raised her head to look straight at Hrafn, who was still smiling silently at her. Rika did not like his expression; it made her feel as if a snake was climbing underneath her shirt.

But she held some sort of power in her hand, so she appealed once more to the masses: 'Who is this man? Of what significance is this priest called Hrafn?' There was a reaction this time, but only from the priest himself as he took a step closer. She faced him, dangerous electricity crackling between the two of them. Neither of them moved and Rika could feel sweat beading on her brow. She kept her hand on her knife.

Hrafn made a small gesture and took another step forward and Rika saw why he was so confident. With him came a young male berserker, complete with a stinking bear-shirt and drug-addled eyes. The younger man bore an enormous double-headed axe in his hands and a sick feeling curdled in Rika's stomach. Frozen in place, she watched him raise his hands, slowly, ever so slowly, to bring the double-headed axe high, high into the air –

'Stop.' Someone's voice, low and gentle, broke into the moment, and Rika exhaled in relief as the berserker lowered his axe. Hrafn had slunk back to his previous place. Light-headed with fear but grateful, Rika turned to look at her saviour.

It was Arje. The woman was dressed in a ceremonial robe of the *góthi*, a full priestess of the Old Ways. But under the open robe she was naked. Her hair was uncovered, shining as violently silver as the blade of the berserker. 'Come,' she said, holding out a hand to Rika. 'It is no time for senseless bickering. We have more important tasks that await you, my child.'

Her grasp was surprisingly firm and if Rika had wanted to stay she would have been hard-pressed to force her position. For a moment, as she was half dragged away, she turned back to the silent crowd. She thought she had caught a glimpse of Pia and her long dark hair. But there was only Hrafn staring at her, Hrafn's face looming malignant and base as Arje jerked her away. Rika shuddered. With dignity she let Arje lead her out of the circle and towards the enormous longhouse Rika had surveyed from the woods. People parted for them as they walked by like a knife moving through the crowd.

'Who is Hrafn? Why is he here?' Rika persisted in a loud voice. Arje kept her wrist firmly in her own and led her up the trail to the longhouse.

'He is a priest,' she said darkly.

'I know that,' Rika snapped.

Arje yanked harshly at her wrist. 'I wasn't finished. He is a high priest of the Old Ways, one of several *góthi* who will never sell their souls to the fish-worshippers, as so many here have done.' She shoved Rika ahead of her, so that the younger girl now stood first before the door of the longhouse.

However, the building didn't interest Rika as much as the answer to her question. 'You don't understand, Arje. I saw that man in Britain. With – Ingrid.' Her voice faltered; she had the feeling she was giving far too much away.

'You think you saw him, or you're sure?' Arje pulled her face into a weird expression, and Rika didn't know how to read it.

'I . . . I'm sure.'

The older woman sniffed and then shoved Rika even closer to the gate. 'Thinking is not good enough, Rika. You said you've arrived only recently from Britain. You said yourself that it took you several weeks to pay your way and arrange your voyage. What kind of old priest could fly as quickly as a raven over the sea? And after a taxing battle, too.' Arje sighed and raked her fingers roughly through her silver hair. 'Now take a look at this craftsmanship before we enter, so that you in part acquaint yourself with the rites that await you.' She pointed to the wooden carving on the door, a design of the huge wolf Fenrir, the bestial son of the god Loki who would one day eat the world at the time of Ragnarök.

Rika strained to catch a glimpse but, in the dim morning, she could only make out the ferocious teeth of the wolf and the fangs of a serpent, plus a beast she assumed to be the Great Ice-cow. The pictograph was the colour of blood and bitter currants, the deep red imbedded in the grooves where the artisan had chiselled. This bright red was traditionally used for runestones; she worried that for her it would now forever be associated with the blood of the battle in Britain.

'It's . . . pretty,' she said, but she was secretly fuming that Arje had ignored her queries just as all the others had outside. The pendant was not the bargaining piece she had hoped it would be. Arje led her through the long entrance hall.

It was dark inside and the little light present soaked through the windows of *skjall*, the stretched birth-membrane that encased newborn calves. The effect was eerie and did not make Rika feel better. Arje's grip was still unrelenting; it occurred to Rika to ponder whom exactly she *could* trust. There were at least two she could count out immediately – Ingrid and old Hrafn. Lina had betrayed her with regards to Ingrid and she began to wonder whether even Pia had been honest towards her. And as for silver-haired Arje – why, she had absolutely no idea whether the woman was pure good or pure, unrepentant evil. Rika sighed and wished for a time when war and friendship and religion did not seem so complex. When she left home there had been easy answers, winners and losers, friends and enemies. It did not seem to be that way now.

She walked through the last steps of short corridor behind Arje.

'And here we are.' Arje pulled her into the warmth of the low-ceilinged room. It was abnormally bare, except for the customary furs and pelts that lined the raised-earth ridges up against the wall. Nor were there any animals in the smoky, poorly ventilated room. It was near the entrance of the longhouse that Arje sat herself down. There were several fires smoking inside and the holes in the thatched roof drew the smoke out. Rika was immediately surrounded by the clamorous shouts of several dozen young women, all beautiful, clad in scant furs or not at all, all touching at her hair, stroking at her flesh, or – most obviously – staring in wide-eyed fascination at her pendant.

'These are my disciples,' Arje told her, with more than a touch of pride. 'They are training for the days when we will grasp back our land from the fish-priests, and for when we will once again worship the old and true gods.' Arje's voice had become solemn and even the grasping girls went silent, as if remembering a more lofty purpose.

Arje walked through the longhouse, sniffing at the air, examining the fires which burnt and clouded up the caul skins, ruffling her fingers through bits of fur as she passed by. Rika's gaze followed Arje and she saw that the longhouse was devoid of the rubbish that would normally line the floor. And though the room was stuffy, it was a relief from the cold.

'Come,' Arje commanded Rika. Rika took a hesitant step forward, followed closely past the gaggle of young women. Rika passed the *skjall* windows as she approached Arje. As she brushed the fingers of one hand along their taut, brittle surface, with the other she retrieved from her pocket the ring she had found. She held it up to the greyish light source. She made her face expressionless, but felt suddenly sad: it was a twin of Pia's ring that Pia had shown her so long ago on the boat. There it lay in her palm, with the writhing little red dragon biting at its own tail. She closed her fingers around it and thrust it back down in her pocket.

Pia had assured her that the ring had been unique; now she knew it was proof that Pia was here, looking after her. She briefly contemplated running out the way she had come in, perhaps straight into Pia's arms, but remembered that Hrafn and his henchmen waited on the other side of the tunnel. It was too late to back out now.

'We begin,' stated Arje when Rika stood before her. She beckoned Rika closer and then guided her to the centre of the longhouse. There was a circular fire-pit there, long since gone cold and dead. 'Do as I do,' Arje urged, removing her clothes to reveal her voluptuous body. She knelt at the pit and began to scrub her fingers in the ashes, rubbing them into her skin until her flesh absorbed the grey flakes and glowed, burnished and polished. She then drank from a long horn lying by the fire and bade Rika to do the same. Rika glanced around, saw that others also drank from horns, and so she accepted the vessel. It was pungent mead and went easily down her throat.

Rika stripped and then knelt and rubbed the ashes hard into her arms and face, as Arje had done. She knew it was a purifying ceremony; she had heard tales of this act before. She thought of her pendant and the ashes it held inside it; perhaps there was some ritualistic connection? She opened her lips to speak of it, but just then an image of Pia cautioning her to hold her tongue entered her mind.

She shut her mouth and instead looked straight at Arje, who had begun to fondle one of her red-headed disciples, slipping her hands on to the curves of the girl's breasts and licking at her neck and ears. Rika wondered if she should be watching, as she observed Arje's bright tongue flickering wetly in and out of the young girl's ear. Her own breasts began to feel heavy, as she watched the shaman's hand rub the pale nipples of the red-haired girl and then rub lower on to the girl's belly, smooth on the copper thatch of pubic hair.

Finally Rika turned her head away and looked behind her. The other girls had also rubbed the ash on to their bodies and now were snaking their polished flesh against each other, rubbing and thrusting and smelling the scent of smoke rubbed into their young limbs. As the girls writhed and moved on each other, Rika turned back to Arje. Everything was building up in her, intensified by the explicit scenes she was now witnessing. She should act before she drowned in this dangerously erotic environment.

Arje was lost in a pleasurable contortion with the red-haired girl when Rika walked briskly up to her, shoved the redhead out of the way and whipped out her scramsasax from the bundle of her clothes she carried.

'I've had enough. I want to know where Lina is and I want to know now,' she said, holding the point at the woman's pulsing throat. Arje lost all semblance of enjoyment and stared directly at Rika, her own eyes not once flickering down to the sharp point of Rika's blade. For a moment, neither of them breathed.

'Lina . . .' Arje began, and then bit her lip.

'Yes?' Rika pressed the blade just gently into the flesh above the woman's jugular vein, letting loose a tiny trickle of bright red blood.

'Lina has a great . . . part to play in our rites.'

'What kind of part?'

'She plays . . .' Arje winced and at last dropped her eyes to where the blade stung at her neck, before resuming her speech. 'She plays Freyja – the goddess of love and sexuality.'

'That's quite a proud and impressive role to play within the

143

rites, with no shame attached – and yet you've stolen Lina away in extreme secrecy. Why?' Rika smiled harshly, her fingers never faltering as they tightened round the knife.

Arje lowered her gold-and-silver lashes. For a moment, she looked as innocent as a child. 'Because she'll be sacrificed, of course, Rika, as I'm sure Ingrid has told you. I know you said you were unsure of your own role, but Ingrid must have informed you what lies in store for Lina?'

Thoughts raced through Rika's head; foremost was the realisation that she couldn't let Arje know that Ingrid had not let her in on the details. Behind her she could hear the moaning sounds of sex between the girls, who had not been distracted by the altercation. Her head thudded; her veins raced with quick blood. Slowly, she lowered her hand from Arje's throat.

Arje was not laughing. She finally reached out a hand to lead Rika further into the depths of the longhouse. 'Come. Lay away your knives,' she said. She motioned as well for the other girls to desist their play and follow her and Rika. 'You've proved your worth as a competent warrior, but now that it's time for you to start your training you'll need to rely on other skills. For the rites.'

They went ahead to the far wall of the longhouse where there was a leather door-flap that led to an even further, darker room, the group following. Rika kept her bundle of clothes, scramsasax, knife and sword clutched firmly under her arm. She felt a surprising sense of satisfaction from confronting the priestess – just as she had had in battle, when she had survived to engage in yet another combat. The rites themselves were not so different from war, after all, she thought. A constant test, a constant proving of self. In a strange way, it appealed to her Viking soul.

Upon emergence, the women converged into a huddled group. The room was a tiny enclosure, lit by burning candles set along the compact walls, with not even a thin oval of *skjall* for additional light. With no caul-window it was disorienting, and despite the fact that it was still morning she began to feel sleepy. Once inside, Rika was the centre of attention, as the young women caressed and warmed her body with their palms, teased her with the brush of their hair against her naked flesh. Arje stood by, watching lecherously.

'She's very beautiful,' Rika heard the red-haired girl commenting to Arje. The redhead bent to run her hands over the tender curves of Rika's breasts and hips and Rika groaned with excitement, despite herself. The other girls cooed and murmured and Arje herself nodded approval, walking a circle around Rika in order to get a fuller look.

'That she is,' the priestess finally responded, laying a hand just above Rika's pubic bone and pressing softly.

A girl with lustrous raven hair meekly dared to speak up. 'Is she . . . is she trained?'

Arje gave the girl a withering look. 'That's an impertinent question. But I'm in a good mood, so I'll answer it. She's been trained enough. I've established that she likes to suck and lick and I've established that she hankers for the . . . taste of certain flavours. There should be no problem with the rites at all, especially not the most popular – which, I am pleased to tell you, will be occurring once again this year – with twenty well-chosen girls.'

To Rika, there seemed immediately to be a mood of some relief amongst the girls, as if they feared that a particular rite would not occur if she herself was not worthy. Their evident relief warmed her; their hands flickered at the inside of her elbow; she let the caresses smooth the delicate bones of her clavicle. But Arje was still speaking and still giving an analysis as to Rika's suitability:

'When it comes to her stoicism and tenacity, we should have little problem there, either. And she can tolerate things for a long time and, considering what the rites are like' – the disciples giggled nervously – 'I'm sure all of you will agree that this is no mean feat. What's more, the girl can hold contrasting ideas in her head at the same time. I think she's very flexible.'

The girls touching Rika all broke out into cheers, and Rika felt warm and beloved and cherished. Perhaps Pia had been wrong to be afraid. Maybe she was fighting too hard against what was only pleasure; maybe she should relax and just enjoy the rites.

'Why are you smiling?' Arje asked, her eyes twinkling.

'I'm rather enjoying myself,' Rika admitted. 'It's true, though; they're the opposite of what the fish-believers promise in their preachings. Here pleasure is sought after, and is considered good and healthy.'

Arje smiled widely and Rika knew that she had said the correct thing. It had never occurred to her that Arje had been carefully observing her even at her cabin, when they had gone through the 'practice' for the rites. Even Pia had never shown her such attention. But Pia and the mission for the Crew were beginning to feel like distant memories to her, half-dreams, as Rika relished the cool feel of flesh on flesh.

'You should relax a little; you look sleepy,' Arje said to her, and Rika was gently lowered to a pile of smooth, silvery wolf-fur by many hands, her belongings still nestled comfortably under her arm.

'No,' Arje said softly, 'we have no holy wars as the fish-believers do, no wars fought solely to convert. Those wars waged by our people in the name of religion have always been by traitors lured to the side of the fish-men. Traitors such as Olaf . . .'

Rika shuddered inwardly. To even speak against the old dead king Olaf was high blasphemy.

'. . . we have not yet stooped to such a level. But there are those among us who want new methods of combating the fish-believers and their reign of terror over our people. People who want to take the fish-believers' weapons and use them against them, and fight our own wars to convert to the Old Ways . . .'

For a moment, an inexplicable vision of Hrafn conversing with Ingrid appeared before Rika's eyes.

'Myself, I am not sure. My interest lies with the rites them-selves and the worship of Freyja, goddess of all that is most sensual. Here,' said Arje, 'you must sleep for a while. We will wake you up when it is time to join our theatre and see the spectacle we have prepared. But for now, you must sleep.'

Rika's stomach rumbled slightly and reminded her that she had had no food since the broth the day before at Arje's cabin. But she felt pleasantly light-headed and food seemed of little account as she sank into the rich pelts. The disciples in turn kissed her goodbye, their lips as soft as the fur on which she lay. The candlelight was extinguished and the darkness made her lids heavy as both Arje and her entourage retreated from her view. The last thing she was conscious of was the simple, dreamlike feeling that someone was quietly slipping her scramsasax away from the bundle in which it rested.

# SEVEN

She woke up only once from her dreams. When she listened in the darkness, she heard only the rattle of many hooves. For a moment she grew frightened that it was Odin himself who sought revenge for some unknown reason, and the hooves she'd heard were those of Sleipnir, his eight-legged steed. But this nightmare eventually passed and soon she went back to a deep, drugged sleep.

Hours later she woke again to the sensation of rough hands scraping over her body. Jerking herself to her feet as Ingrid had taught her, she reached immediately for her scramsasax knife. Gone. She put her hand to where her sword should be. Gone too. And her father's knife. She held her breath and listened in the darkness. It was just a slight sound, but it was enough. She reached her hands out, caught hold of the intruder and they tumbled and rustled in the darkness.

'Stop!' someone said in the darkness. 'At least let me light my torch.'

Rika loosened her grip and a torch was lit, whereupon Rika immediately grabbed it with her free arm. Only then did she see clearly that she had her elbow crooked around the throat of a frightened redhead. In the dim recess of her mind she recalled seeing this red-haired beauty with Arje the night before. Rika felt groggy, as if she'd been stunned or drugged. 'Why did you creep up on me?' she asked the whimpering young woman.

'I had instructions to dress you,' the girl said, scarcely daring to look Rika in the eye. 'I was trying to wake you up.'

Rika had her doubts about that. 'It was the mead I drank, wasn't it? I was drugged.' The girl nodded. 'Where are my weapons?' Rika demanded.

'Arje instructed that we take them last night. She has them under her protection and says to tell you not to worry.'

For some reason, Rika felt only slightly better knowing that they were in Arje's safekeeping. 'All right. Now why did you want to wake me?' Her head ached, as if she'd been drinking whole flagons of mead. She had no idea what time it was.

'I've brought the garments for you,' the girl whispered in a frightened voice, glancing at the necklace round Rika's neck.

Rika put her hand to her pendant and ran her hand over the gem. The girl shuddered slightly and Rika smiled to herself. 'Which garments do you mean?'

'The clothing for the rites.' The auburn-haired girl brought forth a glorious red shirt and leggings, the same colour and material as the dress that Rika had seen once before at Arje's cabin. 'I have to arrange your hair,' she added shyly. Rika let her brush back her blonde tresses and bind them like a boy's, uncovered.

Rika held up the frail material to her slender frame. In fact, all of the clothing was that of a young man. She put on the shirt and breeches, and added to it a woollen belt studded with small decorations of amber and jet that the girl shyly handed to her, along with other body ornaments. Rika bound her wrists with bracelets of bronze and her ankles with golden anklets on which intricate, writhing strange animals were carved. She looked down on herself. In this male clothing, she looked very handsome indeed. She half hoped that red-haired girl had noticed. But she obviously held all the power in her hands already when it concerned this girl and others like her. It was Rika who wore the pendant. Besides, the redhead had politely turned her head away.

'Are you nearly finished?' the girl asked hesitantly. 'Because Arje said we were to hurry.'

Rika ran her hands over the curves of her body, along the flimsy fabric of the blood-red shirt and leggings. 'I'm ready.' And the girl led her forth, through an exit in the longhouse that had escaped Rika's notice before, through a tunnel and out to a wide open space – where an enormous arena had been built into the snow and hills. High impenetrable walls of snow rose up all sides to form the shell of the enclosure.

In front of the arena was a stage, and top of the stage were the stacked logs of a funeral pyre. That much Rika could see even from a distance. But she was not really prepared for the clear sight of the enormous statues behind the theatrical stage. Set high above the arena was a series of sculpted ice-cows, dripping icy water that ran slowly down their luridly carved udders. There was some lewd insinuation of copulation and Rika felt embarrassed just by looking at them – they were incredibly obscene and sexual, and yet disturbing. In one statue, a naked ice girl straddled a teat, using it as a phallus, and in another a man sucked diligently at a swollen udder, while he was anally penetrated by a teat that shot out a frigid representation of milk – or semen.

Mist made it difficult to see more than several paces ahead. Rika took a further step into the vast space and stood for a moment, the winter wind cold through the frail blood-coloured clothing. But there was heat from the assembled crowd. A huge amount of people were present, people of both sexes. Perhaps several hundred altogether, they were all gazing up at the stage and the ice-statues expectantly.

But right then another of Arje's acolytes ran to throw a thick rug of bear fur over her shoulders. The red-haired escort led Rika towards two waiting figures, before falling back into the crowd.

'Rika,' Arje stepped forward out of the mist, 'I'm so pleased that you could make it.' The tone was faintly mocking and a tiny shock of fear began to run up Rika's spine. Her flesh grew goose-bumped, and not only from the cold. 'Did you sleep well?' Arje continued, grasping Rika towards her and enfolding her in a warm embrace.

Rika felt paralysed, as if she were glacial, solid ice herself. She could not run nor fight, and she had no weapons at her disposal. She numbly let herself be hugged by Arje, trying to steal a glance at the other figure. But he – or she – was wrapped in a hooded garment; she could not see the face of the mysterious *gòthi*. Still, she knew somehow that it was Hrafn.

Arje led Rika towards the enormous stage where the marvellous statues of ice dripped. The priestess lightly murmured little details about the artisans and visionaries who had made this spectacle possible. Rika could not bring herself to listen, but she froze her expression into a polite smile and nodded back to Arje whenever it seemed appropriate.

When they reached the oak curves of the edge of the huge stage and the wooden poles that supported it, Arje chattered on about the workmanship, evidently expecting praise. Rika choked out a few words of flattery and raised her eyes to where Arje was directing her attention. She could not believe who she saw lying there on the makeshift bed of a pyre, the logs crossed in careful alternations so that they formed the frame for the slim body at the top. It looked like Lina, and at the same time it looked nothing like Lina at all . . .

'Lina?' she called up, her heart pounding. But there was no answer. She looked dead.

Arje appeared excited; her eyes were glowing. 'You want to see more clearly? Come.' She helped Rika to the stage, and then hoisted herself up as well.

Lina lay there prone upon the tall tower of logs. Her blonde hair curved in pale silk waves on the pillow; her hair was shining and bright. Her delicate face, with its rosebud mouth and finely arched blonde eyebrows, looked flushed and healthy – though the horrible feeling that she was dead did not leave Rika entirely.

151

She was not surprised to see that Lina wore the red dress from the cabin. A weird feeling began to creep up Rika's spine; the sight of Lina dressed in this glorious attire was strangely disconcerting. She thought it was Lina's hands. They curled slightly at her sides, the fingers paused in unfinished movement.

'Does she still live?' Rika asked Arje quietly, dreading the answer.

But it was not what she expected.

'Yes and no . . .' Arje exhaled slowly. 'She sleeps. But we cannot wake her up even if we wanted to. She is still drugged with strong medicines. So I let her sleep, Rika; I let her sleep until the last rites begin. And then, well –' Arje shrugged sadly.

'When is the fire to be . . . lit?' Rika tried to make her voice sound nonchalant.

'It will be the last of the rites, Rika, as I said. Remember? The rune called *perþ*. Let her sleep in peace for now.'

But Rika felt little joy at the thought that Lina still lived – it could not be more clear that she was designated for sacrifice. She much preferred her last memory of Lina, galloping bravely away to new adventures, to her lifeless, frozen beauty. She stood on her toes and touched the young girl's cool red dress, rubbing her fingers on the gossamer-light fabric. She felt like she was going to cry. She could see the edge of Lina's flaxen hair, woven tightly into a cascading fountain of curls and waves. This funeral hairstyle reminded her of a wood rendition she had once seen of Freyja – and ever so faintly of the figures she had once seen carved on Ingrid's mirror – and confirmed that Lina represented the sex-goddess herself, just as Arje had said she would.

But she couldn't bear to look at cold, stiff Lina for a moment longer. She would have to find an antidote. Still, Arje had said that it would be the last of the rites. It would be impossible to forget Lina's lot, whatever the case, with the girl thrust up there on the pile of sticks, looking for all the world like she would be set alight at any moment.

'Come.' Arje moved across the stage and Rika followed after

152

her, steadying herself on Arje's hand. Arje jerked suddenly away when Rika accidentally brushed against her, though it was only the touch of Rika's boyish clothing against Arje's skin. Rika peered at Arje's face as they marched across the stage, but it gave nothing away. She remembered how she had reacted to the priestess back in the cabin when she had been aroused to breaking point, desperate not to look on smooth skin, or think thoughts that would make her face go hot. Maybe – though it was a wild supposition – Arje felt exactly the same of her.

'Arje,' said Rika, 'remind me, why is it that only women participate in the rites?' Perhaps she could make use of the woman's attraction to her. 'Which woman have you picked to play Freyr in his beauty, as you already have an example of Freyja in hers?' She laughed lightly, as if to show that the question was only a mocking one.

She already knew the answer; she knew who was picked to play Freyr, had known it at some level ever since she arrived. The same person who wore a pendant of Freyr around her neck. She had been marked since . . . well, ever since Ingrid had given her the jewel last spring. What she needed to know was whether she was fated to share Lina's fiery destiny. She ran a gentle finger from Arje's wrist to her bicep as they slowly walked along the stage, and this time observed the woman breaking out into a faint perspiration on her brow.

'Who?' she pressed, then, in order to goad, added riskily, 'Why does a man not play Freyr instead?'

Arje stopped dead in her tracks and turned sharply on Rika. 'What, and waste a male in flames? Have a *male* wear the pendant? What would Hrafn say? Don't joke about such things, Rika,' she said in a tired voice. 'You know the answer to that as well as I.'

I'm in danger, Rika thought, and a vision of her burning atop the pyre with sleeping, unknowing Lina in her arms filled her mind. She had to distract herself somehow; in order to survive she had to push back these terrible thoughts. What would a

Viking do? What would a Crewmember do? A Crewmember would save Lina, she knew.

They stopped on the far right corner of the platform, Rika looking wildly around for some escape, something on which to concentrate her attention. Finding no exits, she walked over to the curving side of one of the great ice-cow renditions and placed her hand on the glassy surface of its hoof. She drew it away, dripping. It was colder than the most frigid winter. She began to shiver and turned to Arje. 'These carvings are fantastic.'

'Yes, they are.' Arje sounded very proud. 'We contracted artisans from far north to carve them for us and we paid for them to dredge the northern lakes for ice from which to sculpt.' She pressed closer to Rika to confide a secret. 'They have dual purposes, too; they are not merely ornamental. The artists are highly skilled. Look up.'

Rika raised her head and saw that she stood directly underneath the protruding, four-pronged udder of the ice-cow. Every detail was lovingly carved, so it seemed that the frost-dappled stretched teat skin could indeed be sourced for milk. Or perhaps ice-water would run out instead. 'Very admirable,' she told Arje, who was waiting for her response.

Arje smiled; there was a wild gleam in her eye. 'Just wait and see. It is the first of our rites: *uruz*, or the wild ox called the aurochs. Its purpose is to strengthen will, and let submerged desires rise to the surface.' Arje scratched the rune into the surface of the ice, and smiled at Rika.

'Now that I have written it, it is invoked, you see; we can never go back. Now there is only base instinct.'

Arje whistled, and the hooded figure Rika had recognised as Hrafn led up four naked bound men who had been painted from their shaved heads to their toes in bright oranges, purples, shimmering silvers, blues and vibrant reds. Hrafn deposited the men before Arje and Rika and then drew back some distance, but still stayed on the stage. With a jolt, Rika suddenly knew for what the paintbox she had once used on Pia had originally been intended. Everything was starting to connect: the paintbox, the pendant . . . and Pia's comments that Ingrid sold people for the sacrifices.

Arje's voice was loud and holy. 'You have been convicted for crimes unmentionable,' she told the four men, 'and you have refused to pay a tribute, or to work in lieu of money. Now you must pay the price – you shall suck diligently, for my pleasure and for the pleasure of all who watch. We shall see your true desires emerge.' At these words, a tall bench was brought in by white-clad thralls and the paint-covered men climbed on top of it, underneath the hanging teats of the ice-cow.

Noticing the resignation in the eyes of the four men, Rika vowed to mentally withstand the trials, even if she was on that pyre with Lina. She never wanted to be as empty of spirit as these men before her. In a perverse way, the sight filled her with fresh courage. With no one she could trust, she would have to fight for herself. It was an intriguing thought and it frightened her.

The men brought their mouths up to the dripping, elongated teats and sucked and sucked at them. Even though her mind was racing with various plans of escape, something stirred between Rika's legs at the image. The men looked to be sucking at the end of enormous, huge phalluses and Rika knew this was a forbidden act for men. The brilliant multicoloured paint on their faces and chests began to mix with the moisture melted by their lips; soon the aphrodisiac took its effect. One by one the men crumpled from the bench, holding their stomachs in apparent agony.

'Why?' Rika whispered, wrapping her arms tightly round herself. Arje caught the sound of her words.

'It's not poison as we know it, Rika; it's not like that which

155

Lina has ingested,' she told her. 'There is no sex-spell or poison in the melted liquid, though the men think it is there. It is only frozen water that they suck on. These men have beaten their wives and despise all things they consider womanish; afraid to be kind, afraid to be gentle; they must now learn how to be kind to each other. The liquid that they suck will change their actions, but not their desires. Like everyone else on earth, they have always had those desires – and always suppressed them.' Rika knew the worst humiliation for a man was to be dressed as a woman, but to show vulnerability to another man in acts of lust – well, this was even more forbidden for Viking men. And strangely exciting.

The men rolled around dazed on the wooden floor of the stage, grabbing at their guts as the strange icy liquid worked its way into their bodies. But slowly they began to reach for each other. Rika watched amazed as they began to suck at their neighbour's cock until the four of them formed a strange animal on the stage, jerking and bucking and sucking out the milky fluids from each other.

Rika began to feel hot with lust as she watched and she cursed herself for being so weak to succumb to the sight; if she had not succumbed to Ingrid in the first place she would not be in this position now. But she could smell the musky foreign scent of male sweat as she watched one of the men slowly pulling on his stiff cock until he shot out a stream, groaning with pleasure. Another limber young man, perspiration rolling down his firm muscled body, took the man's softening prick in his mouth and sucked it as avidly as a newly married wife. Rika's cunt swelled at the sight; in her masculine clothes she almost felt impelled to join in the male-only orgy.

Then she looked out over the audience that stood in front of the stage. She was not alone in her reaction. Most of the men, she saw, were stroking themselves beneath their robes, and not a few of the women had jammed their hands down on themselves and were busily working their fingers into their wet pussies, too. But she kept her hands at her side. She had to keep her wits about her; she couldn't get drawn too far into the first of these strange, exhibitionistic rites. She had to come up with an idea that would save both herself and Lina.

Arje smiled at the sight of Rika gripping her hands, willing herself not to succumb to lust; she watched Rika take a quick opportunity to look up at poor Lina in the red dress. She wished Hrafn hadn't drugged the girl; it would have been much more entertaining to watch Freyr and Freyja fucking first. Arje had a lovely dildo that would be just perfect for that occasion, but today Hrafn had insisted that the best way to do it would be to burn them both, and quickly. Still, Arje was enjoying herself. She only hoped that Rika was fully aware of the honour that had been bestowed upon her.

She reached over and stroked the pendant at Rika's throat. 'Ingrid has given you such a gift, Rika,' she said. 'I hope that you appreciate it. To play Freyja's lovely male twin and sacrifice that type of lust to the gods – what an honour.' She left her hand on the sacred pendant. Ingrid had chosen well; she usually did. For a moment, Arje thought uncomfortably of the time seven years ago, when the dark-haired girl Ingrid had chosen had nearly killed Ingrid, Hrafn and herself in a successful bid to get away. But by and large, Ingrid had had considerable success persuading the perfect girls to wear the pendant of Freyr – beautiful, sexual, confident girls. Just the kind that Arje liked. She stroked her fingers over the etching of Freyr. Perfect.

Rika held her breath as Arje's fingers played with the pendant. The best way to glean more information would be just to smile and let Arje talk. But no more information passed from Arje's lips and Rika began to immediately worry about what she had just heard – especially the reference to 'sacrificing lust'. She had always hoped to save Lina, but the thought that she would have to save her own skin too put things in an entirely different, even more frightening light. She looked up again at Lina, saw the girl just breathing slightly: the shallow breaths of the very ill or heavily poisoned. She would go along with the first parts of the rites, and when it came time for the final rite, she was reasonably confident that, somehow, she could save Lina – if not herself.

Below her, the audience had developed into a full-blown orgy, with men and women groping at each other, tongues tickling lips and the wet insides of mouths, breasts pushed and fondled and teased, people fucking and slowly wanking and licking each other as roughly and luridly as the four men entangled on the stage. From where she stood, Rika saw the red-haired girl licking deep into another girl's cunt, while a young man took her from behind as an animal, forcing the redhead's tongue to work even harder on the other woman's pussy.

At least a hundred people – nearly a third of the crowd – were fucking down there; meanwhile, the four men on stage twisted into a sexually explicit spectacle. Only she and Arje and Hrafn stood apart and watched, but the wish to join in was growing in Rika with every second that passed. She still suspected that she would in some way damn both herself and Lina if she partook. So she withstood temptation, but her cunt was so juicy and already leaking moisture on to the red fabric of the light breeches.

She ground her thighs together, but kept her hands at her sides. Arje's hand was still cupped around the pendant and she could feel the woman's escalating breath patterns as she watched the debauchery below. Arje let her hand travel below the fabric of Rika's shirt and stroked her hand over the young woman's soft breast.

'It's glorious, isn't it?' she whispered to Rika. 'Complete excess, complete sexual chaos. Just as I wanted it to be.'

'But it can go further.' Hrafn, still hooded, stood uncomfortably close to both Arje and Rika. 'It *can* go further. Your problem, Arje, is that you always draw the line at sexual chaos. It's fine and good in its place, but we can bring our beliefs to a much wider spectrum – there is life and death outside that of sex – and indeed we must widen our church, if we want to bring on

Ragnarök.' It was obvious that this was an argument that he and Arje had gone over many times before.

Arje sighed, removing her hands from Rika's breast.

Hrafn lurched behind Rika and whispered in her ear, 'Isn't that right, little Rika? Isn't that right, my dear? *Ragnarök*. The end of the world. The chaos when even gods die. But when our own beliefs shall finally triumph once again over that of the fish-believers.' His breath was putrid and Rika whipped around to face him, breaking partially free of Arje's tender grasp.

Hrafn finally drew back his hood and Rika was face to face with the snarling, rabid visage of a madman.

'Chaos?' she heard herself saying. She felt dizzy, unable to make clear judgements, as if she were thinking through a thick fog. Judging from the overindulgence taking place below them in the audience, chaos seemed no bad thing at all. In fact, she wished desperately that she could join the lascivious crowd below and suck and lick and fuck, rather than breathe in the rank breath of this despicable old man and discover a solution to save herself and Lina.

'That's correct.' The old man smiled crookedly. 'Our intervention in the Saxon and Norman wars was only the beginning of attempts to bring on Ragnarök. I shall cause chaos and war whenever I can, and bring back our rituals of sacrifice and blood.'

Rika felt as though she would faint.

'And as always, it has been our Ingrid who has helped the most. Isn't that right, dear Arje? Procuring the sweetest sacrifices I've ever seen.' The old man winked at the priestess, whose own expression was serious.

'You know I don't fully agree with your interpretations of the Old Ways,' the female shaman told Hrafn sharply.

Rika looked from one to the other. Why, they were as bad as the fish-believers were when it came to questions of religious doctrine.

At last Arje drew back from the bickering and released her hand from the pendant round Rika's neck. 'Hrafn,' she coolly

159

informed the hooded old priest, 'we have many more rites before your role is required, or indeed that of any male; so if you'll excuse us . . .'

Hrafn nodded reluctantly and withdrew. 'We can discuss this later, Arje.' He looked Rika up and down, and a wave of disgust hit Rika as she endured his lecherous appraisal of her charms; she began to appreciate the extent to which she would have to go in the lurid and rough rites. But she would bide her time. There was no way she could escape now, with a crowd of hundreds guarding the only way out to freedom.

'I know that you'll be needing Rika for the time being,' Hrafn added, 'but I'll willingly remove her when you are finished. And before she's finished.' He cackled and departed.

Arje stared solemnly at Rika. 'Pay him no attention. He's a zealot; I'm not sure what he means by that, but I'll keep you safe with me until it is time. I'll make sure your exit is respectful and worthy of the warrior you've proved yourself to be.'

Rika swallowed, trying very hard to misunderstand Arje's serious, well-meant words.

'Not like Ingrid, who Hrafn informs me has sold out her entire crew of female warriors, who have now disbanded in Britain. Ingrid's Crew no longer exists. You would never do that, Rika; I know this. You have an honest soul and you will die an honourable death.'

Despite the woman's chilling words, Rika began to feel a little respect for the priestess, who obviously believed strongly in what she said. But of course, so did Hrafn. With horror, the full meaning of Arje's words hit her and she tried not to let the realisation show upon her face. Not only had Ingrid betrayed the Crew with her double-dealings between Godwinsson and William, but she had sold Rika into a certain ritual death as well.

She followed Arje to the edge of the stage and made her way through the orgiasts, whose lasciviousness affected her far less now that the fear of death had fully hit her. She realised she had changed since she first left home, when she used to believe in Valkyries and honourable deaths. After what she had experienced in battle and after witnessing first-hand the hypocrisy of religion, her conclusion was that there were no 'honourable' deaths. Even if everyone around her seemed to think that she was heading towards one herself.

# EIGHT

As they walked back through the crowd the way that they had come, Arje told Rika that the rites would reconvene in a matter of minutes. Rika resolved to keep her mouth closed and listen to all the information she could, preparing for the moment when she would make her break and save Lina, too.

'The next rune is only a taste of pain, but it represents an ordeal which eventually passes, the clearing-out of a bad situation. It is called *þurisaz* – the frost giant from the Cold World.' Again, Arje scrawled the rune on the wall of ice with her fingernail:

'So, the result of the ordeal of the rite is that we are eventually warmed from the frost.'

'The . . . sacrifice is not any time soon, is it?' Rika asked, not especially caring for the particulars of the runes.

'No,' Arje told her, slightly irritated. 'I told you before: the sacrifice is the last rite. It is the finishing touch, the jewel that adorns the necklace of the rites – so to speak.' She left Rika momentarily in the corridor by which they had first entered the arena, leaving the oaken door just slightly ajar, and then disappeared back towards where the audience was revelling in sexual play.

It was dark and uncomfortable. Rika looked behind her for an exit, to where the corridor had connected to the longhouse. But now the way was barred with a huge block of ice; she would never be able to move it. She sat on the hard-packed earth in the cool dark womb of the tunnel. There was not even a *skjall*-window that she could remove. The only way out was the way she came in – back through the arena. She heard a sudden piercing whistle, and then the sound of many people exiting the sphere. She felt a rush of optimism: there must be another exit somewhere, she thought. Perhaps beyond the stage.

When Arje shortly returned, she handed Rika some blueberries on which to munch and an icicle wrapped in fur. 'A little refreshment for you and a little preparation, too,' she said, smiling benevolently. Rika smiled hesitantly back, unsure what Arje meant. The blueberries squished pleasantly in her mouth, the taste tart and sweet; the rivulets from the icicle coolly soothed her mouth and throat. She needed fortification.

Arje watched while the young woman downed the food. She knew full well that complete capitulation often depended on lack of food, senses drugged with medicines and herbs and limited sleep, but she had felt so sorry for the tender young thing that she had let her doze for longer than she would have normally let a pendant-bearer sleep. It was the least that she could do, really; the girl would soon be for the gods alone.

After Rika finished her food, Arje took her by the hand and led her back to the arena, now empty of all but her own disciples – close to a hundred young women. All men had left the arena at the sound of her whistle and she felt the change in the

163

atmosphere, the rising excitement and tension that comes with an all-female environment. She was already growing wet at the thought of what was to come.

She pointed to the twenty young women she had previously chosen, all big tall beauties of child-bearing age, and they stepped out from the crowd. She positioned the girls into a line and bent them over gently from the waist, murmuring encouragement all the time. Then she handed over the spruce branch to young Rika. She was not sure if the girl could do it, but she was surprisingly well muscled for one so slightly built. She felt the young blonde girl would be able to master the challenge. She stole a look herself at the delectable sight of the girls' pink, plump buttocks: shapely, prone and quivering. She sucked in her breath. She would have done it herself, if her role had not been a supervisory one.

When Arje handed a large wide fan of spruce to her, Rika had gripped the stem of it, feeling the rough bark and the sap sticky on her fingers. The sky was dark, but the arena was eerily lit from what seemed like a thousand torches. A huge bonfire was blazing on the ground in front of the stage and she could smell burning pine and oak and spruce. And up above, she could see the beginning of a display of the northern lights: cool glowing shades of blue and green starting to weave together. She looked ahead of her. The girls' bottoms were so round, so willingly vulnerable that her excitement quickly mounted. She would not be faking her excitement, she admitted to herself. And perhaps that would be the best attitude, one that would see her through to the last of the rites.

She brought down the branch from high in the air, rapidly; and it stung the milky-white posterior curves of the girl directly in front of her, bringing a light pink flush to the surface. She then did the same to the bottoms of the other nineteen, bringing the young girls' buttocks up to the colour of a fine, invigorating pink glow. Her arm was starting to ache, but she still felt disturbingly eager to continue.

One flaxen-haired young woman tensed her buttocks in anticipation and Rika felt as if the tingling was rising up through the branch, from the girl's pink arse to her wrist. The girl moaned. Rika raised her hand up again; felt herself growing wet. When she next lowered the branch, she slipped her fingers between the girl's legs underneath her moist blonde curls and felt how wet and sticky she had become. The blonde girl groaned and trembled and when Rika next thrashed down the branch on her tender bare skin, she screamed in delight.

'Rika.' Arje cleared her throat. 'Don't make the other girls jealous.' It's just a performance on my part, Rika thought. Just so I can make it through to the last rite. She looked down the line at the nineteen shapely bodies of the remaining women. Their nipples hung as taut as sweet solid raspberries. She thrashed all of them again in turn: gently at first, just feathering their backsides. The mounds of their breasts swayed with the motion of the lashes. They were moist now and eager for the stinging blushes from the branch that Rika held. Rika knew that she was enjoying the rite too much already.

'Thrash their backs as well,' urged Arje, in a commanding voice. Rika did so, bringing the healthy glow of pink stripes to the sturdy, muscled backs of the girls. She almost began to yearn for the sting herself; she had been told many times how refreshing it was. Spruce-beating was supposed to be good for the constitution.

Arje came up to Rika as the refreshment drew to a close, with both Rika and the other girls exhausted. 'Do you remember how I told you of the rites you would endure?'

Rika nodded.

'And do you remember me mentioning that you would be required to lick and drink?'

Again, Rika indicated that she had not forgotten. Immediately, her mind was full of obscene pictures.

'Well, what follows is the most important rite. In the minds of the girls, anyway. It is the re-enactment of our creation myth. All parts are played by disciples of mine, and you, of course.'

Arje lewdly gripped her crotch and Rika watched fascinated. Arje removed her hand and this time invoked the rune by drawing it in a nearby snowdrift with her finger:

'Bliss through endeavour,' she reminded Rika. 'It is called *wunjo*: glory. And it represents the joy that follows a completed task. Lead her to the stage.' The twenty strapping girls took Rika in hand and marched her back to the raised platform. There was a long log-bench raised to knee-height, and two fur-covered ropes strung horizontally behind and in front of it, all the way across the stage. If a girl sat on the log she could either lie back and be supported by the tender cord behind, or grip the rope in front for balance.

Arje gave one of her piercing whistles once again. The troupe of beautiful young girls walked up the steps of the stage and placed themselves sitting on the long log. She drew close to the stage and motioned for Rika to join the girls. 'Don't sit down with them, though. I want you to remain standing,' she cautioned. 'We need to see how well you finish your given task. You shall do as you are inspired to do and it shall be complete.'

Rika climbed the stage and then stood with her back to the girls, looking at the audience of eighty women – and Arje. In the crowd, there were women of all types: some lushly fat and curvy, some delicately, smoothly slender. Older women, with proud, lined faces, and girls who looked as if they too were young enough to have run away from unacceptable marriages. Most had blonde or light-brown hair, but there were also women with grey and red and jet-black locks. She took the chance to scan the crowd for Pia's own dark head, but she could not see the warrior-woman as she hurriedly searched the audience.

'Begin!' shouted Arje from the crowd. 'Pleasure them as best you can, and if you stop before it is time . . .' She made a motion that indicated that Rika would not have a pleasurable punishment. It looked disturbingly like Arje had indicated her throat would be prematurely cut. Rika turned abruptly to the line of girls, whose backsides she had so recently refreshed.

All twenty of them sat there suspended on the log, their breasts full and plump. They were not quite as varied as the audience who watched – some were voluptuous, some sinewy and sturdy – but they looked to be around the same age. She put her mouth near the sex of the first woman in the line, who sighed and gripped tighter at the rope strung in front of her for balance. She was an extremely pale woman with light brown, silky hair, and her creamy flesh was lovely and soft. Rika wanted to bury herself in all her delicious, abundant curves. The light-haired woman closed her eyes at the feel of Rika's lips tracing her satin-soft pussy and she leant back on the wide fur-covered rope behind her.

Rika bent in closer and again the woman sighed, feeling Rika's warm tongue licking near her clit. Rika could see the surprising vision of ripe plump blueberries at the opening of the woman's sex and, as she looked down the line, she saw that all the other women had their legs open, too, coating the tiny fruits with their warm flavours. Rika's mouth watered as she rested her hands on either side of the woman, moving her face into the moaning woman's honey-sweet pussy. The scent, the feeling of the woman's soft, milky thighs, the dew she lapped up – all were heavenly.

She paused, her long soft tongue seeking out one perfect little blueberry. She took it in her mouth, biting into it, and felt its wild sweet taste spreading in her mouth, dissolving with the flavour of this woman's juice. She swallowed it down with delight, the taste of the woman running down her throat. Something warm and wet pooled down her neck, and she withdrew momentarily.

Small pearls of milk were running down from the lush tight

orbs above her; sweet milk was overflowing from the woman's stiff pink nipples. She had thought the woman was of child-bearing age – but here was undeniable proof.

Heat from the bonfire below the stage flickered at her cheeks. And far higher Rika could see coloured streamers of the northern lights cutting across the sky. She kept the image in her mind when she put her mouth back to the woman's sex and sucked at it, slurping at the remaining berries. Coarse, sweet milk was being pumped out above her; she shuddered with arousal at the thought as she licked at the dew moistening the woman's pussy. The woman sighed and twisted, and drops of milk fell on Rika's back when she ran her tongue near the woman's clitoris.

It occurred to her that the woman's breasts pumped forth more the deeper and harder she licked, and so she sucked hard on the woman's clit and was rewarded with a rain of creamy tit-milk falling down on her; the woman she sucked at was writhing and twisting and slippery. Rika kept on sucking and alternately licking. She thought of the woman's spurting breasts and the ache between her legs increased. She wished she knew how it felt for the pale-skinned woman; but she could imagine: a mouth working hard at her own nipples always made her aroused and wet from tugging sensation, always turned her clitoris hard and tight, and the reverse was true as well. The woman was so slippery, her cunt so wet and lush over Rika's face, milk pumping out from her full, taut tits. A spasm shook Rika's sex and then her whole body as her pussy convulsed. She licked and sucked harder than ever, while the milk flowed over her shoulders and back. It mixed sweet and heavy with the woman's dew in her mouth.

As the brown-haired woman neared her peak, Rika rose up and placed her lips around the woman's stiff, rosy teat – her breast huge as a gourd – and sucked the milk out, fucking the woman with her fingers. The sweet thick taste shot down Rika's throat, the ache between her legs blending over into pure pleasure as she drank. The woman beneath her moaned and gushed into her mouth, her sex spasming in orgasm as Rika's fingers moved rapidly over her clit.

But an acolyte pulled Rika away from the woman's rosy-tipped breasts and admonished her. 'It's the berries that you concentrate on,' the disciple told her. 'And you've got nineteen more women to pleasure.'

Rika looked down the line of women, supported by the odd combination of the spruce-log and the ropes. The woman whose creamy tits she had just sucked was helped down and then escorted several paces away, where she was treated with a female disciple's hand in her cunt and another disciple's wet eager quim atop her mouth. Rika's own sex was still tingling, but she felt well satisfied. She looked over the line of nineteen beautiful and wanton-looking women, plump and lush, with the sweet blue-berry fruits nestling in their even sweeter cunts. She wasn't sure how she would do it, but at the thought of the taste of all these different women – as well as poor Lina – she knew she would find the strength.

All the women were delicious but all tasted different as she sucked and caressed their pussies with her tongue: some were smoky; some were deliciously marine-flavoured; the blonde woman who had been so eager to be thrashed with the spruce had a mouth-wateringly salty cunt. As the rite went on and Rika sucked and licked and swallowed, the only punctuating taste was the feast of the berries, coated and covered with the slightly different taste of each new woman. One particularly pretty girl, with long dark curls, soft lashes like a fawn and skin as soft as fur even tried to touch Rika's drenched sex as she dipped her tongue between the girl's plump labia and drew out the morsel of the blueberry. But this girl was reprimanded with a stern word from the red-haired disciple who was avidly observing. The point, she reminded both Rika and the girl, was the rite, not pleasure for its own sake.

Rika looked up past the girl's pert and milking breasts – she must have given birth quite recently, Rika thought – to the girl's bright blue eyes and received a big wink and a smile. Rika

169

quickly put her head back down to the delicious taste – she had three more women to service, after all, and her jaw was beginning to ache. With her dark hair, the girl reminded her of Pia. But Pia wasn't here, so she went back to the ecstasy of the woman's velvety, creamy sex.

She was half praying for the rite to be over and half hoping that it never finished, as her tongue licked lovingly at a woman's little proud pearl of a clitoris, enticingly erect and bright pink. This was rapture. Her face was covered hot with the come, her shoulders and her hair coated with sweet mother's milk, her mouth stained with blueberry juice as well.

The northern lights were shimmering and waving across the sky when Rika finished pleasuring the last woman and swallowed the last blueberry. She crumpled exhausted on the ground. Her lips and tongue were numb, but she felt marvellous. The ribbons of blue and green rippled above her in the night sky and she watched the colours shift and tremble. There were no stars in the cold air, only these sheets of coloured light, bleeding into each other.

She breathed in a cold breath and then blew it out in the smoke of a winter-breath. She still felt very hot from her exertions in the night air, but at the sight of the glorious *aurora borealis* she also felt refreshed.

'Come down off the stage and closer to the fire for a moment,' the red-haired girl who seemed to be her sponsor whispered to Rika, squeezing a handful of crushed snow down her neck and under her red shirt to cool her hot, flushed flesh. Rika climbed down off the stage and crouched in front of the fire, holding her head in her hands. What was she going to do? She could smell both a heady smoke from the fire as well as the scent of sex that rose from the frail masculine clothing covering her limbs. For several minutes Rika crouched like that, trying desperately to gather her thoughts and to quiet the pounding, unfulfilled arousal in her cunt.

The redhead leant towards her uneasily. 'I'm sorry, Rika,' she whispered, 'but you're not yet finished.'

'Not finished?' Her whole body exhausted, Rika followed the pretty disciple back from the fire to the rope-and-fur log contraption on the stage. 'What more could I possibly do?' Her eyes were nearly closing with fatigue. Gently, Rika felt herself being strapped on to the log herself and then, not so gently, felt blueberries being shoved up her own cunt.

Someone sang out a clear, high note that seemed to soar out all the way up to the shifting blue-green heavens themselves. Almost immediately Rika was surrounded by the flesh of all the women she had attended to so eagerly and carefully. Forty hands now caressed and squeezed her, twenty mouths licked and sucked and searched and, when she opened her eyes, all she saw were twenty pairs of breasts, lush and jiggling, nipples in search of her yearning mouth.

She sucked and sucked and when she opened wide her palms there were soft, heavy breasts laid on to them, which she squeezed while another woman suspended herself on the rope above and thrust her wet sex in Rika's face. Rika could smell her pussy while she sucked at a breast, and when she opened her eyes she could see all the women kissing and fondling and fucking each other. For the first time she felt the exquisite pleasure herself, felt the fruits between her legs being tasted by an anonymous warm, wet mouth. Berry by berry, the succulent ripe little plum-fruits were kissed from her cunt.

She pumped out moisture and she cried out as every spot of flesh on her was touched, or so it felt, touched and licked and kissed and with the blueberries being eaten out, she was sobbing with pleasure, eager and thirsty for milk and come, needing the hands upon her and needing the tickling, slipping mouths at her cunt. At the peak of terrible pleasure, she screamed out. Even when she closed her eyes the blue and green northern lights flashed beneath her lids and inside her skull. The twenty women drew slowly away from Rika, retreating from the stage area, their work done.

★

171

'Good.' Arje stood over her, smiling. 'You've done very well. You can complete your endeavours, and I'm pleased to see it.' She reached down to touch the pendant. 'It's almost a shame, isn't it, that there are greater religious repercussions involved. Rika, I should dearly like to train you properly to work as my apprentice. But you're fated to be sacrificed as Freyr, just as Lina is fated to be sacrificed as your proxy twin, Freyja. And Hrafn says that if this is not completed, Ragnarök will occur unbidden – no matter what we do.'

Her matter-of-fact tone was chilling; Rika had a hard time grasping that Arje was actually referring to her own death. The priestess seemed under the spell of the priest Hrafn and for a moment Rika reflected on the man's charisma.

She watched Arje break off one of the tips of the ice-cow teats and roll it between her palms. The ice had frozen in green, swirling colours.

'Get down on your hands and knees,' Arje told her. 'That was still merely the fourth of many rites.' Rika was so drugged with sex that she had lost track of how many rites had passed, but felt relieved at Arje's words, as she still hadn't come up with a feasible plan. But she still squirmed in disbelief as Arje pressed the icicle against the warm tender flesh of her sex. The cold was shocking.

Arje removed the intruding dowel of ice abruptly and handed it to a disciple. 'That's just a taste, Rika. Now you will experience the banquet.' Rika began to have the feeling that she would never escape the rites. Perhaps she should abandon the hopes of escape, and freeing Lina – or even of finding out what became of Ingrid's Crew. Rika ran her eyes over Arje's full, sensual breasts, and she shuddered, cursing herself: arousal was already pumping through her veins, as it had done ever since she had first seen the grey-haired priestess's lush naked body at the cabin. She watched Arje gird herself with an odd belt, one with straps that descended on to her full, creamy thighs.

Arje broke out in laughter as she saw how eagerly Rika was observing her. 'You should be feeling, Rika, not watching.

Feeling. Feel what I'm going to do to you.' She snapped her fingers and an acolyte handed her the frigid jade-tinted phallus. It was only melting slightly. Rika pretended to shut her eyes, but she kept her lids ever so slightly raised, so that she saw Arje shove the dripping ice-cock beneath a circle in the belt, and then the rounded icicle stood out, protruding triumphant from the scry-woman's pelvis.

'Ice,' said the priestess, and she scratched the symbol on to the frozen wall.

I

'Ice. And that's all it means.'

'You should make sure the woman is hot-flushed,' Arje instructed her disciples, 'for maximum contrast.' Rika shut her eyes.

All at once she felt what seemed to be a hundred warm mouths kissing and licking at her: her breasts, her supple arms and legs, even the outer folds of her sex. Then the dreamy, erotic music of a low-pitched flute began to play and the kisses became more searching and ravenous, the licking more lascivious. Rika's pulse started to race. She was turned on to her back and someone began to sponge hot, near-burning fluid over her face and entire body, and Rika's flesh was easily lured into its promise. Every inch of her flesh was tingling from the constant heat. She began to squirm as the mouths began to have the desired effect on her; her cunt was hot and red and wet and ready. A wet towel was placed on her scalp and her head was gently bent further backwards and wetted with heated water. A third pair of hands began to dry the strands of her hair. Little tickling sensations ran up her spine.

The music continued its low melody and she wiggled back and forth as someone nibbled on her tight nipples. She groaned as hot fluid was poured over her abdomen, then just as quickly rubbed off by the brisk, scrubbing, anonymous hands. She twitched, hoping that the hands would soon stroke at her sex again, but she was left, breathless and warm and panting. She was exposed, her legs wide apart, and she flushed at the thought of the glances that were surely being given to her naked, pink sex.

The music began to rise almost indiscernibly in pitch, the melody making her feel hot and safe and juicy, like a plump ripe fruit. The furs were soft against her back and buttocks, and she tried without success to achieve some titillation by rubbing herself against the soft prickly fur.

All at once the music stopped. As she lay on her back she heard the seer-woman's voice from somewhere near her head. She had entirely forgotten Arje also stood there before her. 'This is how you do it, girls.' Arje plunged the curving ice-dowel straight into Rika's hot, tight cunt; Rika's eyes flashed open.

The pain was momentarily indescribable, but then the chill that first reached her dissipated as Arje slowly fucked her with the strange ice-belt, her hands holding tight to Rika's red-tipped breasts. Rika threw her head back as Arje fucked her steadily and the icicle began to melt inside her. The numbness around her pussy was chafing and exciting, and little thrills ran up her backbone as the round icicle melted in the fragrant, sticky heat of her cunt. The water mixed with her own milky, thick juices and ran slow as spruce-pitch down her legs.

An orgasm was tickling at her, the feeling rising first from the back of her cunt and then spreading through her navel and her limbs. She shifted as Arje rode her and let the warm waves of sensation overtake the coldness in her sex. She grabbed at Arje's tits, swaying and full above her, and as she sucked on them sensations uncoiled deep within her gut, and she clung to them as she came, sucking hard on the enormous red nipples. Arje bucked the dowel deep into her, and the chill hit Rika deep inside, but soon warm juicy responses shivered through her and she came a second time. Arje thrust deep inside her several more times for good measure, then withdrew. The melting stick of ice was noticeably smaller.

Rika panted on the floor while the red-haired girl again dripped cooling icicle drops on her feverish brow. After a minute or so, she was able to get up from the floor, though she still felt very shaky.

By the time she rose, Arje was already lying near the left end of the enormous stage on a red cloth-covered slab from which four poles of birch rose up. Rika shakily headed towards the silver-haired priestess. Several others had had the same idea, though, and there was a circle of five thrall-girls dressed in white with shaven heads, none of whom Rika had ever seen before, around the slab on which the priestess lay. Rika pushed herself through so that she stood elbow to elbow with the other girls, and looked down at Arje. Each of the woman's hands were tied above her head to the birches by a heavily engraved golden chain, and her feet were tied too, separately, so that her legs were far apart. A flush covered Arje's bountiful chest and when she writhed in her bonds, her breasts swung back and forth like slow waves upon a quiet tide. Rika had rarely seen a woman so evidently aroused. Arje's face was flushed, her eyes closed, her mouth slack with desire and her tongue came out momentarily to lick her lips. Though sweat was glistening on her powerfully muscled inner thighs, Rika could make out a trickle of juice escaping from the woman's hot, wet cunt.

'What happens now?' Rika whispered urgently in the ear of the thrall who stood nearest to her. The priestess was exposed in this way for some special act, she was sure.

'We're deciding now who it is who will now entertain Arje,' the girl explained impatiently to Rika. 'Whoever draws the longest straw of wheat from the broom will have the honour.' She rapped a little broom against her palm, to which Rika's attention was immediately drawn. The switch was made of black, lush velvety feathers woven together with ripe pearled sheaths of amber-coloured wheat, bound together by intricate beading.

Arje gave a mighty sigh as if to remind the girls of their

purpose and tried in vain to rub her thighs together. On cue, the thralls withdrew slightly and each drew a long stalk of wheat from the broom. The girl whose straw was longest so far turned pale, but one of the other girls handed the broom to Rika, too. When Rika reached to collect it, her pendant tumbled out from her red shirt so that it was completely in view. The other girls gasped and drew back. It was obvious that they had not been aware that Rika bore this particular pendant.

'There's no need to draw a straw,' a thrall told Rika. 'It is your privilege.' She grabbed the little switch from the girl who would have otherwise won, thrust it quickly in Rika's hands and stepped back, as if Rika could infect her with a strange disease. Rika saw a slack-jawed sigh of relief forming on the lips of the girl who had previously held the wheat broom, but the decision seemed unanimous; she had no choice. It was Rika's glory to tease the priestess. Rika coiled her fingers round the switch and turned to face the magnificent, aroused vision of the priestess Arje.

'First you make the sign,' one of the girls hissed. 'On the ice wall, in this shape.' She traced it in the air for Rika and Rika replicated it on the ice.

'*Inguz* means fertility and harvest,' the slave girl told her, assuming correctly that Rika had no clue to its meaning. The thrall glanced at Rika's necklace. 'It can even mean Freyr. Now you must stroke her with the wheat.'

Arje sighed at the girl's touch. She had never known a quicker student and for a moment she again regretted that this one was chosen for the sacrifice. But Hrafn insisted on frequent offers to the gods, and it really wasn't her place to disagree – though the sacrifices were a bit merciless for her own tastes. Her favourite slave had once gone that way, and ever since then Arje had lost her taste for gory rites. Not that she wasn't a traditionalist, of course; the rites were still a necessity. But there were some aspects that she chose not to oversee.

Rika drew the feathers in circles over the tender underside of Arje's inner arm and the priestess trembled.

'Am I doing it right?'

Damn, she wished the girl would just be quiet. She closed her eyes and felt the fringe brushing on her pubic mound. At the thought of the velvety black feathers and soft sheaths of grain sweeping across the silver bush of her pubic hair, she smiled. Arje enjoyed titillation, particularly when she didn't have to work too hard herself at figuring out what to do next. The wheat was delicately beautiful as it was stroked across the fragile skin of Arje's eyelids. Yes, she was going to miss the girl.

Rika ran the switch down Arje's body, swirling it over the mounds of her large breasts and over the soft flesh of her inner thighs. She placed her hand under the woman's hips and signalled by touching her that she should raise up her pelvis slightly, so that Rika could stroke the feathers and wheat under her eminently squeezable buttocks. Rika tickled Arje against the fine hairs of her neck, not enough to make her laugh, but enough to make her breath come more quickly. Arje was reacting and it made Rika feel very good inside to see that she reacted with shivers and sighs. A pulse began to beat against all places in Rika's own body where blood rose quickly to the surface: wrists, neck, chest, cunt.

Despite every instinct she had for self-preservation, Rika knew in her heart she had not yet come up with a plan to leave this atmosphere of twisted eroticism. Part of the reason was that she was finding the rites far too pleasurable, even knowing Hrafn's plans for violence concerning Lina and herself – and even though she knew the extent of Ingrid's treachery.

Her fingers vibrated the lush little feathered quills against Arje's waist, tracing the sharp inward curve as if her own fingers were there. The woman's breasts were so huge that Rika had an uncomfortable feeling that either she had ignored them through embarrassment or not done them justice. She leant over and placed her lips around Arje's soft, fleshy nipple, lightly teasing it up into a ripe, firm mound, and then she sucked on it for near a minute. She snaked a finger down in the warm wet crevice between Arje's legs and then brought to her mouth some of the taste of the sweet cuntjuice. She let the taste swill in her mouth and then swallowed it down before returning to Arje's teat. Eventually she withdrew her wet mouth from the priestess's now achingly stiff nipple.

Everything felt tight inside Rika, but she knew that her release would be limited – if it occurred at all. She gazed at the beautiful priestess with the silver hair, thrusting back and forth on the red cloth, her bound limbs tanned and strong, her colour clear and flushed. For a short moment she pressed herself against the flesh of Arje's breasts. The soft unending expanse felt peaceful. Then she withdrew and began to draw the beaded strand of wheat and feathers slowly across Arje's body once again.

As Rika stroked the switch into the woman's lush breasts and soft body, a warm glow seemed to emanate from the priestess. Curious, Rika continued to stroke her, but around her all the other girls stepped far back and drew away. So engrossed was Rika and so transfixed with the heady rush of sexual power she had over the priestess, she did not think anything when the woman's whole body began to shimmer and change. Her hand faltered with the switch and dropped it, so she laid down her hand to slowly stroke the soft swell of the seer-woman's belly. When her hand touched fur, Rika's eyes grew wide, for it was then that she saw what she later swore was the furry body of a she-wolf, snapping and vicious and spitting-angry. Rika screamed and fell back, wanting to keep her distance as the other girls had done from this terrifying shape-shifter. But when she looked again, the wolf vision was merely Arje, voicing her pleasure as an orgasm evidently came upon her. Cautiously, Rika approached and as the woman shouted out her satisfaction, Rika carefully touched the woman's hot wet cunt and inserted two fingers, pumping and thrusting into the woman. She had never really fucked Arje, so it was a delight to feel her tightening around her hand and to feel the juices running down to her wrist as the woman came. Still, Rika could smell the disconcerting scent of a wild animal. If she hadn't known better, she would have thought it was the musk of a wild, silver-haired wolf.

As soon as the priestess seemed completely satisfied, Rika withdrew some distance to where the other girls were, sat herself down on the ground and slowly licked at her fingers, relishing once more the little thrills that started in her cunt at the mere taste of the older woman's liquid. She was giving in to the rites – and the worst thing was, she was enjoying it.

# NINE

The rites went on and on and Rika began to feel she didn't know where her own body stopped and another began. She once raised her head to look above the sea of skin: all the way across the arena she could see only bodies fucking, hands wet with come, backs soaked with sweat. But then a new woman's quim came close to her mouth and her crotch grew tight with arousal. She nibbled at the woman's cuntlips, before dipping her head down to sip at her soaking pussy. She ran her tongue out to the tip of her partner's clit and licked at it, then she put her hand out and rubbed the stiff little nub slowly, and then more and more quickly.

She put her face to the woman's sex and sucked at the tiny perfect clit, trilling her tongue against the hard little bead. Rika's face was already soaked when a stream of juice shot out, the liquid lovely and clear. Rika climbed on top of the woman and thrust her hand deeply into her pussy, wet and tight. She kissed this beautiful person roughly, their mouths wet against each other, tongues intertwined. Rika reached down to roughly fondle her partner's small breasts, and in return her own plump nipples were squeezed until they were red and engorged. But the anonymous woman was soon supplanted and Rika was fucking an entirely different woman. Everywhere she looked she could see taboos being broken: languid twenty-year-olds fucking wiry old women; people in groups of three or more screaming with pleasure; a tall woman slowly and erotically licking at a diminutive beautiful girl who was obviously menstruating, the tall woman revelling in the blood in her face and hair.

At one point the girl with the red hair came looking for her and stole Rika away from an embrace with the promise of a fresh kiss. Their tongues touched lightly, then the redhead withdrew to relay her message. 'Arje wants to see you. The rites are nearly complete, and she says that you are to eat the meal prepared for you and then be purified, before joining her. I will be escorting you.'

Drunk with sex, Rika did not immediately respond, but instead pulled the red-haired girl closer and deeply kissed her. They rolled around on the floor, not caring whom they bumped into or offended. They were both shivering with lust and the redhead had already forgotten her errand when a curious woman walked by. She was proudly naked, but she also had a little upturned tail such as a goat might have. Rika and the redhead raised their heads momentarily from the passionate kisses to stare, but the woman had walked by too quickly for them to confirm what they had seen. It was a strange enough sight to draw them both back to the real world.

The red-haired girl cleared her throat. 'Rika . . . we really do have to go now.'

Rika's thoughts were sluggish; she was so dazed with lust that the plans she was trying to form were unlikely or foolish at best. Pia had been right to warn her off these intoxicating rites. She thought of knocking down Arje and running for it, but she knew she would quickly be captured by the hundred disciples. The only sensible thing that entered her mind was the fact that there had to be a door behind the stage from where all the men had exited. Once she was up there she would escape, before they cut her throat or did whatever they planned to do to Rika.

She thought uncomfortably of Lina, who would still be drugged and asleep above the pyre.

Reluctantly, Rika raised herself to let the girl lead her to a corner of the arena where food and refreshment had been prepared. The delicious scent of boar being baked in an ember-filled pit made the mouths of even the most dedicated devotees water. Those who had tired momentarily of the orgy tore at pieces of the meat which had been baking in the coals, hungry for the salty, sweet taste of the rich flesh. The huge savoury wild boar had been roasted with onions and dried cherries, and there were piles of rye breads moistened with soft cheese, as well as venison, buttermilk, mutton and common beer. Rika rushed to the table to devour the food, but the girl caught her arm and stopped her.

'It's not meant for you, Rika. You are special; you receive sacred food in preparation for your journey.' The redhead directed Rika to a far more impressive, if smaller, table. It was laden with a wide variety of dishes; some were foods Rika had never seen before. There were goblets of mead, raspberries, pearled sheaths of fresh wheat, small bowls of wild honey. The morsels were arranged in lewd shapes: half revealed figs, juicy fruit-pods open and exposed, fruits arranged to look like lush genitals, breasts shaped from edible flowers and the whole feast was encircled by horn-shaped ice blocks of golden frozen beer, removed from the antler moulds into which they had been placed.

'How is it that the fruit looks so fresh?' Rika asked, curious despite herself.

The red-haired girl smiled with pride. 'These morsels – summer-grown – have first been transported and then frozen in the lands far to the north. The skilful northern artists who carved the sculptures brought the frozen fruits down with them for the rites. They are very eager, you see: they have been promised that in exchange for their helpfulness they will receive their own sacrificial thralls.'

'What do you think about that?' Rika said in a sharp tone. 'Do you think it's right to sacrifice thralls?'

The red-haired girl stared at her. 'I – I'm not sure,' she stuttered. 'Here, you had better eat.' She pointed to the straining bounty of the table. The vessels on it were silver and coloured glass as opposed to the normal bowls of ashwood. No one else touched the food on this table; it looked as if it was reserved for Rika alone. And there was a single pinkish-orange pomegranate on the table, too. The sight of it reminded her again of Lina and she turned away from the feast.

The red-haired girl was waiting for her to eat. 'Aren't you hungry?' she asked Rika. 'It is required that you partake, you know.'

The whole meal was probably poisoned, but if she tasted only a little bit . . . She raised an antler-horn of mead to taste. She licked her lips: the honey liqueur was strongly familiar, and not because it was berry mead, either. It tasted faintly of . . . She blushed; it was impossible. But the thought of mixing a woman's juices with a liquor was an embarrassingly intriguing one.

The disciple, evidently feeling she could confide in Rika, bent close to her and whispered, 'Can you imagine becoming drunk on it? Of course, you're the only one who is allowed to taste it.' She moved even closer and softly squeezed Rika's buttocks. Rika's whole face was burning. She raised the little horn to her lips once more and let the taste swim in her mouth. This time the subtle taste of cunt was more evident, and she swallowed down the decadent liquid.

She dipped her middle finger into a goblet of honey and tasted that, too; the same flavour was there. Such delicacies at a sacrificial feast, she thought. It seemed no expense had been spared. She carefully polished out the little antler drinking horn with her shirt and replaced it. The fact that she was enjoying the sex-mead was made more poignant since it could be her last taste of food and drink – ever. She shut her eyes and thought of Lina. 'I'm not hungry any more,' she told the disciple.

The girl looked uncertain, but then her face cleared. 'Well, you tasted it, and I suppose that counts for eating. I only hope Arje agrees. Now we must cleanse you in snow – Arje's told me that you've already practised for it?' With a sinking heart, Rika realised that the girl was probably referring to the occasion when she had nearly frozen her feet off outside Arje's cabin. But she had no choice but to follow the girl to the side of the arena. There, snowdrifts were piled higher than houses, but thankfully she was motioned towards a hut near the piled drifts, still inside the inescapable walls of the arena. 'Here you shall be cleansed,' said the girl, and it was she who drew the next rune in a bank of snow.

'Technically it means birch,' the girl said, '*berkana*. But generally, it means to purify.'

Rika entered the little hut behind the girl, grateful that she wasn't meant to walk barefoot in the snow this time. She was pleasantly surprised to realise that it was a sweatlodge, complete with wooden benches and a rock fire already hotly burning. There were perhaps ten others crammed into the small interior, including the poor thrall whose job it was to periodically douse the heated stones with water. This caused billows of steam to rise up in hot waves, near choking the occupants and making Rika's eyelashes sting with heat. She removed her ceremonial clothes shyly, leaving only the jewelled pendant round her neck.

The red-haired girl patted a seat below her, the one empty place in the whole room. The other women already within shouted at them to close the door behind them, for fear of the heat escaping. Rika closed the door and sat on the wooden slats beneath the disciple. Immediately the girl's hands were on her shoulders, pressing and kneading them, as Rika felt the sweat that had built up on her skin begin to slip away with the grime.

She was sweating so much that the girl's hand slid easily over her back and Rika leant back, closing her eyes and relaxing her head in the girl's lap. She could just feel the redhead's springy pubic hair tickling at her neck and she detected the familiar musk of sex. She would concentrate on the feeling of the red-haired girl's hands on her body, she decided, and reserve her energy for her escape. She tried this, but would have dozed off several times were it not for the almost unbearable fresh dousings of water on the rock stove, fed with crackling spruce and birch logs.

'Nice, isn't it?' said the red-haired girl. Rika thought to ask her name, but she was so comfortable she could not muster the energy to speak. It came as no surprise at all when the girl brought her fingers down to Rika's sex and rubbed softly at her wet, tender clit. Rika let herself relax back in the disciple's arms as she was brought towards an incredibly sweet orgasm in the sweat-house. But right in the most passionate moment of orgasm, as Rika began to twist in the arms of the red-haired girl, the door of the sweat-house was thrown open and the shock of the cold air made Rika's whole body freeze. Her body was in such turmoil that she had no idea whether she was enjoying herself or not. She was pushed, shoved naked through the door, though she tried to withstand it and not enter into the cold. For a moment she was poised at the door, panicked and not knowing what would happen next, and the next moment the redhead took her hand and pulled her into the fresh drifts of snow.

For a moment Rika thought her heart had stopped. It was like falling into lake-water; she could not catch her breath and she was gasping as the enveloping cushions of snow touched her hot, still-sweating body. Pure rage was running through her, as adrenalin pumped through her veins, to the very tips of her fingers and toes and scalp. But just as quickly the fury receded and an ecstasy came over her, the sheer delight of being here naked in the snow. And the red-haired girl's mouth was upon hers, kissing her cold lips with a warm tongue, and Rika slipped into the delirious embrace and rubbed her hands over the body of the other girl, crushing the snow against her back and limbs. This was no torture; this was bliss.

For a long while they kissed, then the girl took Rika's hand and held it. 'I have to bring you to Arje now; I'm sorry. You understand, don't you?'

Rika nodded. What else could she do? She retrieved her clothes from the sweatlodge and dressed.

'Listen,' the other girl said. 'I meant that. I'm sorry, I really am. I don't want to be here myself, but my family owed a debt to Arje and I was "volunteered" to train as a priestess. I'm working my way up; that's why it is I who assists you. But I've decided I'm leaving soon. My sister's going to help me escape.' The girl thought for a moment. 'I have something that can take the pain away,' she said finally. 'You'll have some time between meeting Arje and when you go on stage for the final perform- ance. If you meet me back here in front of the sweat-hut then it will ease your passage into the next world.'

Rika was about to answer, but at that moment Arje caught sight of them and called to them from the middle of the arena.

'Bring the pendant-bearer forward,' she commanded the red- haired girl in an austere voice. Arje was looking straight at Rika. Everyone else seemed to be avoiding the gaze of the priestess, but Arje held out her arms to Rika; there was very little chance that she could graciously refuse to advance to Arje's frightening embrace.

On the floor of the arena near Arje a stand had been placed, several feet high, made of new grey iron and just long enough for a person to lie down prone. Arje motioned for Rika to hoist herself up on the stand.

'If only,' the priestess said to Rika, 'something would convince me that true religious sexual ecstasy could exist, then I would try to put a stop to these sacrifices of Hrafn, these blood-lettings he orchestrates purely for the sake of spectacle. But I've not seen a true blend of religion and sex yet at the rites. It's a shame,' she told Rika again, looking down at her with kindness. 'I would possibly have had hopes for you. Never mind.' Rika was transfixed with fear as the priestess slowly pulled off Rika's red breeches and left her legs and cunt bare.

'Spread open your legs as far as they go,' Arje told Rika, then brazenly circled her index finger lightly in the wetness of Rika's crotch. 'Do you wish my tongue was there, Rika? Do you? My tongue, careful and slow on your pussy? Is that what you want most?'

What did she want most? Rika thought, eyes closed. Arje was stirring her. Rika knew that all the women in the entire arena were watching Arje dip her fingers into her sex. Did she want Arje's tongue slipping inside her? Or did she want to save herself and Lina? Maybe she wanted both, she thought, as Arje's fingers swirled erotically through her cunt.

'Lick me,' she said. 'I want you to lick me.' She opened her eyes and saw Arje smiling.

'And licked you will be, Rika,' the woman said calmly. She drew her hand out and painted Rika's lubrication on Rika's stomach.

'Self-sacrifice,' she whispered in Rika's ear. 'And *teiwaz* also implicates the presence of a wolf.'

Arje watched Rika on the stand; watched the beautiful appearance the torches and the bonfire made when the shadows of the flames quivered on the girl's body. She wanted to lick the girl herself, lick her out until she screamed with pleasure and came with gushing prowess. She wanted to taste the sex between the young woman's legs, but she would have to wait.

She could still take a certain amount of pleasure in observation, anyway. She began to feel a pulse between her legs. Her pussy was growing slick and her clit was growing stiff; wetness would soon be moistening her pussy all the way up to its little head. She ran her hands down the sides of her body, feeling her smooth skin, then sighed and snapped her fingers.

An acolyte came running, a raven-haired beauty, and Arje looked at her approvingly. She massaged the dark-haired girl's rosy nipples until they stood out in stiff red peaks from the girl's small pale breasts.

Then she whispered to the girl, pressing her fingers into the soft flesh of the girl's arm before pushing her forward to where beautiful blonde Rika was lying. Rika was far too eager, Arje thought, marking how Rika's breath was already coming short and quick; it was obvious that her fingers were aching to spin circles in her cunt.

Arje watched the dark girl's pink, clever tongue begin to taste Rika's honey and she watched Rika shudder in gratification. The girl steadily lapped and lapped at the blonde woman, drinking her up as Rika had once drank from Arje's own sex with that long, delightful spoon. Arje's mouth watered, but the best was still to come.

Rika lay back on the iron slab and let the girl slowly lick her out. Her senses gathered into a coil in her pussy, then began to uncurl in waves of slow, sensuous pleasure. She gripped the metal with her hands and spread her legs even wider, feeling the girl's rasping tongue tickling at her wet sex, slurping and licking like an aroused dog. The picture came unbidden to her head, and she grew even more aroused at the image of a dog slowly and roughly licking her, the tip of the tongue just lightly beating on her clit. It was even starting to feel like the uneven lapping of a canine, she thought, and she pushed her cunt further into the girl's face, whose face was soft as fur but whose tongue was rough and bestial.

★

Arje watched the entrancing vision of the girl licking and licking and licking, then she made another quick hand-motion. The girl ceased her movement and pulled away from Rika's cunt, her face dripping with the sweet, thick juices.

'Now,' whispered Arje and her cunt tightened in excitement. A new group of women huddled around Rika, touching her, and the raven-haired girl was led away by the red-haired disciple – one Arje suspected of having become a little too fond of an intended sacrifice. This worried her: the redhead already had a bad precedent to follow, considering who her sister was. But she was happy to observe that the redhead threw the brunette on the floor and started eating her out with no preamble, and the sex-cries of the dark-haired girl almost rivalled those put out by Rika in frustration. She knew she was being overcautious, worrying about trivial matters. But she wanted everything to be perfect.

Arje watched her women soothing Rika with cool hands and she smiled. Her girls had been very well trained. She looked behind her, and saw that the subject of this rite was right on time, as well. A disciple led in a silver-furred she-wolf, one with flashing eyes and white teeth. Its lead was handed over to the high priestess. The female animal itself was obviously on heat; it nosed at Arje's crotch obscenely and roughly. All except Arje, who was pleased, and Rika, whose eyes were closed, trembled and drew away from the wild animal. It was evident that this was not a wolf that had been temporarily tamed.

Arje herself led the wolf up to the groaning, writhing blonde girl on the slab and smiled at the sight of one so lost to sex. Rika was moaning and shoving her hands against her crotch, rubbing herself as quickly towards an orgasm as she could. But Arje gently placed Rika's hands back to her sides.

'Wait,' she said. She gingerly pushed the wolf up to the woman's sex and the wolf began to lick at her.

Rika moaned in pleasure and it was all Arje could do not to shove her own pussy on to Rika's face and have the girl lap and lick at her as well right then. But she withheld the pleasure and watched the silver wolf lapping and lapping and lapping up the

189

girl's copious milky juices. It was obviously a very randy animal and that was exactly how Arje felt herself.

Rika felt the girl return and her tongue was even more rough and uncompromising, seeking out all the crevices in her sweet folds and tasting, licking off the moisture. She grew steadily more wet and the earlier fantasy returned; she imagined a dog's smooth pelt pressed up against her sex. This time her fantasy was so intense she could really feel the fur and she thrust against the probing tongue at the forbidden thought, and still the great tongue licked at her slowly and purposefully.

She opened her eyes and the image remained with her, only this time it was a great silver wolf lapping at her sex, which was even better than the thought of a dog had been. She screamed in delight at the thought of a beast doing such private things to her and felt relieved that no one could read thoughts. She threw herself back on the metal slab, her heartbeat slowing, and she felt the girl withdrawing from her sopping-wet cunt.

When Rika finally pushed herself up on her elbows, she was amazed at what she saw: Arje on the floor coupling with a huge female wolf, the muzzle of the beast pressed tightly into the sexual organs of the priestess and vice versa. Arje's face was screwed tight with pleasure as the two rolled about on the floor in the most debauched combat imaginable. The priestess's silver mane ran into the pewter fur of the wolf. More than one onlooker was given the impression that there were two she-wolves there, locked together and rolling around in the most urgent of primal acts.

The disciples stood a good distance away and trembled in fright. Rika merely exhaled slowly and threw herself back down again on the slab. This had been the Fenrir rite to which Arje had referred. The situation was beginning to feel more than a little dangerous.

For some time, Rika was left alone on the iron table, looking up at the stars in the colourful sky. She assumed that she would soon be called up to the stage, but no one came to fetch her and orgies of all descriptions continued around her. Eventually she remembered that she had promised to meet the red-haired girl. No one seemed to be paying attention to her at the moment, so she wandered over across the arena to the sweat-hut. Meet me here, the girl had said. The girl had not yet arrived, so Rika took a look around while she waited. Nearby on the ground she could see a woman stretched beneath the careful hands of two tattoo artists, who painted her in as many colours as were in Arje's paintbox with the cruel tip of a needle dipped in colour.

For a while Rika watched fascinated as the designs grew intricate and curving on the woman's back and backside. There was a green wolfhound that spat out a spray of red-and-gold fire, and whenever the colour entered deeply into the soft flesh of the woman, the assistant wiped away the bright blood that rose up with a dampened cloth. Rika longed to look at the woman's face, but her head was covered with a square of material. Rika knew why: both Viking men and women hated their expressions to be vulnerable. Stoicism was such a virtue that some opted to keep their faces covered in painful situations such as tattooing, scarring or branding, in case their grimaces revealed weakness. She suspected that the woman's teeth would be gritting. But probably her face would be calm; no wrinkles scarring her brow. Stoic, a true Viking. Rika saw it in the way the woman strongly gripped her fists against the pain.

'Do you want to try?' one of the artists asked Rika, deferential at the sight of the pendant round the young blonde woman's neck. The artist shifted to make room for Rika on the ground. Rika knelt and held the sharp point of the needle in her hand, and eventually pierced the woman's olive-coloured flesh with it. She added a gold shimmer around the head of the wolfhound and the hint of blood on its fangs, before handing back the needle and thanking the artist for the privilege. After the artist wiped the blood away, Rika admired her handiwork on the woman's well-muscled back. She would like to see the tattoo

191

when it was complete. If she survived these rites, she resolved to find the woman.

There was still no sign of the red-haired girl. Impatient and attempting to distract herself from what lay ahead, Rika went around to the other side of the sweatlodge. The thrall that had been inside was taking a well-deserved break; she was obviously overheated and overworked. For the first time, thraldom left a bad taste in Rika's mouth, the idea of ownership or manipulation through promises or circumstance. That was how she found herself here today. She resolved that she would never own a thrall, nor hold another to a blood-oath herself.

Someone tapped her on the shoulder. 'Do you want to come with me, then? I've got something that should relax you a little.' It was the red-haired girl, her face friendly and open. Rika felt grateful for her friendship in the midst of all the double-dealing and secrecy of the rites. She followed her to another group of people sitting on the floor of the arena, near the sweatlodge. Knowing that it was only a matter of time before she would be called to the final rites, her heart began to race.

The group sat in a circle, sucking in dried herbs in little clay pipes. Rika knew immediately what the effects of this particular herb would be. Her village raised hemp as most other villages did, but it was rarely used for clothing and was usually smoked for relaxation or woven into rope. And she needed to relax, that was for sure. The red-haired girl sat at Rika's left, inhaling in the precious fumes and eventually she handed the lit, glowing little pipe to Rika.

Rika felt the least she could do now was ask the girl's name. 'What do they call you?'

'I am Sigrún Gunnarsdóttir.'

She had heard the family name before, once long ago on a boat. She stared at the red-haired girl. 'Do you have a sister?'

'I do.' The girl watched Rika levelly; even her gaze seemed familiar. 'She's a member of Ingrid's Crew and I will be too, someday. She's recently returned from battling in Britain, and you should hear the tales she tells –'

Rika interrupted Sigrún. 'She's recently returned?'

'Yes.' But before Rika could press her, Arje called Sigrún back to the centre of the arena. Rika sucked at the clay pipe, her sensations pleasurable but distorted. It felt strangely like being drunk. Pia's sister. Why wasn't Rika more surprised? She had even said her sister fought in Ingrid's Crew. The herbs Rika smoked were pungent and green; when she inhaled she drew a heady smoke into her lungs. A moderate amount of smoked hemp always relaxed her. She had already forgotten several times that she was trying to devise a plan. She would start by musing over Pia's possible whereabouts, then would lose track of what she was thinking altogether. She barely heard the first time Arje commanded them to break up the camaraderie of their momentary circle.

'Rika!' Arje called again.

'Is this the last rite?' Rika whispered to a goatish old crone from the group of women that sat and smoked with her.

'No,' the old woman said, 'but it is not long now. Be strong.'

No sooner had she returned to the centre of the arena than more hands pressed her into sexual service down on her knees in the dirt, with her breeches pulled down to expose her once more. Specifically, Sigrún returned and skilfully oiled up her arse under Arje's watchful eye.

*Berkana.* Arje marked the purification rune in the dirt with her toe this time and spat out the word quickly. It was as if she wanted to hurry, to move quickly on to something else.

Rika sighed in reluctant enjoyment as the smooth end of a polished birch branch entered her cunt and as another smoothly slid into her tight arse. It was too much, too soon; and she felt an orgasm approaching far too rapidly from this dual pleasure. She panted, telling herself to enjoy the sensations and to keep her wits about her as she lay prone to Sigrún's advances. Tiny premature pussy-willows stroked her most intimate places at the same time as the wooden dowels were pushed into her. She willed the thick rounded branches to go even deeper and rubbed desperately at her red nipples, groaned as red-haired Sigrún twirled the round stick in her arse. Rika found herself wanting to touch Pia's sister's cunt, and the desire was somehow exciting. The other birch dowel was fucked skilfully into her pussy, juicy and tight, and she was now very close to coming. *It won't be long now*, the old woman had said. But Rika was lost to the pleasures of sex once again.

She wasn't too aware when the branches were removed, but eventually she became conscious that she was lying on her back and that Sigrún had left her alone on the floor of the great outdoor arena. The arena had filled up with men again and Rika cursed herself for not paying more attention – if she had not been dozing in a sleepy sexual haze, she could have seen how they entered. Out of the corner of her eye she could watch the ongoing additions to the fiery bonfire below the stage. The branches that had satisfied her so thoroughly were bound into an upright bundle with other sticks and added to the pile. She stayed upon her back, watching branches being fed into the huge bonfire; she watched the preparations as if she was still caught in a disturbing dream. Perhaps this was already Ragnarök; perhaps this was already the end of the world. She sighed and lay back again. She was so satiated she almost did not care. But in a tiny corner of her mind, she still thought of escape.

The great bonfire, consisting in small part of branches which had recently penetrated her, burnt rapidly and the red and gold flames reached up towards the heavens where the northern lights swelled more than ever. The combination of fire-colours and the curving curtains of blues and greens overhead was striking. Rika could feel the heat from the fire on her face, though she lay many feet from where the fire burnt. Dispassionately, she watched as several women took up torches from the fire and marvelled as they ran the sticks of fire over their bodies in a slow erotic dance, skirting the flames dangerously close to their vulnerable sexes and mouths. One of the girls even took another in her arms and teased her with the searing torch, before finally releasing her.

Rika raised her eyes to the stage where she could see Lina hitched high on the logs, drugged and awaiting her fate. Near the pyre on the stage lay another single pomegranate, polished to a high sheen, cut in half. Even from a distance it was disconcertingly sexual. Perhaps it was the exact same fruit she had refused from the sacrificial meal. Her eyes flickered back to Lina atop the pyre and, though her head was still fuzzy from the herbs she had inhaled, she found herself remembering how Lina had pressed the little pomegranate into her hand. From a merchant named Hrafn, Rika now remembered, and in terror she rapidly sat up, knowing full well the source of the poison that now drugged Lina.

'Rika. Soon it is time.' Arje stood over her and guided her to the stage, up the steps and next to an insanely grinning Hrafn. Arje's acolytes followed, though Rika could not see Sigrún anywhere. Rika's teeth chattered with fear and she couldn't stop her eyes from darting to the strange fruit. Escape. She had to think of an escape.

'How well you look,' the old man said. 'I trust you are relaxed? Purified and fed with holy food? Invigorated from the all-female proceedings?'

'Yes . . .' Rika shook her head to lift the fog that had settled since she smoked the herbs with Sigrún. The stage on which she stood seemed incomprehensibly vast. There were no exits that she could see.

'Good.' Arje's tones were at their most decisive. 'Then it's time for you to eat the fruit.' She picked up the open, exposed pomegranate; Rika could now see that it was full of juicy little red pips all nestled together. 'As before with the taste of blueberries I offered you, the taste of pomegranate is both refreshment and preparation.'

Rika looked from the little fruit to Lina to Arje and then finally to Hrafn, thinking as quickly as she could under the circumstances. Hrafn had to come from somewhere. Wherever he had come from was the exit. She took a deep breath. 'No.'

'What?' Hrafn's face was blank and shocked.

Rika looked quickly at Arje; the woman's smile was hesitant; Rika vowed to use this to her own advantage. 'No. Hrafn, I need to speak to you privately.'

'No! You little slut!' Hrafn was so angry that he was nearly frothing at the mouth.

'Please, Arje.' Rika appealed to the priestess. 'As I'll be making my sacred journey so shortly, anyway. Just a short moment alone with Hrafn.'

The face of the head-priestess softened; she was obviously thinking of the skill and devotion the girl had shown to the rites. It was highly unlikely that she would betray the cause, not having endured so much. She turned to Hrafn. 'I don't think it can do much harm.'

The man's face was dark, but Rika knew that it would be difficult for him to deny a simple wish to a soon-to-be-sacrificed victim without seeming extremely petty. He glared at Rika, but he nodded acquiescence.

Arje seemed relieved. 'Why don't the two of you discuss what you need to behind there?' She pointed to a fold within the sheet of ice that Rika had not previously seen; the glare from the ice curtain and the statues had hidden it. Rika felt drunk with relief. There it was. 'I'll wait for you both here.'

'I'll be back within three hundred heartbeats,' Rika assured her.

'It depends on how fast your heart is beating,' Rika thought she heard Hrafn mutter as she and he walked towards the little opening, neither looking or touching each other, but neither moving too far out of the distance of the other, either.

They exited through the fold in the icy backdrop and for the first time since setting foot into the stump-circle, Rika tasted freedom. She was standing just next to the hill; a very narrow trail led up to the woods, on the other side of the thick wall of ice. Hrafn didn't have his berserker goon with him this time and she doubted that he could outrun her. But for some reason, her feet stayed flat on the ground, even when she commanded them to run faster than she ever had before. She knew why, as well.

Lina.

She felt Hrafn's hand gripping her shoulder. 'Don't think I don't know what you're playing at,' he snarled. 'You've been sold, my dear; I paid a high price to Ingrid and you're not leaving now, no matter how much you try to delay the inevitable.'

He was right. She *was* delaying the inevitable. A thousand reasons why she should immediately run came to her mind, but she could still see Lina atop the pile of kindling. It was as if the glassy ice curtain separating Rika from the stage wasn't there at all. The values of leadership; the reasons why she had aspired to the Crew in the first place; the qualities that she had first admired in Ingrid – all were questions of bravery and valour. She could run away, or she could go back and die with Lina. Either she was a true Viking, or she was not. Lina's family would be shamed by Lina's passive death and Rika did not want this for her friend. She could wake Lina somehow and the girl's family name would not endure the shame of a passing that came with sleep. Rika realised suddenly that there would be no exit for her after all and that there was only one escape: back to the rites, and death with honour for both her and Lina – but mostly for Lina. Rika hoped that there would be a beautiful Valkyrie to bear her away afterwards, but she suspected that there probably wouldn't be.

She looked down at herself and the sex-stained red clothing, and then batted her eyelashes up at Hrafn coquettishly. 'I just wanted to tell you personally how much I have enjoyed myself.'

'You're not fooling me for a minute,' the old man said sourly and correctly.

Maybe not, but it was buying her a few seconds to sift

thoughts through her smoke-addled brain. It was enough. 'Have others worn this pendant before me?' she asked, pointing to her necklace. 'Have others had this honour?'

Hrafn's expression mellowed; he was susceptible to flattery, after all. 'Many,' he said, 'and only one was not successful. The fact that she got away was a public disgrace for Ingrid; it showed her up. By the will of the people Ingrid was forced to grant her freedom and release her from the blood-oath. Another of Ingrid's lovers, too, and I don't think she's ever forgiven poor Ingrid.'

Rika was not too surprised to hear it. How could she distract him? In desperation, she removed the necklace, clicked her fingers on the little carved metal curls, and opened the locket to reveal the grey ashes inside the pendant. Thankfully, it did not stick this time. 'Do you know that this gem is a locket?'

'What? But this is marvellous! Those are rumoured to be ashes from the Great Fire itself! We have always used that very pendant in our rituals; Ingrid has never spoken of this.' The old man was almost gibbering with excitement and bent closer to see the sight that Rika offered him.

It was the moment she had been waiting for. Quick as a raven, Rika snapped shut the locket and thrust the chain over Hrafn's head, twisting the metal coils tight into his throat, choking him. 'Tell me the antidote.'

Hrafn could barely rasp out an answer. 'I don't know what you're talking about.'

'That's the wrong answer. I want to know the antidote for Lina's sleep and I want to know it now.' Hrafn's face had gone ashen and he felt as frail as snowflakes in Rika's hands. It occurred to her that he was a very elderly man. But she still tightened the chain. 'Tell me.'

'I have never known there to be a cure.' The man croaked the words out and Rika's heart fell as she saw that he spoke the truth. 'But,' his voice came as a whisper and Rika bent closer to his mouth to listen, 'they say that ashes from the Great Fire will cure any diseases that exist. Perhaps?' With a roll of eyeballs, he indicated the locket suspended from the chain that choked him.

Rika released her grip, just slightly, just enough for the man to breathe a little. She had only a minute or so left before Arje came to find them.

'Where are Ingrid and the rest of the Crew?'

'The Crew has disbanded,' the man stuttered, 'and some have returned to Norway. Ingrid is long since gone, nowhere to be found, and the remainder of the Crew wait in a little town in Britain near York, in hope of some leadership.' It was a mouthful and he fell silent, exhausted.

'Tell her to extinguish the torches.'

'What?'

'You heard me. Scream it out to Arje. She'll love the suggestion; she likes atmosphere. It will add to the suspense of the whole thing.' Rika was hoping this was true.

With Rika's fingernails pinching at his larynx, Hrafn walked to where the fold in the ice was and raised his voice, commanding in a sepulchral tone that all light be put out and not lit again until at his command. His voice echoed out to the arena, hollow and dominant. Rika couldn't see the reaction of the priestess, but Arje apparently liked the idea, for within half a minute all the lights were doused. There was only the glow of the bonfire below the stage and it did little to illuminate the environs.

'You're no warrior,' Hrafn sneered. 'You don't even have the spine to kill. You're soft and stupid and if you're not killed this time at the rites, you will be at the next. That scar binds you for ever, you know.'

Rika looked wildly around as he croaked the words, her hand still twisting the chain around his throat. Finally in desperation she reached for Hrafn's knife, which was tucked under the old man's belt. Hrafn's back was to her.

'Stupid,' he repeated in his harsh sarcastic whisper. 'That's why we only choose girls for the rites.'

For a second Rika paused, then she plunged the knife deep into his back, deeper than when she had cut off the man's hand in Britain, deeper than she had ever fucked, past muscles and sinew and flesh, the knife scraping on bone. She thrust her hand into him and pulled out his lungs. It was an old Viking punishment for traitors, one which was aptly called a blood-eagle. She felt some pity for the cruel old man, though, so she slashed his throat to let him bleed quickly, then took his knife and tucked the blade into her belt.

Her hand bright red already, she bent to Hrafn's body and then replaced the necklace round her neck and ran for her life, faster than she had ever run before – faster even than she would have run away from it all only minutes ago – straight back to the funeral pyre which had promised not only Lina's doom but her own.

She climbed up the pyre in the darkness, scratching and rasping her clothing on the rough branches. She would die as a Viking dies, with honour. And she would not let Lina go unaware and sleeping to a coward's death, woken only by the death-filled flames. Rika would wake her and comfort her first, so that she knew love and no dishonour. Then she would stab her straight across the throat with Hrafn's knife; Lina would only know brief pain before she died. Following which Rika would join her in death, within the inferno of heat and smoke and blood. She made it to the top just before the simultaneous flames of many torches jolted once more across the whole of the arena.

Arje had been growing steadily impatient. When another minute had passed without Hrafn's command, she had shouted out herself for the torches to be lit again. Then the blonde figures of both the fertility god and the sleeping goddess of love and sensuality lay atop a high pile of logs. Arje was startled to see that Rika had already climbed up, but she noted with pleasure a detail that had previously escaped her notice: the pile was alternately criss-crossed with different woods – ash, alder, spruce, yew, pine and oak – each placed carefully so that they would either burn quickly or slowly. The fastest burning logs, such as narrow twigs of spruce, were placed at the top of the pile. Her acolytes had done an impressive job.

Arje was in her element; she was sure no other high priestess had ever looked so glorious or so beautiful. Her silver hair hung in ringlets to her waist; beneath her open robe her naked body was powerful and commanding. She could have played the lush fertility goddess Freyja herself, she thought, had her presence not been necessary to direct the delectable proceedings. With a wave of Arje's fingers and another of her strange, high-pitched incantations, the twenty bosomy women who had participated in the rites of lactation and blueberries came forward. Each was holding a small torch taken from the bonfire that had burned below the stage, and they encircled the pyre on the platform with the bonfire flames at their feet.

She gave them the signal to step back. Someone in the audience shouted, but the sound was overpowered by the scream that rose from the pyre. Arje stepped up to the mound of branches grimly, intent on slitting Freyr's throat so that the blood would fall like crimson rain and anoint the holy fire. Her eyes flickered up to the top of the pyre. The girl was afraid, Arje could see that clearly, afraid and mad-eyed despite the honour bestowed on her. And despite the imminent slaughter, 'Freyr' still held the sleeping woman up before the others in his arms. Tears ran down Freyr's face as he stroked at his sister's throat, fondled and kissed her beautiful flaxen hair, ran his hands down under her bodice and revealed the rosy little peaks of her breasts to the masses. Those who enjoyed blood-spectacle – the vast majority – leaned forward with eager eyes and tongue-moistened lips.

Freyr rubbed carefully at his sister's lips, almost as if he wanted the girl to feed from his fingers. The crowd watched as Freyja began to stir in his arms. Never had they seen such a beautiful representation of the goddess, her cheeks flushed and beautiful, her lips like strawberries, her eyes bright green. They watched as the two blonde deities kissed and the crowd sighed as if they were being told a great love story by the best scaldic bard ever. It was a pity that the two would soon be sacrificed, but that was ordained by the high priestess and so it was so. Still, they liked this new, invigorated Freyr, stroking and kissing Freyja. They liked it, and Arje did too.

But her groin was stirring with excitement and the audience was starting to grow impatient; Arje could sense their urgency. Freyr, in his red male clothing, should have had his throat slit by now. And where was Hrafn? Arje cursed and took a disturbingly narrow knife from the pocket of the open robe that revealed all of her nude splendour. She looked up at the two of them. Such beauties; it was a pity, really. But she snapped her fingers and one of her acolytes brought a ladder of tacked birch logs up to the pyre. Arje looked out at the crowd. The odour of adrenalin and sweat was rising. Even the acolyte priestesses drew back when they saw the look in their mistress's eye. The proxy Freyr made his way to his feet and looked down at the crowd as Arje had just done. A wave of gasps shuddered across the arena – the audience could now see that one of Freyr's hands was already bleeding, wet and red.

'Stop! You don't have to let this happen!' Freyr screamed out, appealing to the crowd, his girlish voice echoing throughout the snowbound environs of the rites. But the crowd cared little for Freyr's protests, so he reached down and abruptly dragged up his newly woken sister Freyja, and the similar blonde girl was also exposed to the hungry eyes of the crowd.

'Please!' he pleaded. 'You can save both of us.'

Arje smiled. This plan of Hrafn's was better and more effective than she could have devised herself. He had obviously convinced Rika to make the sacrifice more dramatic before the flames were lit. A little resistance always pleased the crowd. Or perhaps that had even been the girl's idea; what she had pulled him aside to request. Beautiful. Arje closed her eyes and gripped the knife, relishing the scent of wood and blood.

Methodically she stepped on each rung of the birch ladder pressed against the pyre, rising up until she was level with the divine twins. She could see the terror in Rika's eyes. She held high the knife in the air, so that all who watched could see its sharp lethal glint, and then quickly cut the last and ninth rune into Rika's arm, below an already-healing scar.

*Perþ*: Cunt. Vulva. Sexuality and fulfilment. The girl remained still and stoic, her arm scarcely trembling as she was marked, and Arje smiled slowly, secretly pleased. Rika was a credit to the rites, a real treasure of a thrall. Scarlet pearls welled up from the cut and then became red threads running down the soft white flesh of Rika's arm; became temporary runes spelled only from liquid that in turn finally evolved to blurred but normal blood-rush. Arje closed her eyes again in triumph, savouring the moment before she drew the knife along Rika's lovely throat.

'Listen.' Rika grabbed and held Lina tightly. 'Don't say anything – I know you don't know where we are, but just kiss me and hang on.' It was the only thing she could think to say – doomed as they now were, at least Lina's last moments would not be filled with dread. The bloodlust of the crowd had become an almost physical presence. Arje stood over them on the ladder, grinning like a madwoman, eyes closed, hand folding over a long knife that Rika was reasonably sure was meant for her. Her arm stung from the rune-cutting but it hardly mattered; she had shown strength to the last and her memory would not be shamed.

Lina looked at Rika with alarmed eyes. 'Where are we? Who have you been shouting to? Rika, the last I remember, I –'

'Shh,' said Rika, desperately trying to keep her caresses of Lina's body sensual, for the girl's sake. The knife was still in her belt; she couldn't yet bring herself to use it on Lina. She briefly considered making a lunge at Arje, but quickly realised that both she and Lina would be torn limb from limb within minutes by the dangerous crowd. There was less pain for Lina this way. But still she could not yet force her hand down to clutch at Hrafn's knife. Blood dripped down from the *perþ* symbol to her wrist. She glanced up; Arje had begun to intone a chant again. Rika would distract Lina with pleasure and then she would enact the deed. 'Please, Lina, just trust me. Actually, you don't have to trust me; you just have to kiss me.'

Lina's green eyes were confused, but Rika's hands were stirring violently sensual feelings in her. And it all felt so lovely, like an extremely erotic dream. 'All right, Rika,' she said, 'but I trust I'll have an explanation later.' And Lina gave herself up to Rika's kisses, while something in Rika's breast rose and sank. Now all was doom and blood; all she could give the girl before her death was pleasure and lust.

The twins kissed and caressed each other's body so passionately that Arje paused in awe, though she was still intent on drawing blood from the pulsing vein in Rika's throat. But when she finally made the move forward, the crowd hissed at her; shocked, Arje drew back momentarily to see what the audience was evidently enjoying. The twinned pair were making love with what looked like the most desperate craving ever before seen at the rites: nearly eating each other alive with desire, tearing their clothes half off, hands fucking hard, mouths biting and nipping, cunts as avid for flesh as starved, libidinous animals. It was a miracle, the onlookers – even her own acolytes – were murmuring, the spirits of the gods Freyr and Freyja had magically risen to participate in the sexual rites. They were truly blessed.

'Arje.' There was a voice from where her disciples stood behind her, and Arje began to shake with violent fury. The voice sounded familiar even before she whirled around on the ladder. Which of her acolytes would be so stupid as to interrupt the most holy of rites? When she saw, she fell back in surprise and nearly had to brace herself on the amorously entwined couple. The one who dared to speak was the same who had once betrayed the rites seven years ago. And here she was again; here to interrupt at the worst possible moment.

'What are you doing here, Pia?' Then, in the next breath, Arje commanded: 'Light the fire.' The girls could have had the knife but now, she thought sadly, they would burn with pain.

The scent of mixed woods, the acrid perfume of burning shoots and bark began to grow, small whorls of smoke curling and licking through the thick crossed logs at the bottom of the pile. Arje slowly made her way down from the pyre, but kept one eye on the twins.

'Arje,' Pia's voice was crooning, 'look at me.' She held up her hand with the little white rune scar. It was indiscernible to the audience, but there was no doubt what she was revealing; some could even remember her escape seven years before. 'I am a sold object, a thrall for ever. I know better than anyone else how cruel these rites can be, and yet I've come back to tell you that it doesn't have to be like this. It can be what you want, Arje – sex. Sex instead of Hrafn's dream of sacrifice.'

Arje stared at Pia as if she were a ghost and tried to make her face unreadable. She acknowledged the truth of the dark-haired woman's words: only a fool or someone extremely brave would venture to return, having once escaped the rites. The burning scent of sacred yewwood filled her nostrils.

'Isn't this what you want?' Pia nodded her head up to Rika and Lina on top of the pyre, the flames licking ever higher. Pia took another step forward, but Arje quickly withdrew the long knife and held her off. But the woman's voice carried on, slow and confident: 'Look at them, Arje.' Even as the fire rose, the two blonde figures were joined, mouths between each other's legs, cuntjuice running over their cleavages, over their arms and backs and down their thighs. 'That's the closest example of sexual ecstasy you could ever hope for, Arje. Isn't that what you've been trying to move the rites towards for all these years?'

'Stay away.' Arje slashed out the long knife in front of Pia. The crackling sound of the fire was growing; the heat of the flames was causing the frozen statues behind the stage to melt slightly, icy water dripping down. And still Freyr and Freyja drank from each other up above, licking and slurping, hands running over each other's hot body.

Pia moved still closer, nearly touching the knife. 'That's it, Arje; that's what you want!'

Arje glanced up again and the knife shook as a shiver of uncertainty ran through her. The sight above the heaped wood embodied all of the hopes she had ever had for her religion. Where was Hrafn anyway? Rika had had a chance to escape when she had taken Hrafn aside; the girl had obviously made a choice between life and sex – and chosen sex. A thought occurred to her regarding Hrafn's whereabouts, but she pushed it back. The fire was starting to rear as the wrist-thick kindling began to burn and pulse with orange and blue flames. Yes, Rika could have run away, but she had returned. For once Arje was glad Hrafn was lingering outside the exit; the decision was hers alone. Panic began to throb in her and she closed her eyes for just a split second.

It was enough. Pia kicked her foot up, dislodging Arje's grip so that the knife clattered to the floor. Then just as rapidly she grabbed at the priestess, wrestling her, wrapping her arm tightly around the silver-haired woman's neck.

Arje could not breathe; there was only the scent of fire and death. Pia bent down to retrieve the bloody knife, never loosening her hold, and now it was Arje who had a blade held to her throat.

The crowd stared dumbfounded. If they lunged to the stage, the priestess would be killed. And up on the pyre, the vision of Freyr and Freyja was now nearly masked by the sheets of bright searing white-orange fire. Everybody held their breath.

'If you do not accept this display of excess before you as sufficient for the rites; if you do not accept that there is no need for blood sacrifice,' Pia hissed in Arje's ear, the long blade skimming the flesh of the priestess's throat, 'than you deny your whole religious ethos.' Though Arje now feared for her life,

Pia's words were rapidly sinking in. 'You stultify your creed into a sexless religion like that of the fish-believers.'

Shame rose in Arje, greater than fear; greater than the heat of fire. She twisted suddenly in Pia's arms, biting and scratching and clawing herself away. She was panting, her eyes bright, her hair wild. 'I make no decisions under duress, thrall,' she spat out, but in her mind she was already considering the dark-haired woman's words.

Pia stood tensely facing her, hand on the hilt of the blade. Arje glanced up at the pyre, and the shame she had felt came back in waves. The fire had nearly reached the girls, and yet they licked and kissed. What the thrall had said was true: there was a better way to chaos than mere violence and she had known it all along. A sensation of regret grew in her at the sight of Rika and Lina, fucking as if their lives still depended on it. She felt sorrow for the girls and sorrow for her own religion, the full pain of a faith suppressed by foreigners who knew nothing of the Old Ways nor of sex, those who cared nothing of the martyrs killed because they would not convert to the fish-religion. She had been wrong concerning sacrifice, but perhaps she could still reward this woman's courage.

'It's too late for them,' she told the dark-haired thrall. The blonde couple's bodies were already obscured by smoke and flame. She turned to the audience. 'Do not hurt this thrall on my behalf,' she called out, 'she has great courage and she has convinced me of the truth of our religion. The rites are meant to be celebrated in sexual chaos, not blood-sacrifice, and –' But Arje never finished her words. Pia was racing across the stage to the fire, stumbling in her haste, rushing towards the flames as swiftly as a salmon slips through rivers.

Rika could feel the heat beginning to tongue at the thin branches directly underneath her, but she continued to kiss Lina deeply. Sleepy Lina was lost in a dream of lust and Rika finally put her hand down to her belt. In seconds, the near-intolerable heat would turn to pain, to the grotesquely branding heat that charred flesh. Lina would be spared that. Even in the enormous fire, tears ran down Rika's face. She said a quick prayer to the real Freyja, not the false one she held in her arms, that Lina's passage would be speedy. Her own red garments were starting to smoke and burn; she was choking on the smoke; her knuckles curled round the hilt of the knife still sticky with Hrafn's blood. She raised it high. Lina's eyes were closed; she would never know.

'No, Rika!' There was a rush of sound and a scream, and Rika felt the whole glowing structure of sticks and logs toppling, felt a hand around her waist. The knife flew into the fire and she was being pulled away, she and Lina both; the whole scorching pyre was imploding on itself. Then she and Lina were lying on the floor and gasping. She and Lina, and the woman who still held her tightly round the waist with one strong arm, beating at their smouldering red clothes: Pia.

# TEN

The crowd and Arje gaped at the three of them lying there, their breathing slowly becoming regular. Lina was obviously still dazed, still unaware that her life had been in danger. She seemed to think that this was still an erotic, exciting dream and she squirmed and stared at Rika with a moist open mouth, moaning and spreading her legs further apart. She began to move her fingers on herself deftly, slowly wanking, drawing Rika's attention to the folds of her lovely, still-moistened pussy. Lubrication was oozing from the woman's sweet cunt. But the smell of smoke was still in the air, and Rika shuddered. Lina had no idea how close her throat had come to being cut by the hand of her best friend.

'Now! Now Freyr comes!' screamed Arje and kicked Rika surreptitiously.

'What?' Rika looked up and realised that Arje had had a change of heart. She also quickly realised that this would be a substitute for the sacrifice, so she had better start fucking seriously if they were to be a spectacular replacement. She ran her hands under the ceremonial garment and over Lina's breasts, her hands hot on the flesh underneath the now-ravaged, fire-crisp red dress. But her heart was singing, *Pia, Pia*. Pia was here. Rika felt the warrior's hand plunge into her own sex and then felt it slowly withdraw. Rika's heart had not stopped racing for a good hour now, but fear was slowly tightening into sexual excitement. She drew Pia's hand up to her lips, kissing the taste of smoke and come. Pia pressed against her from behind; Rika could feel every hair of the warrior's bear-shirt pricking at her back through the torn burnt shreds she wore. Rika began to slowly trace the shapes of Lina's breasts. If Arje wanted spectacle, then that's what she would get.

Something flickered outside the range of Rika's sight as she lowered her lips to Lina's and as Pia's fingers stroked between her legs. From the corner of her eye, Rika saw a familiar face watching from behind the ice curtain, saw her figure standing in the exit. It was Ingrid.

Rika withdrew from Lina for a moment, detaching herself from Pia. 'Come out here!' Rika screamed to Ingrid. 'If you're so brave, come out on stage and tell me and everybody else why you and Hrafn offered women's lives for sacrifice.'

But Ingrid, who must have been standing near to Hrafn's body, looked stunned. She shook her head and then stepped back, disappearing from sight. It was a complete contrast to what was courageous Viking behaviour. Ingrid had never been a hero, Rika realised, she would never choose honour above all else. Not like Pia – or even she herself – had done. Rika's anger drained from her, but she was left with a momentary sensation of deep sadness.

'Faster!' snapped Arje, uncaring of whatever unfinished business Ingrid and Rika had together. She lashed at Rika's bare legs with a charred spruce branch she had retrieved from the collapsed, still-burning fire.

Rika put all thoughts of Ingrid from her mind. The sting and the evergreen scent of spruce-needles in the air filled Rika with excitement, and she began to slowly feel lust rise in her again. Eventually she started to slowly fuck the former Freyja; Lina was beautiful around her hand, more beautiful than a goddess ever could be. And at the same time Pia's fingers danced across Rika's wet cunt to rub steadily on her clit. For some time Rika was happily fucked in this position before Lina rotated and spun herself so that her lovely arse now faced Rika, and Rika pumped her fingers into the girl's pussy from behind. Rika could hear Pia groaning in her ear, knew that Pia saw what she herself was seeing: Lina so lovely and so lush; transformed from a docile, sleeping maiden to a rearing, lusty woman, desperate for pleasure. Lina drove all other and more sombre thoughts from both of their minds. The former Freyja's fair hair was sweat-sodden, her cheeks red; with her hand on her clit she panted with exertion, wriggling obscenely as she twisted into an orgasm, and the audience broke out in spontaneous applause.

For nearly quarter of an hour the three of them lay there. Rika knew that a spectacle of sex had probably been the only way to convince Arje, though she was not sure how Pia had somehow convinced the priestess of this. She wrapped Lina in her arms, holding her old friend tightly. Pia detached herself respectfully, understanding that they wanted a moment of privacy.

'Rika,' Lina whispered. 'I don't remember anything.'

'Did you sleep with Ingrid?' Rika was irritated with herself for the momentary jolt of jealousy; she knew that she would still need some time to recover from Ingrid's influence.

'No! Never, Rika. She only told me to keep an eye out for that old merchant and make sure I spoke with him. Which I did, remember? The one from whom I stole the horse. After the woods, I rode to the villages you told me to, and then that old merchant was there; he told me to eat one of those pretty fruits that I gave you. I remember almost nothing since, except you kissing me on top of the pile of logs, and me dressed in this thing . . .'

They both looked down at Lina's garment and laughed. The marvellous red dress was torn and burnt, bedraggled almost beyond recognition. Well, thought Rika, the point of beauty is that it should be used, not preserved. She felt exhausted and, in retrospect, more than just a little traumatised – over Hrafn's death, evil though he was; over the fact that she had nearly cut Lina's lovely throat.

'Rika, I'm not sure what happened . . . Why have we been making love before this huge crowd? Why is the captain from the ship here?' Lina referred to Pia, who was standing some distance away and trying not to listen.

'Shh,' Rika told Lina. 'I'll explain later, once we've left this place.' It would take some explaining.

That was enough to content Lina for the time being; they got up, stickily raising themselves to Arje's warm embrace. A chill ran through Rika, but she endured the hug.

'I could use another one of those steam baths,' Rika said, 'but without the snow this time.'

Arje smiled. 'Well, I supposed you've earned it. Where, by the way, is Hrafn?'

'He's dead beside the exit,' Rika stated baldly. There was a sharp intake of breath from both Lina and Pia, but Rika kept her eyes fixed firmly on Arje's face.

'I thought he might be.' The priestess smiled faintly. 'I didn't think your hand began spontaneously to bleed – the image seemed far too Christian for my tastes.' The woman paused to choose her next words carefully. 'I just want to thank you, Rika, for the most inspirational rites I've ever attended. It was pure enjoyment and I think our ranks will swell now, as we seem to have gained quite a few converts back from the fish-believers after they saw what they were missing in their torrid, stale religion. Chaos has triumphed after all, but it is the chaos of the gods, not chaos according to human manipulation. With your lovely example up there on stage, you certainly gave them the idea that they had another option than eating stale bread.'

Pia muttered something under her breath. It sounded like 'many revelations come at knifepoint', but Rika could not be sure.

'Thank you,' Rika said hesitantly. She was not comfortable with the strange priestess who had ordained her own death – and the woman's apparent callousness over a former cohort's death bothered her slightly. Also, the thought of shape-shifting had always made her nervous, even though she was convinced that the priestess had orchestrated the wolf-illusions with smoke and mirrors. She was fairly sure, anyway; it was better than thinking that Arje had made love with the Fenrir wolf itself.

Rika looked out over the arena. Released from the strict sexual codes over which Hrafn had presided, the atmosphere had once more turned bacchanalian. She still felt sweaty. 'Do you want to come with me to the steam bath?' she asked Lina and Pia. 'I'll try to explain it all to you, Lina, after we've cleaned ourselves up.'

'Of course.' Lina was in a relatively good mood and was nowhere near as tired, not having experienced the emotional peaks and troughs that Rika had. Her fatigue resulted from the normal physical exertion associated with sexual matters. She padded after Rika through the great arena, people moving away in awe to let the three of them pass by. Rika could feel Pia's hand on her back and her whole body felt warm. Sigrún had chosen not to join in with the sacrificial ninth rite and had been watching with Pia from the crowd. When she saw the three of them pass, she ran up to embrace her sister, then she made her way to the sweatlodge, too.

Rika stood in the sweltering sweat-house with her back to the door, as Lina slowly lifted up her hair from the nape of her neck and poured cool water over her, causing the steam to rise even more within the hut. The filth and blood had slipped off Rika's skin quickly, and she found that she was now only able to recall the pleasurable aspects of the rites. Pia sat on the benches behind them with Sigrún, watching with some bemusement.

'You've still got this, I see.' Lina fingered the pendant. 'What are you going to do with that?

Rika removed the necklace and looked grimly at the pendant, its glassy red surface made cloudy by the steam. 'I'm getting rid of it as soon as we scrub ourselves up,' she said. 'I don't want it near me.'

Lina nodded, not quite understanding, but accepting that the necklace had had something to do with the reason that they had found themselves in the middle of these strange rites. She swabbed and scrubbed at Rika's tender muscles with the damp cloth.

'Rika.' Pia's voice was so beautifully low and familiar. Rika didn't immediately turn. Some others entered into the sweat-house, neglecting to close the door. But when Rika's name was softly said a second time, she detached herself from Lina's caresses and turned round.

Pia was smiling at her, her eyes filled with tears. She gently took Rika in her arms, and for a moment Rika immersed herself in the kiss, as joy filled her heart and Pia's arms went tightly around her in a strong bear-hug. Rika breathed in Pia's clean, familiar scent before she raised her head to look the warrior straight in her deep blue eyes. 'Well, you're nearest; close the door. You're letting in the cold.'

She had come back from Britain so that she could ensure Rika would come to no harm, Pia told her in the hot sauna, and she had watched the whole proceedings. Even though she had hoped Rika would not become involved with the rites, she had realised that the only way of being sure was to come back to Norway herself.

'I found your ring,' Rika told Pia shyly. 'The one you left for me. That's how I knew you were here. It's with the rest of my clothes and belongings.'

'You found my ring?' Pia said. 'That's wonderful, but I've not lost it.' She showed Rika the ring still on her left hand, then chuckled. 'You must have found Sigrún's ring; she was complaining over its loss. It's slightly different to mine, but they were made by the same artisan.'

Rika was puzzled. 'And your mark in the woods . . . I saw that, too.'

'What mark in the woods?'

Rika pointed to the cutting now swelling the flesh on her arm

214

and explained to Pia that she had seen the same *perþ* rune carved into a tree. Pia laughed out loud this time. 'No, Rika. I have a feeling that was someone's anonymous invocation for the Great Thing, a spell to ensure that they would be getting what the rune represented. I didn't carve the tree, either.'

For a while Rika pondered the fact that she had been relying on evidence built on a shaky foundation – evidence that was false but which had proved reliable anyway, in a curious way. Then she listened to Pia excitedly talk, but Rika was drifting in the heat until she noticed with a start that Pia was still, dangerously, wearing her great bear-shirt in the hot sauna. She immediately urged the warrior to remove her clothes. Pia, certainly overheated but overcome with her need to talk, obeyed and stripped off the heavy clothes. Rika saw the green wolfhound tattoo on Pia's back that she herself had helped decorate, and put her hand to her mouth. Why had she not revealed herself? she asked. Did she not know that Rika had helped to tattoo the extraordinary skin-painting?

It turned out that Pia, so absorbed and dazed from the waves of heat running through the needle to her flesh, hadn't known that Rika had participated.

'You see,' said Pia, 'after telling you to investigate Ingrid, I felt uneasy and set sail several days later in order to judge the situation for myself. I bided my time during the rites, thinking you had a plan and worried that you would be executed if I made my move too early. But by the time I shouted right before the pyre was to be lit, I felt doom settling on me. It occurred to me that I might not reach the stage in time.'

'Well, I didn't exactly have a plan, but I survived anyway,' Rika said, with not a small amount of Viking pride: cunning might be held in high esteem, but so was courage. Behind Pia's tattooed back, she was almost sure she could see Sigrún introducing Lina to the pleasures of the sauna.

'Yes, you did.' Pia looked at her admiringly. 'I noticed that you have quite a deft hand surviving long sexual tasks, as well. I can't stay here long in the sauna, Rika. Sweat is not so good for new tattoos.' She smiled at Rika. 'Perhaps you'd like to show me an example of such endurance in the future?' As they exited to find some privacy where they could talk, leaving Lina and Sigrún behind in the sauna, Rika's eyes told Pia that this was a strong possibility.

As they walked outside near the stump-circle, Rika remembered that there was something important that she had to do. 'One moment,' she told Pia and, grabbing her hand, they made the long trek through the longhouse and its corridor to the sexual arena. The wide place had almost completely cleared, with just a few couples and threesomes making languorous love in an atmosphere of post-sexual bliss. There was a still quality to the whole place, as if something solemn had happened.

Rika continued to lead Pia towards the stage but, as they made their way there, their paths crossed that of Arje. She looked bemused and told them that Ingrid had just sworn a solemn oath before a great crowd in the Thing circle.

'What sort of oath?' Rika asked tensely.

'She said she planned to meet with some upstart noble revivalist named Sacrifice Sven, who intends to start up a whole new push towards the Old Ways, and force on him the lessons she learnt here today. In fact, she swore that she would ask him to tone down the number of deaths by sacrifice the next time they claim Ragnarök is imminent. She says she has learnt better, more pleasant ways of pleasing the gods.'

'She probably just thinks that in matters of filling her hand with coins, sex will bring a higher price than death,' Pia said, rather grumpily.

Rika couldn't bring it in her heart to hate Ingrid, try as she might. As long as her sacrifices didn't involve any of the human kind, she wished Ingrid all the best in her endeavours. She rather suspected that Ingrid's own goals would involve sexually initiating as many young *góthi* priestesses as she could get her hands on.

And what was wrong with that, Rika reminded herself,

thinking of how much she had enjoyed the rites. Surely it was better than the crusty fish religion where women had no say whatsoever. Rika sighed. She knew that no religion was truly for her, but neither was the life she would have been consigned to as a village wife.

She and Pia bid Arje good-night, but only after the priestess had extracted a promise that they would soon come to visit her in her cabin – 'the *two* of you,' the priestess had said with emphasis. Rika smiled to herself nervously. It had sounded promising – if slightly frightening.

They reached the stage and climbed up, Rika realising how much her limbs were aching, though at least she had been sufficiently rubbed down by Lina in the sauna. The stage had been swept clean, but the coals of the ceremonial tower still simmered with tremendous heat.

She held Pia's hand gently in her own. 'Do you know what I have to do?'

'I have a good idea.'

Rika looked closely at Pia. 'That was you, wasn't it? The one whom Ingrid had promised once before? That was the blood-oath you once spoke of and the promises you referred to?'

Pia nodded. 'It was. I don't think she'll be promising many more girls to sacrificial stints without permission. I have a feeling that, strange as it sounds, that you near broke her heart when you raised that blade at her back in Britain. Apparently, if what I overheard from gossip during the rites is correct, she's never recovered from the shock.'

'What did Arje mean when she spoke of the "next time" Ragnarök is imminent?'

'It's a little trick they picked up from the fish-worshippers,' Pia told her. 'In the time of your great grand-sire, in the year one thousand by the way the fish-believers count, the fish-believers claimed the world would end soon and they gained quite a few converts. I think the fanatics in our own religion have taken up the same strategy – claiming that Ragnarök is soon to come. But as with the fish-believers, it suits only their own purposes. It sounds like Ingrid intends to personally initiate every girl she converts.'

For some reason, the thought amused Rika. But she cleared her thoughts of questions of religious interpretations and approached the pyre, Pia's hand still firmly in her own. The stage already felt empty of significance; she found it hard to believe that not much time had passed since she had been in grave danger here. Now there was only the sound of the statues slowly dripping as they melted.

She turned to the heavily tattooed, dark-haired warrior. 'Do you have some flint?'

Knowing full well what the younger woman intended, Pia lit a spark on a piece of twig she broke off from the pile and handed the tiny branch to Rika.

Rika set fire to the pyre of logs as quickly as she could. The acrid scent of burning quickly filled their noses. When the flames at the top of the inferno shot up as high as she stood herself, she closed her eyes, removed the necklace for the last time and flung it to the top of the fire, where it fell down into the pit formed by the frame of logs. The ashes inside the pendant were already absent, the silver would melt, and all that would remain would be the little red jewel with its bindrune and its etching of Freyr. If someone found it, they could polish it and take it home, keeping it as a souvenir of the time they had once had at the Great Thing. She doubted it would ever return to its original purpose of identifying a sacrificial victim. With her eyes still closed, she listened to the crackling flames, felt the heat scorching her face. Pia still held her hand, she realised, and at last she opened her eyes and stepped away from the fire.

Later, after Rika had retrieved her belongings and weapons from Arje, they sat on the snow-covered hill that overlooked the proceedings. There they could watch the men below arguing out judicial questions on the last day of assembly. It seemed as if the rites were already forgotten, but at least some good had come out of them other than Arje's new-found conversion to the idea that perhaps human sacrifice was not always the best religious act. From where they sat, they could see Sigrún and Lina walking by hand in hand. It seemed that Sigrún's physical tastes were very similar to those of her sister, considering how similar Lina and Rika looked. The two looked very sweet walking there below, and Rika nuzzled in closer to Pia at the happy sight of the young lovers.

She kissed Pia's hand and the little rune-scar of now-obsolete promises. Pia looked at her questioningly, but Rika continued to press her case, gently removing Pia's top, covering her with the wolf rug so that she did not shiver. Her hand ran down the high, round breasts of the warrior and lingered at their sensitive tips. Pia sighed and Rika stroked her fingers between Pia's thighs, just gently skimming the source of dew that dampened the wolf-fur.

'Thank you for coming back for me,' she told Pia, running her hands over the dark-haired woman's smooth, muscular thighs. She carefully pressed Pia back against the fur and dipped her head down to delicately kiss the woman's sex.

'Rika . . .' The dark-haired warrior's protest changed into a sigh of pleasure, and Rika raised her head and kissed Pia, wetly and slowly on the lips. She lay on top of the older woman, grinding her pelvic bone slowly against her and then gradually slipped her cool hand below to Pia's slippery sex. She began to deliberately move her fingers in the woman, touching her dew quietly and almost gracefully as arousal tightened in her own groin.

When they finished, they lay there on the pelts, covered by heaps of warm furs and by the heat generated from their own warm bodies. They slept that way and woke up to a frosty morning, one where snowflakes glittered in the frost-tightened trees. Rika's exhaled breath and chattering teeth told her that it would be best to soon retreat back to the greater mass of people.

But for a short time she treasured this moment alone with Pia, warming her nose against the warrior's neck, running her hands against the warmth generated from the fresh tattoos on her back.

219

Pia groaned, waking up, and turned to Rika. 'What now?'

Rika had been considering that question ever since she woke up and when she spoke it was with certainty: 'I want to go back to Britain and find the Crew, just as I had promised when I left them.'

Pia looked at her in amazement. 'You're serious?'

'Yes. There's nothing for me here in Norway; I'm not the marrying type.'

'I've wanted to suggest that you join the Crew for quite a long time, but of course I knew that you were Ingrid's girl – and I worried about dividing the Crew by challenging her. And then of course I wondered whether a religious life of erotic rites with Arje might prove more tempting than one with the Crew –'

Rika interrupted her. 'I don't think you'll have to worry about that too much, Pia. I don't think the religious life is for me. Not when I've almost been a sacrifice. Of course, there has to be some truth to the old legends. Otherwise, why would Lina wake up when I rubbed the ashes in her mouth?'

'Maybe she woke up because you're such a good kisser,' Pia suggested. 'Or maybe because ashes don't really taste all that good.'

'Hmm,' said Rika. She paused, thinking. 'Though I'm not sure that a warrior's life is the right one, either. I didn't particularly like chopping that man's arm off, nor killing Hrafn, and I'm not sure if I want to constantly put my life on the line, either. I've had enough of that here.'

'Rika.' Pia paused. 'I'm not sure whether you can remain here anyway. The mark on your left hand, like mine, means that you're now designated as a thrall – a sex slave to the rites. Arje might be willing to let you go now, but she'll want you back eventually. You may not wear the white clothing and your head might not be shaved, but you will be recognised as a thrall nevertheless. It never was the mark of a "blood-oath".'

Rika found Pia's assertion hard to believe. 'Then why didn't anyone recognise it for that the whole season I bore it in my village before I left home?'

Pia smiled gently. 'You did say it was a bit provincial. By Loki, I certainly thought so when I was trying to fuel up, back when we first met.'

'Why were you there, anyway? You just said the scar meant you couldn't return.'

'It's not universally recognisable,' Pia admitted, 'but it's not too safe, either. Besides, I was trying to convince my family to make my sister leave her training as a priestess – something I've not succeeded at until now.'

Well, thought Rika, that settles it. I have to leave home anyway. Strangely, she didn't feel too sad about it.

'Well, we'll have to think of some solution.'

'Yes.' But Rika was already remembering the thrill before the battle, the excitement as she began the rites, the adrenalin rushing through her veins. How could she ever do anything that would compare to what she had experienced over the last two months? Then she smiled to herself, remembering a story her grandfather has once told her. There was another avenue left, but she would have to discuss it with the rest of the Crew – once she and Pia returned to Britain.

'Come on, lazybones, get up,' she told Pia, tousling the dark hair of the sleepy warrior. 'We've got plans to make.'

After breakfast, she and Pia made plans to meet the firmly besotted couple of Lina and Sigrún in Kaupang within three days and gave their apologies to Arje. They promised a visit the next time they were in Norway, explaining that they were off to new adventures, so it might not be for a very long while. And probably never, Rika thought with relief.

'Well, if that's the case I'll have to come and search you down myself,' the eccentric priestess told them. The gleam in her eye told Rika that she was not joking. They left it at that, and after many hugs and tears and toasts from Arje's nubile disciples, Rika and Pia threw their legs over a young frisky mare donated by an anonymous admirer in the audience, swung their packs up and were off, galloping down the coastal trail where Rika had once struggled in the cold.

They stopped at Rika's village for a brief but heartfelt reconciliation with her father. He had rebuilt the longhouse entirely, and thus his wrath at his daughter had mostly faded – and he acknowledged that by rights the dowry had been Rika's, particularly as she never planned to marry. True, he was still as quick-tempered as ever but overjoyed to see his daughter. He was even sternly kind to Pia, after inspecting her carefully and dropping veiled hints that it would be in her best interest to treat Rika well. They had a tearful farewell, but it was exhilarating as Rika and Pia rushed towards the great dock of Kaupang to sail to Britain once again; the wind whistled violently past Rika's ears as she directed the horse with Pia clinging tightly to her waist. Pia had come up with a suggestion and, after mulling it over for some hours, Rika realised that it was an exciting proposal. She felt confident that she had learnt what it meant to be a leader and she was now ready to put those skills to use – as the head of Rika's Crew.

# EPILOGUE

The sun had not been up long and the remnants of a warm hazy glow spread across the horizon. On the beach, the Crew assembled their belongings in a heap and the newest members – Sigrún and Lina – helped to pull the boat up on the sand. The older members of the Crew watched them, admiring how their young muscles flexed and surged with effort, and remembering how they too would have been first to jump at the chance to pull the boats up when they were only twenty years old.

Rika took a deep breath of the clean air of the new land that she had travelled to with her Crew. Great trees stretched across the banks that rose up from the wide beaches. White sand sloped gently down to the edges of the tide, and the calls of strange birds filled her ears. One walked by a little too closely for comfort; it was a monstrous-looking large bird, with an ugly, malformed head with a red fleshy wattle. But it had an array of feathers that looked nearly as impressive as the descriptions she had received of peacocks from exotic southern lands. It made an odd clucking, gobbling sound and she steered well clear of it when she walked a little way ahead of the others.

She had heard many tales from her grandfather of this place

called Vinland, and she was sure that they had found it. It was supposed to bear thick clusters of grapes and the grass was supposed to grow rich and lush. She had consulted maps in some of the villages in Britain where Norse was spoken, and checked them against the accounts of old, old men whose fathers claimed to have sailed with Eirik and with his son Leif. And though the voyage had been tough, the Crew had made it. The tales of Freydis, the brave berserker daughter of Eirik the Red, must have been true after all. Rika looked over the hills with a certain amount of trepidation. She had heard tales of the Skraelings, too, the people of the land.

She wasn't sure if the vicious tales were true; but she had still brought a great deal of the red cloth she had heard they would trade for milk and furs. With the Crewmembers she had found in Britain, and Lina and Pia's sister Sigrún, they numbered nine once again. Rika had explained to them that, while she craved adventure, she wasn't keen on killing too often; and, beaten down by the aftermath of the war, the others had independently come to the same conclusion.

Just as she was thinking this, she caught sight of a dark-haired, dark-skinned woman walking proudly towards their temporary site. All other eight members had unconsciously put their hands to their blades. Rika motioned for them to lower their hands to their sides, and she saw how the face of the Skraeling woman became less tense.

Rika approached, carrying the red cloth that was purported to be so valuable in Vinland. She held it forth to the woman. 'For you,' she said.

The woman showed her empty hands, and at first Rika thought she meant that she held no weapons. Then it dawned on her that the Skraeling meant she had nothing to trade. This puzzled Rika; she had never heard of someone greeting people without weapons and without stock to trade. Rika thought for a minute; it was best to get off on the right foot. It occurred to her that it was more she and her Crew who were the strangers, not the Skraelings, so perhaps it was best to be respectful and generous. She held out the soft madder-stained cloth to the woman, who took it in her hands, then graciously handed it back.

She was being stared at with a look that was unmistakable. The woman beckoned for Rika to come with her. Somehow Rika felt she could trust her, but as she looked over her full strong body, she realised that there were other reasons why she was so eager to accompany the stranger: strong and capable hands, and a glint in the eye that reminded her, oddly, of Ingrid.

Rika looked behind hesitatingly at Pia. The Skraeling woman saw her looking and quickly registered what the glance meant. The dark-skinned woman looked Pia over and smiled. Rika could see why she looked pleased – if anything, the warrior-woman was better looking than ever since she had relegated herself to a life of adventure instead of war. The tension had left Pia's face and there was a tolerance and a light in her eyes that had not been there before.

Suddenly, the Skraeling stroked the gentle flesh above Rika's breast and Rika felt a familiar tingling start therein. 'I won't be too long,' she told the rest of the Crew as the stranger motioned that Rika bring Pia, too. And the three walked on silently together, feet crunching on the ground laden with pine-needles, towards an adventure that Rika was sure was going to have a very pleasant beginning.

# ALREADY PUBLISHED

## BIG DEAL
*Published in May 1999*   Helen Sandler

Lane and Carol have a deal that lets them play around with other partners. But things get out of hand when Lane takes to cruising gay men, while her femme girlfriend has secretly become the mistress of an ongoing all-girl student orgy. The fine print in the deal they've agreed on means things can only get hotter. It's time for a different set of rules – and forfeits.

£6.99                                         ISBN 0 352 33365 0

## RIKA'S JEWEL
*Published in June 1999*   Astrid Fox

Norway, 1066 AD. A group of female Viking warriors – Ingrid's Crew – have set sail to fight the Saxons in Britain, and Ingrid's young lover Rika is determined to follow them. But, urged on by dark-haired oarswoman Pia, Rika soon penetrates Ingrid's secret erotic cult back home in Norway. Will Rika overcome Ingrid's psychic hold, or will she succumb to the intoxicating rituals of the cult? Thrilling sword-and-sorcery in the style of Xena and Red Sonja!

£6.99                                         ISBN 0 352 33367 7

# SAPPHIRE NEW BOOKS

## MILLENNIUM FEVER
*Published in July 1999*   Julia Wood

The millennium is approaching and so is Nikki's fortieth birthday. Married for twenty years, she is tired of playing the trophy wife in a small town where she can't adequately pursue her lofty career ambitions. In contrast, young writer Georgie has always been out and proud. But there's one thing they have in common – in the midst of millennial fever, they both want action and satisfaction. When they meet, the combination is explosive.

£6.99                                         ISBN 0 352 33368 5

## ALL THAT GLITTERS
*Published in August 1999*   Franca Nera

Marta Broderick: beautiful, successful art dealer; London lesbian. Marta inherits an art empire from the man who managed to spirit her out of East Berlin in the 1960s, Manny Schweitz. She's intent on completing Manny's unfinished business: recovering pieces of art stolen by the Nazis. Meanwhile, she's met the gorgeous but mysterious Judith Compton, and Marta's dark sexual addiction to Judith – along with her quest to return the treasures to the rightful owners – is taking her to dangerous places.

£6.99                                         ISBN 0 352 33426 6

------------✂------------------------------------

Please send me the books I have ticked above.

Name ..............................................................................

Address ..............................................................................

..............................................................................

..............................................................................

.............................. Post Code ..............................

Send to: **Cash Sales, Sapphire Books, Thames Wharf Studios, Rainville Road, London W6 9HT.**

US customers: for prices and details of how to order books for delivery by mail, call 1-800-805-1083.

Please enclose a cheque or postal order, made payable to **Virgin Publishing Ltd**, to the value of the books you have ordered plus postage and packing costs as follows:

UK and BFPO – £1.00 for the first book, 50p for each subsequent book.

Overseas (including Republic of Ireland) – £2.00 for the first book, £1.00 for each subsequent book.

We accept all major credit cards including, VISA, ACCESS/MASTER-CARD, DINERS CLUB, AMEX AND SWITCH.

Please write your card number and expiry date here:

..............................................................................

Please allow up to 28 days for delivery.

**Signature** ..............................................................................

------------✂------------------------------------

## WE NEED YOUR HELP . . .

*to plan the future of Sapphire books –*

Yours are the only opinions that matter. Sapphire is a new and exciting venture: the first British series of books devoted to lesbian erotic fiction written by and for women.

We're going to do our best to provide the sexiest books you can buy. And we'd like you to help in these early stages. Tell us what you want to read. There's a freepost address for your filled-in questionnaires, so you won't even need to buy a stamp.

---

# THE SAPPHIRE QUESTIONNAIRE

## SECTION ONE: ABOUT YOU

1.1 Sex (*we presume you are female, but just in case*)
Are you?
Female ☐
Male ☐

1.2 Age
under 21 ☐ 21–30 ☐
31–40 ☐ 41–50 ☐
51–60 ☐ over 60 ☐

1.3 At what age did you leave full-time education?
still in education ☐ 16 or younger ☐
17–19 ☐ 20 or older ☐

1.4 Occupation _____

1.5 Annual household income _____

1.6 We are perfectly happy for you to remain anonymous; but if you would
like us to send you a free booklist of Sapphire books, please insert your
name and address

_____

_____

_____

_____

---

## SECTION TWO: ABOUT BUYING SAPPHIRE BOOKS

2.1 Where did you get this copy of *Rika's Jewel*?
    Bought at chain book shop ☐
    Bought at independent book shop ☐
    Bought at supermarket ☐
    Bought at book exchange or used book shop ☐
    I borrowed it/found it ☐
    My partner bought it ☐

2.2 How did you find out about Sapphire books?
    I saw them in a shop ☐
    I saw them advertised in a magazine ☐
    A friend told me about them ☐
    I read about them in _____ ☐
    Other _____

2.3 Please tick the following statements you agree with:
    I would be less embarrassed about buying Sapphire
    books if the cover pictures were less explicit ☐
    I think that in general the pictures on Sapphire
    books are about right ☐
    I think Sapphire cover pictures should be as
    explicit as possible ☐

2.4 Would you read a Sapphire book in a public place – on a train for instance?
    Yes ☐    No ☐

---

## SECTION THREE: ABOUT THIS SAPPHIRE BOOK

3.1 Do you think the sex content in this book is:
    Too much ☐    About right ☐
    Not enough ☐

3.2   Do you think the writing style in this book is:
Too unreal/escapist          ☐          About right          ☐
Too down to earth            ☐

3.3   Do you think the story in this book is:
Too complicated              ☐          About right          ☐
Too boring/simple            ☐

3.4   Do you think the cover of this book is:
Too explicit                 ☐          About right          ☐
Not explicit enough          ☐
Here's a space for any other comments:

# SECTION FOUR: ABOUT OTHER SAPPHIRE BOOKS

4.1   How many Sapphire books have you read?

4.2   If more than one, which one did you prefer?

4.3   Why?

# SECTION FIVE: ABOUT YOUR IDEAL EROTIC NOVEL

We want to publish the books you want to read – so this is your chance to tell
us exactly what your ideal erotic novel would be like.

5.1   Using a scale of 1 to 5 (1 = no interest at all, 5 = your ideal), please rate
the following possible settings for an erotic novel:
Roman / Ancient World                                    ☐
Medieval / barbarian / sword 'n' sorcery                 ☐
Renaissance / Elizabethan / Restoration                  ☐
Victorian / Edwardian                                    ☐
1920s & 1930s                                            ☐
Present day                                              ☐
Future / Science Fiction                                 ☐

5.2 Using the same scale of 1 to 5, please rate the following themes you may find in an erotic novel:

Bondage / fetishism ☐
Romantic love ☐
SM / corporal punishment ☐
Bisexuality ☐
Gay male sex ☐
Group sex ☐
Watersports ☐
Rent / sex for money ☐

5.3 Using the same scale of 1 to 5, please rate the following styles in which an erotic novel could be written:

Gritty realism, down to earth ☐
Set in real life but ignoring its more unpleasant aspects ☐
Escapist fantasy, but just about believable ☐
Complete escapism, totally unrealistic ☐

5.4 In a book that features power differentials or sexual initiation, would you prefer the writing to be from the viewpoint of the dominant / experienced or submissive / inexperienced characters:

Dominant / Experienced ☐
Submissive / Inexperienced ☐
Both ☐

5.5 We'd like to include characters close to your ideal lover. What characteristics would your ideal lover have? Tick as many as you want:

| | | | |
|---|---|---|---|
| Dominant | ☐ | Cruel | ☐ |
| Slim | ☐ | Young | ☐ |
| Big | ☐ | Naïve | ☐ |
| Voluptuous | ☐ | Caring | ☐ |
| Extroverted | ☐ | Rugged | ☐ |
| Bisexual | ☐ | Romantic | ☐ |
| Working Class | ☐ | Old | ☐ |
| Introverted | ☐ | Intellectual | ☐ |
| Butch | ☐ | Professional | ☐ |
| Femme | ☐ | Pervy | ☐ |
| Androgynous | ☐ | Ordinary | ☐ |
| Submissive | ☐ | Muscular | ☐ |

Anything else? _____

5.6 Is there one particular setting or subject matter that your ideal erotic novel would contain:

_____

_____

## SECTION SIX: LAST WORDS

6.1 What do you like best about Sapphire books?

_____

6.2 What do you most dislike about Sapphire books?

_____

6.3 In what way, if any, would you like to change Sapphire covers?

_____

6.4 Here's a space for any other comments:

_____

_____

_____

_____

*Thanks for completing this questionnaire. Now either tear it out, or photocopy it, then put it in an envelope and send it to:*

**Sapphire/Virgin Publishing**
**FREEPOST LON3566**
**London**
**W6 9BR**

*You don't need a stamp if you're in the UK, but you'll need one if you're posting from overseas.*